BLOOD

Francis Owen was born in Peterlee, County Durham. After leaving school he began working as a reporter for his local newspaper. Over the years he has worked for regional and national newspapers in Britain, Japan and Hong Kong, as well as for the BBC and the Reuters international news agency. *Beijing Blood* is his first published novel. Francis has been shortlisted in the annual awards contest organised by the UK Crime Writers' Association. He met his wife Iris in Hong Kong and they have two children. The family now lives in London.

A *PETER DUGGAN* crime novel

BEIJING
BLOOD

Francis Owen

ASIA **CRIME**

HONG KONG and LONDON

First published in Hong Kong in 2009 by Asia Crime, an imprint of Dancing Tiger Publishing, 1338 Lai Kuk House, Lai Kok Estate, Cheung Sha Wan, Kowloon, Hong Kong. First published in the UK in 2009 by Asia Crime, 25 St Mary's Road, London, NW11 9UE.

Copyright © Text Francis Owen.

ISBN 978-0-9563024-0-3

A CIP record for this book is available from the British Library.

Set in 12.5/14.5 pt Garamond.
Printed and bound in Britain.

For my mother

1

TYPHOON WEATHER.

Rain spewed from an ash-coloured Hong Kong sky and scudded across the road, sending mist curling into the air like smoke from a funeral pyre.

On Catchick Street, police officers wearing waterproof capes turned rubbish bins on their sides to stop them from spiraling away. Workers hauled protective netting over the glass doors of Shanghai Commercial Bank and over the windows of Kuen Fat Seafood Restaurant. Shoppers stampeded up and down the pavement, jostling each other with umbrellas; waving franticly at crimson-coloured taxis as they sped past churning spray into the air.

I parked the Daihatsu around the corner from the office then reached over and grabbed my umbrella from the back seat, silently congratulating myself that for once I'd shown sufficient foresight to bring it, only to discover on closer examination that my foresight had not extended to ensuring the damn thing worked. Three metal spokes were broken — before going ten metres I was drenched.

Cursing myself for my stupidity and the heavens for the unjustness of it all, and still clutching the useless umbrella, I splashed across the road, jinking to the right to narrowly avoid a truck full of squealing pigs bound for the slaughter-house.

I was less successful with the minibus travelling in the opposite direction. A side-shuffle prevented it from hitting me, but nifty footwork couldn't stop the bus spraying me head to foot with water. Well this was just bloody typical. I plan an afternoon off for the first time in eight months and what happens? Hong Kong only goes and gets battered by its worst typhoon for fifty years. Maybe I should change my name and start calling myself Lucky instead of Peter. There couldn't be a man alive who encountered more good fortune.

My plan had been to stop work at noon and then go fishing. A friend had recently told me about the perfect place half a mile off the coast of Sai Kung, where the sea heaved with yellow tail and garoupa: even a hopeless fisherman like me would catch something. Fishing was out of the question now, though. Only people with a death wish put to sea during typhoons.

I reached my office block.

I shoved open the glass entrance door and tramped into the lobby, oozing water over the white tiled floor. Mei, the matronly-looking fifty-six-year-old I share as a secretary with fourteen other businesses in the block, glanced up from her desk. She gave a cursory once-over to the drowned rat standing two metres in front of her, before returning her gaze to the papers lying on the top of her desk.

"You're soaked," she said tonelessly as she scribbled something down on one of the pieces of paper.

"In case it escaped your eagle-eyed attention, Miss Yeung," I retorted, brushing lukewarm rain from my face, "a typhoon has started to kick seven bells out of Hong Kong. And my umbrella happens to be broken."

Mei glanced up from her work again.

"Never heard of raincoats?"

"I forgot to bring one," I said. "When a man reaches the age of ninety, his memory starts to go."

She shook her head slowly and at the same time gave me one of those tired, mother-knows-best sighs that I knew so well. Then she reached into a drawer under her desk, and with that magical efficiency that never ceased to amaze me, produced a large pale blue towel.

"Well make sure you remember to dry your wet hair before you go upstairs — Alan Yip wants to see you."

She handed me the towel. I started to dry my hair.

"*The* Alan Yip?"

Mei nodded. "I showed him up to your office ten minutes ago."

I frowned. "You let him in without me being there? Why did you do that?"

Mei gave me the sort of look which a patient teacher might give to a student who always tries his hardest to do well in class, but who despite his best efforts invariably manages to screw things up.

"Because *you* asked me," she said. "It's part of your latest efficiency drive. You said last month — if a client arrived early I should let them into your office to wait."

"Did I say that to you?" I wracked my brains to try and recall the occasion. "Oh yes, of course I did. Sorry, Mei, I remember now."

I finished drying my hair, gave her back the towel, and then took the lift to the eighth floor. I got out here

9

and turned right on to a long, narrow corridor. My office lay at the far end. I chucked my useless umbrella into the rubbish bin by the office door, pushed open the door and went inside.

Film producer Alan Yip sat by my desk, smoking a cigar and gazing out of the window. He had obviously got used to the office during the ten minutes he had been sitting there. Because when I came in he turned abruptly away from the window and shot me an angry, proprietary look. A look which said that this was his headquarters, not mine, and what the devil did I think I was playing at barging in and disturbing him like this.

I'd seen him often enough before, of course — barely a day passed without his bruiser-type features staring out from the glossy pages of some entertainment magazine or other — but this was the first time I had encountered the king of *kung fu* films in person.

He appeared smaller and fatter in the flesh. So fat that he risked bursting some buttons on his double-breasted grey jacket, which although it had probably cost a fortune at a top store like Lane Crawford or Shanghai Tang, still couldn't prevent him from looking slightly seedy: a bit like a third-rate sumo wrestler who had been out of training for ten years.

He leaned forward in the chair and jabbed a finger at my face.

"Are you Duggan?"

"Guilty as charged." I peeled off my soaked canvas jacket and hung it on a metal hook behind the door. I walked over to the desk and sat down opposite him. "How can I help you, Mister Yip?"

"I could have sent someone over from my studio." Although he had escaped from the Mongkok tenements forty years ago, Yip's voice had retained the hardness of the tough working-class area where he had grown up. "But I came here myself because Alan Yip is a man who thinks that personal business should always be settled *personally.*"

"Personal business?"

"I've decided to hire you to do a job, Duggan. How much is it going to cost me?"

"I haven't decided I'll take the job yet. What is it?"

He took a puff from his cigar then blew out a silver-blue cloud of smoke. He searched the desk for an ash-tray, but couldn't find one; I stopped smoking eight months ago — I don't provide ash-trays. Yip refused to let technicalities stop him enjoying his Havana. He tapped ash on the floor.

"That's right, don't worry about the carpet, Mister Yip," I said. "I've meant to replace it for ages; it must be all of two weeks old."

"I'm hiring you to find one of my actresses." Yip deposited another half-centimetre of ash on the floor. "When she didn't turn up for work six days ago I sent someone to her home in Sham Shui Po to check out what had happened, but she wasn't there."

He pulled a black-and-white photograph from his pocket and handed it to me. The photograph showed a girl who looked to be in her early twenties. Not a standard beauty — the ears were a bit too large for that, her eyes set slightly too closely together — yet something about her face intrigued me. Maybe it was the broad, girl-next-door smile. I've always been a sucker for friendly grins.

"I don't recognise her," I said. "What films has she starred in recently?"

"None," Yip answered brusquely. "I only said she was one of my actresses, I didn't say she was a star. I've given her a small role in the latest Alan Yip production and if she does well it could lead to bigger things. But at the moment acting isn't her main job. She works as a secretary at my studio."

"I charge clients four hundred US dollars a day, plus expenses," I said. "But maybe you shouldn't really be hiring me. Have you any reason to think this actress-secretary of yours is in danger?"

"Why?"

"It would be better to contact the police. They've got a lot more resources than a one-man outfit like me."

"I don't want to involve the police."

"Any particular reason?"

He stiffened. "I'm not paying you to question me, Duggan."

"You aren't paying me for anything, Mister Yip." I got up smartly from my chair and moved to the door. When I reached the door, I swung round. I said: "I'm sorry but I can't help you."

He almost swallowed his cigar.

"You mean to tell me," he spluttered, flecks of spittle flying from his thick lips, swamp-grey eyes bulging in disbelief. "*You're turning me down!*"

"I always like to know exactly what I'm getting myself into." I opened the door. "If you can't tell me the truth, I'm afraid we'll have to call it a day. I suggest you contact other investigators. They might feel differently about—"

Yip interrupted.

"All right, all right," he said gruffly. "We'll do it your way." He made a brusque gesture with his hand that told me to close the door. "What exactly do you want to know?"

I returned to my desk. I sat down and fixed him with a level stare. Then I said slowly, "Why do you really want to find her?"

He took a puff from his cigar. "She stole papers from the safe in my office."

"Papers?"

"The script for the next Alan Yip blockbuster film project and documents concerning my financial operations; if my rivals get their hands on just a few pages ..." He shuddered at the thought.

I sat back in my chair and nodded thoughtfully. Alan Yip-type big-shots like you to nod thoughtfully. They think it means you're hanging on to their every word. I realised now why he had been anxious not to get the police involved. Those documents must reveal how he fiddled his taxes — or perhaps worse. If the police read them, Yip's next blockbuster might be a court-room drama. With Asia's leading movie producer struggling to beat a fraud charge.

"What do you aim to do to this girl if I find her?"

"No harm will come to her."

"You're sure about that?"

"Once she returns all of my papers, and satisfies me that she's made no copies, she can do what she wants to do."

"Supposing that what she wants to do is to keep your important papers?"

"She won't," Yip said confidently. "Not when you tell her I'll pay for their return. Everyone has their price. Kam Sau's no different."

"That's her name? Kam Sau?"

He pulled a key from his pocket. "My people have already checked her flat." He handed me the key. "They found nothing to give any hints where she might be, but they're not professional snoopers." He shot me the sort of stare that probably had the minions at his studio sprinting for fall-out shelters. "I expect better results from you."

"I don't get it," I said. "Why do you have a key?"

I did get it, of course. At least I thought I did. The thought of him sleeping with a girl about the same age as my daughter made me feel sick.

"Kam Sau kept a spare in the office, in case she mislaid her other key." Yip pulled a leather-bound cheque book from his pocket. "Twelve hundred," he announced. "That buys you for three days — if you haven't found her by then, I hire someone else." He scribbled in one of the pages of his cheque book, tore out the page and handed it to me. "And you report daily." He jabbed a finger at my face. "Understood?"

I thought about telling him to go and screw himself. I didn't like how he had pushed his weight around; I've always disliked big-shots throwing their weight about, that's partly why I quit the police. On top of that, I felt he'd still not told me the entire truth about the girl.

I thought about how satisfying it would be to tear the cheque into tiny pieces, then haul his two-hundred-and-twenty-pound frame from the chair and boot him down eight flights of stairs. Then I thought about my bank account and the lack of money in it, all the unpaid bills and the Rolex watch I wanted to buy Kathy for her nineteenth birthday. I put Yip's cheque in my pocket.

2

I GOT YIP to tell me everything he knew about her, which wasn't much. A twenty-year-old from China, Kam Sau had worked for him for five months. Both parents were dead and she had no brothers or sisters. Yip didn't know if she had a lover and had no names of friends. After reminding me again that he expected a daily report, he swaggered out.

Immediately the office door closed, I had doubts about taking the case. Could I trust him not to harm her if she refused to return his documents? No, I couldn't risk handing her over. My dilemma was that I didn't want to hand that cheque over to him either; I needed those twelve hundred dollars.

I could pocket his cash, of course, and not bother looking for her. That would probably be the smart thing to do. It would also be unprofessional. And I pride myself on being professional in my work. A psychiatrist would probably say it's to compensate for my personal life being such an amateurish shambles.

After mulling things over for five minutes, I drew up my master plan. I would spend three days looking for

Kam Sau. If I hadn't found her by then — and it would be tough if she had crossed the border and entered China — Yip would hire someone else and I would be twelve hundred dollars richer.

To protect her from him after he yanked me off the case — he would no longer be a client, so it wouldn't be unethical — I would call my ex-partner, Detective Sergeant Frank Ching, and explain what Yip was doing. If, on the other hand, I managed to find Kam Sau in the three days, I would return Yip's money and keep her away from him.

Nothing unethical in any of that, was there? No, I assured myself, my plan seemed perfect. Except that a dim-wit called Peter Duggan risked ending up twelve hundred dollars poorer. To hell with ethics! If I found that girl then I would keep her away from Yip *and* keep his money!

The phone rang: "Inspector Duggan?"

It was a man's voice; early twenties.

"It's *Mister* Duggan. I quit the police force last year; how can I help you?"

"It's me who can help you — with good advice."

I stiffened; I always tense up when someone offers good advice. It reminds me of that part in *The Godfather*, where Don Corleone makes someone an offer they can't refuse. Experience has taught me that when people say they want to offer good advice, they often would like to break both my legs.

"Who is this?"

"Drop the Alan Yip case, Duggan. Or you'll never work another."

The line went dead. I hunted through my memory bank; had I heard that voice before? Could I put a name or face to it? No. After a few moments I realised the caller was a stranger. Why tell me to drop the case? Would he make good that threat about me never working again?

I sat back, blew air from my cheeks. If my instincts had urged me to steer ten yards clear of Yip before that phone call, they now screamed at me to run a mile from him. It would be safest to return his cash — another client would turn up soon — go home and bomb my brain cells watching TV.

Instead, I trooped downstairs and borrowed Mei's umbrella and then headed for the missing girl's flat.

As I drove in my ten-year-old Daihatsu down Kennedy Town's waterfront, I saw that the weather had worsened. Waves pounded against the sea wall and showered the road with spray. The wind tore advertising boards off a tram as it clanked along ahead of me. Across the harbour the fourteen-hundred-metre long Tsing Ma suspension bridge, which links Kowloon to the airport on Lantau Island, had vanished in a swirling mist of rain.

I drove through the cross-harbour tunnel, then moved on to a traffic-snarled Nathan Road and headed towards Sham Shui Po. I switched on the radio. The main item on the RTHK news was the typhoon and how it would be the biggest to hit Hong Kong for years. It was global warming, the newsreader explained. The sea's temperature level had risen dramatically so typhoons had grown much more savage. He moved to a report on British government minister Ian Jeffries, who would arrive in Hong Kong the day after tomorrow and then visit China to sign a trade deal. In business news, Hong Kong's stock market had ended a shortened day's trading one per cent higher, while share prices in Japan and Singapore had also made some slight gains.

I parked the car about twenty metres from the girl's apartment block, which was as close as I could get, and then battled my way over there through the wind and rain. I shoved open the double glass entrance doors and sloshed into the lobby. Rows of shiny metal postal boxes were studded into the wall on either side of the lobby, like miniature lockers in a gymnasium changing room. Open Kam Sau's box and check her mail and I might find something there that would help me find her. But a skeletal-faced old man in a white vest and baggy blue shorts sat by the lobby's window monitoring the storm outside. Yip had only given me a key for her apartment. To access the mail box meant smashing the lock, and no way would I do that. Not with this old boy hanging around.

I took the lift to the tenth floor. Kam Sau's flat stood near the end of a long, dingy corridor. The door to one flat on the corridor lay open. A man inside the flat bowed to a picture of Buddha hanging on the wall. Wisps of silvery-blue smoke curled from the joss sticks which the man held. A sickly-sweet smell of burning incense drifted through the air.

Kam Sau's flat was as small as all homes are in the government-built blocks. Apart from a cramped and windowless living room, which doubled as a bedroom, she had a tiny kitchen and a tiny bathroom and toilet. The place seemed hardly big enough for one person, let alone the large family groups who inhabited this block. In an effort to make her home appear bigger, she had painted the walls an airy light blue. Hanging from these walls were pictures of a middle-aged man and woman — perhaps her dead parents — and six postcards displaying views of China. I pulled the postcards from the wall and checked to see if any of the senders had written their addresses on the back — perhaps Kam Sau had holed up with one of them.

The only address was for this flat.

The living room had a sofa, wardrobe, chest of drawers and coffee table. It also had a small fish tank to add an element of water to the room and hopefully bring good *feng shui*. The phone rested on the coffee table, its winking red light announcing that someone had left a message. I played the message to hear a girl named Giselle ask if Kam Sau — Giselle called her 'Shooter' — could play basketball on Saturday.

Judging from her name and her melodic-sounding voice, Giselle was one of the twenty-odd thousand Filipinas who worked in Hong Kong as maids or child minders. Giselle was replaced by the robot-like tones of an operator, who explained that to save the message I should now press button two. To get in touch with the message sender, I needed to press button three. I pressed button three.

"Wild Cat Club," a man said almost immediately.

"Is Giselle there?"

"Gone home, mate; we're closed tonight on account of the typhoon."

"Have you her home number?"

"Not allowed to give them out, mate. Mosey on down here tomorrow if you want to meet her. The dancers are due in at half-seven."

He hung up. So Giselle was not a maid or child minder. She worked in one of Wanchai's red-light bars.

19

I moved to the drawers and dragged open the top one. Empty. The second drawer was the same, and the third and fourth; nothing in the wardrobe either, or underneath the sofa. I checked the kitchen and bathroom: again, nothing. It looked like Yip's secretary had moved out for good.

The doorbell rang. I opened the door to a hunched-up old woman, probably in her seventies, maybe eighties. She wore one of those awful Chairman Mao pyjama suits, made of cheap crimplene and decorated with a dowdy floral pattern, which for some reason I'll never understand, Hong Kong women seem to wear all the time once they pass the age of sixty. She clutched a wooden walking stick in what looked more like a claw than a left hand, while the arthritic-curled fingers of her right hand pointed at my chest.

"You're a policeman, aren't you."

It was a statement rather than a question and made in a voice surprisingly firm and croak-free, a voice which belied the frailness of her physical appearance.

"Well, grandmother," I started to say. "I'm really—"

"I knew it! I knew it!" she cried, congratulating herself on her cleverness, leathery face cracking into a grin which showed that she had four yellowing teeth remaining. "I'm never wrong about these things. I could tell you were a policeman just from how you walk. I live down the corridor in number twenty-six — I spied you coming out of the lift."

Spied was the right word to use. She was probably the tenth floor's self-appointed Secret Police officer, a job that would suit her perfectly if initial impressions were anything to go by; she looked like your typical nosey-parker. Probably she monitored people coming

20

out of the lift all day. But I shouldn't be hard on her. Living here, unable to walk without the aid of a stick, and even then not far, there wouldn't be much to do but watch the comings and goings. And if she had spied me she would have spied others. In fact those shrewd little eyes probably glimpsed everything that happened in this corridor: making her an ideal person to quiz about Kam Sau.

"Policemen always walk funny. That's how, when I saw you coming down the corridor, I knew that you were a policeman. It's the way policemen walk so fast and roll their shoulders — what's your name?"

"Inspector Duggan; do you know the girl who lives in this flat?"

"No, no," she said, shaking her head.

"She's a twenty-year-old who—"

"Not *this* flat!" The old woman pointed her gnarled fist at the apartment on the opposite side of the corridor. "That's the one you want. You're too late, though. The other policemen searched it last week."

"Sorry, grandmother," I said, puzzled. "I—"

"It's *that* one!" She rapped me on the foot with her stick. "That flat there! That's where the woman who was murdered lived."

3

"MURDERED!" I EXCLAIMED, and was about to ask her the victim's name and when it had happened, until I remembered she thought I was a policeman who would know these details.

I nodded judiciously, and said in what I hoped was an official-sounding voice, "I know it's that flat."

Her eyes narrowed. "So why search this one?"

"Ah, well." I wracked my brains for a reasonable explanation. "I'm a special policeman, see, and—"

"Did the girl who lives here strangle Ah Chung?" Her face lit up at the possibility. "Is that it? Is that why you're searching her flat?" She couldn't keep the delight from her voice. This would really be something to tell the neighbours. It would keep her in business all week, maybe a whole year.

"I think it's unlikely that she is connected in any way to Ah Chung's death," I said. "But in such a serious crime of this nature all possibilities must of necessity be explored." I assumed a facial expression which I hoped contained the right mixture of intelligence and sincerity, while cringing inwardly at all my clichés.

"She's called Kam Sau."

"Friend of yours?"

"She's a friend of Ah Chung's daughter."

"Is Ah Chung's daughter home?"

"She went back to China two weeks ago." The old woman's eyes narrowed suspiciously again. "You told me you were a policeman."

"That's right."

"So how come you don't know about Ah Chung's daughter going home to China?"

"Ah well, I—"

"And how come you speak such good Cantonese? If I wasn't looking at you, I'd think you were a local."

"I am a local."

"You look like a westerner."

"Have you got an address for Ah Chung's daughter, grandmother?"

"I only know she lives in Beijing. That's how her and Kam Sau became such good friends."

"They knew each other in Beijing?"

"I don't know. Will you arrest Kam Sau?"

"I only want to talk to her."

"It's Ah Chung's girl you should really arrest. It's criminal how she's not come back home for her own mother's funeral." The old woman shook her head in a mixture of disbelief and sorrow. "But that's our selfish young people today for you. No sense of duty."

"When did you last see Kam Sau?"

"Two weeks ago."

My face must have registered disappointment that her grasp on the activities of the tenth floor wasn't as all-encompassing as I had initially assumed it was, because she quickly added, "She goes to work early,

23

when I'm sleeping, and comes back late. So I only see her at weekends. Last weekend I had to go to hospital."

The lift doors jerked open at that moment and an extremely fat woman emerged, weighed down with two large striped shopping bags; she walked, or rather she waddled, to the far end of the corridor.

"That's my neighbour," the old woman announced. "I'll have to go and tell her what's happened with Kam Sau, but ..." Indecision flickered on her weathered face. She was torn between a desire to reveal the latest news about Kam Sau, and an eagerness to stay with me, to make sure she missed nothing. "You won't go away, will you?"

"I'll be here for at least another twenty-five minutes," I assured her solemnly.

But I had squeezed all I could from her. After she had gone inside the neighbour's flat, I tramped downstairs. The grandfather in the baggy shorts still hung about in the lobby; I would have to leave Kam Sau's mail box for tomorrow.

Traffic was more congested than usual due to the typhoon and it took me forty minutes to drive the three miles from Kowloon to my apartment in Hong Kong. It was dark when I emerged from the cross-harbour tunnel. The sea had become a cauldron of swirling tar. Lights flickered in waterfront skyscrapers. I got stalled in more traffic near the Excelsior Hotel. I pulled the mobile phone from my pocket and punched out the number for my friend, Sergeant Frank Ching.

"So you *are* alive," Frank said.

"What are you talking about?"

"Oh, nothing much," Frank said tonelessly. "Just the small matter of an hour I spent twiddling my thumbs waiting for you in that Irish pub over in Tsim Sha Tsui on Tuesday."

"Murphy's Bar?"

"We were meeting there for a drink — remember?"

"Didn't you get my message?"

"For the first time in your life you actually sent one?"

"Sarcasm doesn't suit you, Frank. I need some details on a woman killed last week — her name's Ah Chung. She lived on Lee Kuk housing estate in Sham Shui Po; any chance of you checking her on the station's computer for me?"

"I don't need to check her on the computer," Frank said. "I'm personally working on that case with your old friend Kwan — as you would already know if you had bothered to turn up on Tuesday night."

A gap appeared in the traffic. I jabbed the accelerator and moved into second gear but only got thirty metres down Gloucester Road before a red light halted me.

"So what's it all about?"

"Why the interest, Pete?"

"She may be linked to something I'm working on."

"She was a dishwasher at that big new Shanghai restaurant in Ocean Centre."

"Imperial Gardens?"

"That's the one," Frank said. "And before you start asking me, we found her body in an alley about a mile from her flat, and no we haven't arrested the killer yet. Probably he didn't mean to strangle her — I reckon he just wanted her money. But she struggled ..."

"That's Kwan's angle on this? A street robbery that got out of hand?"

"We found no money in her handbag," Frank said.

"Have you talked with the dead woman's daughter?"

"She lives in China."

"I know. What's her address?"

"Why do you want the *daughter's* address?"

"Now, now, no need to sound so suspicious."

"With you there's every need."

The traffic lights went green. But the road remained congested. I still couldn't get the Daihatsu any higher than second gear.

"I've just told you," I said. "I'm looking for a girl. There's a chance she might be staying with … Do I get the address, or not?"

He gave me the address. Then to show he had no hard feelings over our missed drink, he supplied me with the girl's mobile number too. Business done, we turned to social affairs. We chatted about whether the police station had managed to survive without me: it had; very nicely in fact. Then Frank suggested that instead of having a beer at Murphy's Bar, I drive over to his place in Lam Tin for dinner.

"The wife's always nagging at me to bring that nice Peter Duggan home. For some reason she thinks you're wonderful."

"She's a wonderful judge of character, Frank."

"So it's a date then, yes —Saturday?"

"I'll be there."

I GOT HOME at ten-fifteen.

Old Yuen, the so-called security guard for my apartment block, sat at his desk in the lobby, fast asleep as usual. Which was just as well, considering that he was pushing seventy. The firm which manages my block likes to hire pensioners because they're prepared to work for near-starvation wages, it doesn't seem to matter that they also happen to be the world's worst security guards. If Old Yuen woke up then he might have to confront an intruder. No way would he win that contest. He would only hurt himself, perhaps seriously. Better that he caught up on his beauty sleep — I closed the door gently in order not to disturb him. But the sound of the lift coming down woke him.

"Hey! What ... Oh, it's you, chief ... You're soaked!"

"In case you hadn't noticed, a typhoon's kicking seven bells out of everything outside. Go back to sleep, there's another four hours before your shift ends."

He rubbed bloodshot eyes. "Getting a wink of sleep's impossible in this lousy sweat hole," he grumbled. "Those tight-fisted management bastards turn off the air-con at night — then there's all the lousy mosquitoes. I've got no coils to burn to keep the mosquitoes away. The minute I shut my eyes they're buzzing my head, biting my face and neck — last night one cheeky little bastard even flew up my trousers and bit me on the balls! ... Don't laugh, chief! It's true!"

"I've got a few spare mosquito coils in my office," I said. "I'll bring them back for you tomorrow."

With a loud hiss, the lift's steel doors opened. I said goodnight to Old Yuen, stepped into the lift and jabbed the button for the fourteenth floor.

"Hey! I nearly forgot," Old Yuen shouted as the lift doors began to close.

I opened the doors. "Forgot what?"

"Your daughter came in an hour ago."

"Kathy's upstairs?"

"Unless she grew wings and flew out the window."

"Don't joke," I told him. "With her you can never be too sure."

27

4

"I'M BREWING COFFEE," Kathy called out from the kitchen. "Want one?"

"If it's not that rocket fuel you usually make," I called back to her.

I tramped into the bedroom and phoned the Beijing number that Frank Ching had given me for the murder victim's daughter.

No reply.

I peeled off my wet clothes and put on some dry ones, then went into the living room where a tall, spiky-haired Kathy lounged on the sofa. She wore a college rebel's uniform of grey Bruce Lee tee-shirt, camou-flaged army pants and cherry-red Doc Martens, but it was the hair that really grabbed my attention.

Was this latest dramatic look *completely* new — it was hard to keep track with someone who changed their hairstyle almost every week — or an old one brought back to life? Most teenage Hong Kong girls wore their hair long and conservatively straight. Kathy had had her hair cropped short, then covered it with about half a tonne of industrial-strength hair jell and combed it so that it spiked upwards, the spikes so sharp you could have pierced apples on them.

"Here you go, dad." She leaned over and handed me my hot coffee so clumsily that she slopped half of it over my outstretched fingers. I danced around cursing and spilled most of what remained in my cup. Oblivious to my suffering and the fact that she had caused it, Kathy calmly explained why she had done me the honour of calling in to see me: "Missed the last train because of the typhoon, so I … Oh, stop prancing around like a ballet dancer! You're making me dizzy!"

I had trouble hearing her: she had tuned the television to *Justice Pao*, a soap opera about a kindly and learned judge who travelled around ancient China punishing evil landlords. As usual, she had the volume loud enough to awaken the dead.

I settled into the chair opposite her and drank what remained of my coffee. I like my coffee strong as a rule, but this stuff was beyond a joke; it tasted like treacle.

"You overdid the coffee granules again."

"Oh stop complaining! It's not that strong."

"It's strong enough to send me into orbit!" I shoved the cup to one side. "And for Christ's sake turn that TV down — it's giving me a headache!"

Grudgingly, she pressed a switch on the remote to reduce the volume: from a level that would arouse the dead to one which only destroyed brain cells of the living. "If only Queenie was sitting here now and could see the tyrant you've become," Kathy sighed, shaking her head. "I bet she wouldn't love you any more."

"Queenie?"

"Her real name's Po Tse, goalie on our school team."

"The little fat girl with the pigtails?"

29

"You remember, huh?"

Kathy sounded surprised, but of course I remembered her friend; the world's worst goalkeeper, but a girl who had played with such endearing passion. Yet so timid off the pitch that she had blushed whenever I'd spoken to her. Thoughtful, too; at one season's end she had presented me with a home-made trophy for being the team's best supporter.

"Had a mega crush on you," Kathy said. "Because you were the only parent dumb enough to watch every single game that we played. She reckoned there was something really noble about a man prepared to torture himself week in week out like that."

"It wasn't torture. I've always enjoyed watching a good game of football."

"Bullshit!"

"I beg your pardon!"

"Watching us lot get stuffed six-nil every week was as exciting as watching paint dry!" Kathy levered herself up from the sofa and yawned. "Tonight's *Justice Pao* is total garbage too — I'm going for a shower. The TV's all yours, dad."

I watched her move to the bedroom, walking in the confident bouncy way she always did, head bobbing from side to side. She toe-punted the bedroom door open, then back-heeled it shut. Cupboard doors banged open and closed; she never did anything quietly. I heard her whistling and singing; she sang badly, couldn't reach the high notes.

On television, wise old Judge Pao informed an evil landlord who had ravished a peasant's teenage daughter that he would suffer the death of a thousand cuts, and what remained of his body would then be fed to the fishes. The kindly and learned judge added that he was sorry and all that, but ... well, rules were rules.

A framed picture rested on top of the television: me clutching a newly-born Kathy. Wrapped in a large bath towel, yellow from jaundice, she stared up wide-eyed at an even wider-eyed father, who seemed scared he might drop her. It triggered memories of her birth: three-thirty on a typhoon afternoon: sky the colour of cigarette ash: rain lashing leaden streets. I had spent ages rushing about like a headless chicken, trying to hail a taxi, before calming down and summoning a police car. Kathy had weighed in at a hefty eight pounds twelve ounces, with chocolate-button eyes and as po-faced as Lantau Island's Buddha statue.

She re-emerged from the bedroom. A pink towel was in her hands and blue running shorts had replaced the camouflaged combat pants. She gave the sort of shout *kung fu* film stars give when they chop their enemies, kicked the bathroom door open so hard she almost broke the hinges, and lurched inside. I heard sounds of running water, then of her jumping around and cursing — blaming me because the water was too hot.

I glanced at another photograph.

A shot of Kathy with school friends, I'd hung this one on the wall. Stood in the middle of the back row she towered above the rest, and if she had possessed the poise to go with her height then she might have avoided those taunts. But she had been awkward and ungainly, so kids had picked on her. It seemed like only yesterday when she had run home weeping after class-mates called her the 'Ugly White Giant', and said she wasn't a proper Chinese but a half-caste. Together with Suk Fan — my wife and I had done everything together

31

in those days — I had dried Kathy's eyes and told her not to get upset.

"They called me half-caste too. It's only a name."

In hindsight, all the taunts had helped her. They had made her granite-like resilient, had encouraged her to develop a razor-sharp tongue with which she could cut her tormentors to pieces. But perhaps her tongue had become a little bit *too* sharp. Unless you knew her well, it was hard to realise these days just when she was joking and when she was being deliberately rude.

The phone rang: Old Yuen from the lobby.

"A guy here wants to speak to you, chief."

"Tell him to come up."

"Wants you to come down here — says it's really urgent. Says it's about the woman whose home you went to tonight."

"I'm on my way."

5

TWO MINUTES LATER I stood in the downstairs lobby, staring at a skinny dishevelled-looking character with dark brown shifty eyes. He wore a short-sleeved green shirt and baggy jeans. A navy blue baseball cap was perched on his head and Nike jogging shoes covered his feet. I put his height at five foot six or seven, about the average for a Cantonese man, and his age at twenty six or twenty seven.

"Inspector Duggan?"

I stiffened. The person who had phoned to warn me off the case had also called me *Inspector* Duggan. Were the caller and my visitor tonight one and the same man? No. Judging from the sound of his voice, this afternoon's caller was a confident, assured type. My visitor seemed nervous.

"How can I help, Mister ...?"

"You've got something that's mine."

"Something that's yours?"

"You took it from Kam Sau's and I—"

"Hold on," I interrupted. "Who are you?"

"Joe Chan: a freelance journalist."

"And what makes you think that I've got something that's yours, Joe?"

"You were in Kam Sau's flat."

I feigned ignorance. "Kam Sau?"

"I saw you," Chan blurted out. A nervous tic had developed on the left side of his face. "Yes — yes ... First, I followed Alan Yip to your office. Then I — I followed you to the flat."

"Being a journalist gives you a right to follow people, does it?"

"I want that package."

I had spotted no package in that flat; all the drawers had been empty. There had been nothing in the wardrobe either, or under the bed, or in the cupboards — what was Chan talking about? To find out would require me asking serious questions. Better to ask them in my apartment. That way the flapping ears of Old Yuen would not hear things I didn't want them to hear. And being on home turf would give me more control over Chan.

"It's in my flat. You need to come upstairs to get it."

He shook his head. "I want you to bring it here."

"Too heavy," I protested. "You'll have to come upstairs to get it."

"Liar!" he shouted. "You're trying to trick me!"

He spun on his heels then darted for the door. He yanked the door open, dashed out into the pouring rain. I charged after him, but only managed three strides before slipping on the soaked pavement and almost putting my hip out of joint. By the time I had picked myself up he was thirty metres away.

His blue baseball cap flew off as he bolted across the road, zigzagging between two taxis whose drivers blasted their horns as they swerved to avoid him. Safely on the pavement at the other side, he shoved past an old man and woman who were hurrying home to escape the typhoon, almost bundling the old man to the ground.

I grabbed a deep breath and gave chase.

As he ran past Hang Seng Bank, Chan tried to flag down a taxi. The cab driver drove past. I lengthened my stride and started to gain on him. Our gap narrowed to about twenty metres. He swung left at the Wellcome Supermarket and then left again, fifty metres further on, at the Chinese medicine store. I followed and found myself in an alley about six feet wide with high walls on both sides. The alley was dimly lit by two lamps positioned at either end.

At the far end, about twenty metres away, stood a wall roughly a metre high. A pile of cardboard boxes rested beside the wall. But no Joe Chan. Either he had lied to me about being a journalist, and was really a magician who had made himself disappear in a puff of smoke, or he had climbed the wall. I ran over, put a hand on the wall and began to haul myself up.

Chan emerged from behind the boxes and butted me in the kidneys. As I gagged for breath, he shoved me in the back. The floor was slimy with rain and food waste. I slipped and fell. He aimed a kick at my face. I jerked my head aside and his foot only grazed me on the shoulder. He launched another kick. This time I thrust out my right hand and caught his leg. I yanked hard at the leg and upended him.

We rolled over in the stinking food mess. One moment I was on top, yelling at him to calm down, protesting that I didn't want to hurt him and only wanted to talk. Next moment I lay sprawled on my back, gasping for breath as hands tightened around my throat — he certainly wanted to hurt me.

An elbow in the ribs broke his grip. I tried to seize hold of his neck and restrain him. He would have none of it and bit me on the wrist. I gave a cry of pain and yanked my arm away. Then I felt a whoosh of warm air as his fist brushed the side of my face. I heard bone snap as the fist slammed against the concrete floor.

Chan gave a shriek and his weight was lifted off me — the fight had ended. Breaking his hand was enough agony for one night. Still yelling with pain, he lurched towards the alleyway's entrance. I got to my feet and caught him before he reached it. I grabbed his hair and dragged him around to face me.

Then I belted him three times in the guts.

He collapsed on the floor in a crying heap. I stood over him, gasping for air, oblivious to the rain that drenched me. Chan continued to writhe and scream. The fact that he had tried to strangle me a few moments ago made me less sympathetic than I would normally have been. When I had sucked sufficient air into my lungs, I said aggressively, "I'm going to ask questions. And ..."

I halted in mid-sentence.

He had struggled into a sitting position. His unbroken hand had something in it; something slim, silver and shiny.

"Get away, Duggan! Get away or I'll use it!"

I've always hated knives, even more than I hate guns. Death is something that I have never considered to be a barrel of laughs, but at least a gunshot is usually clean. And if you die from a bullet, unless you get hit in the chest, it's often quick, whereas in the hands of a skilled operator a knife can carve you apart. I did not think that Joe Chan was one of these skilled operators, but I wasn't prepared to take a chance on it.

So I just stood there and watched Chan as he staggered from the alleyway; I made no effort to follow him — why put my life at risk? Alan Yip had only hired me to find his secretary, not to go and get myself killed. This was a straightforward missing person's case, not a matter of life and death. At least that was what I thought as I stood there in the rain.

6

A BLAST OF noise from the living room jolted me awake as my daughter switched on the CD player. True to form, Kathy had the volume turned up to an ear-splitting level: then came the thump, thump of her jumping up and down as she performed her morning exercises.

In case all of this was insufficient to give me brain damage, the phone helped out by ringing. I glanced at the clock on the bedroom wall. It was eight-fifteen as my secretary Mei came on the line.

"What's all that terrible noise? It sounds like you're in a disco."

"My daughter stayed the night. She didn't like what I cooked for dinner so now she's repaying me by demolishing the living room ceiling."

"Alan Yip's office just phoned," Mei said. "He wants you to quit the investigation."

I sat up more straight. *"He wants what?"*

"You're to do it immediately too — his assistant was really keen to stress that bit."

"You're sure about this?"

"Of course I am."

"I don't get it," I said, "why the change of heart?"

"His assistant didn't tell me," Mei said. "But Yip's letting you keep all that money he paid up front."

"It wasn't the great man himself you spoke to?"

"I just told you, it was his assistant."

"Maybe it was someone pretending to work for Yip."

"It wasn't anyone pretending," Mei said. "The Miss Choi I spoke to definitely works for your friend Alan."

"How come you're so sure?"

"Because after I finished talking to her the first time, I realised she'd said nothing about you keeping that money he'd already paid. So I called the film studio back to get it cleared up and got put through to her. When are you coming in?"

"Probably about half-nine," I said. "And thanks for sorting out the money stuff for me, Mei."

I replaced the phone in its cradle. A mosquito buzzed my head. I snapped at it with my right hand but missed; whatever had happened to those lightning-fast Duggan reflexes of old? Perhaps they had never existed. Were they a myth, like Yip's missing documents? Why order me to drop the case? It was strange how he had changed his mind. Stranger still that he would let me keep the twelve hundred dollars he'd paid me; misers like him usually guarded every cent. Why not this time?

I moved to the window, tugged open the pale green curtains and gazed at the office tower across the road, as if doing so might answer my questions about Yip, as well as solve all the other mysteries of the universe. When Suk Fan and I had moved into this flat, a lifetime ago it now seemed, I'd stared from this window and seen ships and junks chug in and out of Victoria

Harbour. The estate agent with the alligator smile had sold the place on the strength of its postcard view.

"Oh! if I only had enough money," he had sighed, sea-grey eyes misting over dreamily; "I would rush out right now and buy the place myself!"

"You're absolutely sure?" I pressed him. "You're certain no tall office buildings will be put up in front of us? The harbour view's why we're keen on this flat."

He placed a calming hand on my shoulder: "One hundred percent certain, my dear sir!" His smile grew so broad it threatened to burst from his face. "May Buddha strike me dead if I'm lying! They're building a sports centre — only four floors high with some tennis courts on the roof. You'll keep your magnificent view."

So, like an idiot, I had persuaded Suk Fan to buy it. Six months later, with the estate agent no longer smiling — he had just begun a two-year jail sentence for fraud — construction workers had arrived to erect a forty-storey office tower, slap bang in front of our picture-postcard home. I smiled wryly. It never ceased to amaze me that someone who claimed to be intelligent and street-wise could act so naively so often.

The view was not helping me to answer questions about Alan Yip, or solving any other mysteries of the universe. I got dressed. Then I phoned the number that Frank had given me for the murdered dishwasher's daughter. As had happened last night, no one answered.

I tramped into the living room and signalled for Kathy to lower the volume on the CD player. Amazingly, she obeyed without protest. She flopped onto the sofa, sweating from her exertions.

"Sorry, dad, did I wake you?"

"Whatever gave you that idea?"

"You have to play rock music really loud. It sounds crap otherwise."

"Do you also have to wreck the living room ceiling doing aerobics?"

She raised her hand in a gesture that told me to relax. "I'll be quieter tomorrow."

"*Tomorrow?*"

"I thought I would stay another night."

My eyes narrowed with suspicion. "Why? Have you and your mother had an argument?"

From her dramatic reaction, you would have thought I'd just accused her of dancing naked on top of Deng Xiaoping's tomb.

"Absolutely and most *definitely* not!" she sniffed haughtily, her over-the-top response instantly confirming all my suspicions of a new mother-daughter row. "Mum and I never have arguments. We always ... Hey! Where are you off to?"

I was opening the entrance door: "Over the road for a newspaper."

"Well nip into the food market for me and get a nice big fat lobster for dinner."

"Never mind lobsters," I hectored her. "Call your mother about tonight. I don't want her to be worrying."

I BOUGHT A newspaper from a shop on King's Road.

The typhoon was the main item on *Ming Pao's* front page. It had failed to live up to all of the experts' predictions that it would be the worst storm to batter Hong Kong for fifty years. At the last moment it had veered away and battered the Philippines instead. We had still had heavy rain, of course. But apart from some homes in villages in the rural New Territories, up by the

China border, no buildings in Hong Kong or Kowloon had been damaged. The newspaper also carried a story about the forthcoming visit to Hong Kong and China of the British government minister Ian Jeffries, and one about how the United States had finally accepted that something urgent needed to be done to tackle the problems of climate change.

But the fourth item on the page was the one which really gripped my attention. It concerned a man who had been killed in a hit-and-run accident late last night: journalist Joe Chan.

7

I WENT INTO a noodles shop and ordered coffee. I had to make sense of what was happening and caffeine boosts my brain cells. Not that there would be much caffeine in what the shark-faced shop owner placed in front of me. He swore on his mother's life that it was the best Italian espresso, but it looked like liquid mud. I took a sip; not even hot mud, only lukewarm.

I pushed the cup to one side. My brain would have to work without the aid of a stimulant. Had Joe Chan's death really been a hit-and-run accident? According to the *Ming Pao* report, he had been sprinting home to escape from the rain. He had slipped over on the road and then been hit by a taxi.

Supposing the driver had hit him deliberately?

Chan had been scared last night, charging off like a rabbit caught in car headlights when pressed about the package he thought I'd taken from Kam Sau's apartment. Did the package really exist? Did it contain Alan Yip's stolen documents? Had those people Yip had sent to Kam Sau's flat before hiring me found it — was that why he no longer required my help?

No. His flunkeys had searched Kam Sau's place days ago. If they had discovered anything Yip would not have hired me. So if those stolen documents had still not been found, why was Yip suddenly eager to dispense with my expert services?

My phone rang. "Peter ... Oh, it's you, Kathy ... What's that? ... No, I haven't forgotten about your bloody lobster."

I replaced the phone in my pocket and tried to refocus on Alan Yip. No good. Kathy's call had broken my train of thought. I decided to return home, brew some real coffee and start again. Not before I bought a lobster, though. Fail to return with my daughter's favourite dinner-time treat and life would not be worth a dog biscuit.

The indoor market was as crowded as it always is and stank of raw meat, a smell that invariably makes me imagine dead bodies on the mortuary slab. I tried to think of some more pleasant things. But it's hard when butchers are carving up pigs barely two metres from your face, and then tossing heaps of entrails into baskets which ooze blood.

At one stall, a leathery-faced grandmother jabbed a finger at a rack of scrawny-looking chickens. The fat butcher dragged out a squawking bird then broke its neck with a flick of his wrist; the grandmother smiled — one more satisfied customer. I trooped over to a stall which sold seafood. The squat, pug-faced woman on guard behind the counter grinned, displaying teeth that contained enough gold to fill a small bank vault.

"*Aheya!* You're getting as fat as me!"

"You always say the nicest things to me, Ah Jun. Got any lobsters?"

"And your face! It gets more like a bruised mango every day!"

"I think you're beautiful too, Ah Jun. Have you got any lobsters or not?"

She gestured impatiently to the large tank beside her. "What do you think these are in here — silk pyjamas?" She thrust a mottled arm into the tank, fished out a lobster and bound its claws with twine. She paused before handing it over. "Know how to cook it?" She stood back and eyed me slyly.

"Was Mao a communist? Of course I know."

She gave a raspy chuckle. "Make sure you've got the phone number of Tung Wah Hospital handy, Peter Duggan. If you're as good a chef as you are a liar, you're heading for food poisoning."

"Not before you cut yourself with that tongue."

KATHY WAS TAKING a shower. I stored her lobster in the fridge and then brewed coffee. Then I went into the living room, flopped down on the leather sofa and tracked back over everything that had happened since Alan Yip had swaggered into my office.

When I reached the part where Joe Chan had visited me last night, I realised that it was crazy; I had been hauled off the case. Why waste time on something not my concern? A smart man would bank Yip's cash and await a new client. So why did I itch to rush to Kam Sau's flat and hunt for Chan's mysterious package?

Because you're not a smart man, I could hear my wife whisper in my brain, you're a fool. Once you've got your teeth in something you never let go. I'd had to let go of her, though, despite wanting us to stay to-gether. My own stupid fault, of course; I had promised

45

to put family before career: then broken that promise as effortlessly as I had broken countless others. So ten months ago Suk Fan had upped sticks and left me. She had not demanded a divorce yet. But it wouldn't be long before the solicitor's letter landed in my mail box.

The bathroom door burst open and Kathy emerged, a pink towel draped around her hair like a Sikh's turban.

"Did you get my lobster?"

"Will you shut up about that damned lobster?"

"But did you get it?"

"It's in the fridge; what did your mother say about you staying here tonight?"

"That everything's cool," Kathy replied, as though the answer was obvious. "Why would she say anything else? You don't think she would deliberately try to screw things up between you and me, do you?

"Of course not."

"She's not like that, dad."

"I know."

I went into the kitchen and poured a cup of coffee. Kathy sloped off to her bedroom to get dressed. She emerged two minutes later in Barcelona football shirt, black jogging pants and trainers.

"Going for a run in Victoria Park," she announced.

"Take your key with you. I'll be out when you get back. And close the door quietly."

She left, slamming the door behind her so loudly that the wall shook. I drank my coffee and struggled again to work things out. But I remained as puzzled as I had been in the noodles shop. I needed Joe Chan's package. Once I had it everything would become clear.

I drained my coffee, patted my pockets to make sure they contained car keys, mobile and Swiss pocket knife, and was getting up from the sofa when the doorbell rang. I thought it was Kathy, returning to announce she had forgotten her key. It proved to be Grandfather Chow, the sixty-year-old coin dealer who lived in the flat across the corridor with his teenage grandson. Grandfather Chow stood in the doorway, looking as dignified and sincere as he always looked. But what was he doing with a football tucked under his arm?

"I have come here to make a most sincere apology, Mister Duggan," my grey-haired neighbour announced, speaking with all of his trademark formality. "My grandson Ah Yat promised to return this ball to you after one week. Yet he has kept it for many months."

Of course! I understood now. Three months ago, the old man had turned up seeking advice on how he could steer his only grandson away from street gangs. I'd been rushing out to work, so I'd not had much time to talk, but had promised to ask Frank Ching to enrol the kid in the Police Sports Club. Membership formalities would take about a week, but Ah Yat could get in some practice while he waited. I had handed over the ball, rushed off to work and forgotten all about my promise to contact Frank.

Grandfather Chow had not reminded me, of course; he was way too respectful of a person's dignity to do that. Even the slightest suggestion that I had broken my word would cause me to lose face. And for a Chinese person, especially one as old and traditional as my coin dealer neighbour, not even mass murder was as bad as losing face. That was why I couldn't mention the sports club now. Doing so would imply the old man had been stupid not to remind me about my forgetfulness weeks ago — and then he would lose face.

I said, "Thank you most kindly, grandfather. But my football days are long gone. Please keep the ball. Tell your grandson it is a gift."

"I told him to apologise in person, but he refused."

"He's shy. Perhaps he thought I would be angry."

The old man shook his head. "Not shy, Mister Duggan, disrespectful. It is the fault of the Americans and their hamburgers."

"Hamburgers?"

"American meat contains many poisons that can cause disruptive behaviour," my neighbour explained. "Since they began eating such food, all of our Chinese children have grown stubborn with their elders. When our children ate noodles they were not disrespectful. Your own daughter, I well recall, was never stubborn with her elders."

I stifled a smile. I was about to say: "Are we talking about the same girl? In an Olympics for stubbornness, Kathy would win gold." But my neighbour was such a serious and proper character that he would take the remarks the wrong way and think I was calling him a fool. I said: "Wasn't she? It's so long since she was a child that I've forgotten. But please keep the ball. Tell your grandson it's a gift."

"You do not require it yourself?"

"My football days are long gone."

"Yet you once played the game?"

"Long ago."

"And I have often heard it said that you were indeed a most exceptional player."

I hid another smile. Who had told him that? Probably me after a bottle of rice wine. He obviously hadn't spoken to any of my ex-team mates, though. Two left feet and the pace of a crippled tortoise was how one of them had described me. And he had been my closest friend on the team. No way would I say this, of course. The old man was flattering me. It would be disrespectful not to accept the flattery. I said as graciously as I could: "You are most kind. And please assure your grandson I am not angry."

"Goodbye, Mister Duggan."

"Goodbye, grandfather."

We shook hands. He turned and walked back to his flat, went inside and closed the door.

I pulled on my canvas jacket, checked my pockets again to be cast-iron sure that I had my wallet, mobile phone and keys, and then headed for the lift. I could hear Suk Fan whispering in my brain: forget this case, I have really bad feelings about it; go to your office and wait there for a new client; please, Peter, do it for me; just this once. But I closed my mind to her this time, just as I had closed it to her so many times before.

8

THE TRAFFIC PROBLEMS were even worse today than yesterday. It was a nose-to-tail crawl all the way from Tsim Sha Tsui to Sham Shui Po. It took almost forty-five minutes to get there.

If I'd thought that was rough, it was nothing compared to the parking problems that awaited me. Yesterday I'd been forced to leave the Daihatsu twenty metres away from Kam Sau's home. Today I couldn't even get that close. Workmen had begun digging up the roads to lay a new water main. The nearest I could park to Kam Sau's apartment block was two hundred metres away.

I climbed out of the car, locked the doors and started walking. I had to pass through an Urban Council playground to reach the apartment block. A group of teenagers in running vests and shorts were enjoying a game of football on the park's seven-a-side concrete pitch. Other youngsters strutted their stuff on the adjoining basketball court.

Skeletal-like grandfathers with sunken faces hunkered down on wooden benches by the sides of the football pitch and basketball court, watching all the youngsters play; dreaming of the time years ago when they too had been young enough and mad-brained enough to go charging after a football or basketball. Some of the old men clutched wooden cages. Trapped inside these cages were tiny colourful birds. Keeping such sorts of small birds is a popular hobby with a lot of the older folk in Hong Kong. Personally, I've always thought it's a bit cruel. I don't think anything should be caged up like that.

Not all the old men in the playground were sitting down. Some were standing up and performing *tai chi*, the ancient system of physical exercises that helps make Chinese pensioners some of the fittest in the world. As he completed his exercises, one silver-haired grandfather gracefully waved a wooden sword above his head.

At the far end of the playground by the exit gate, an old woman poked about in a rubbish bin with a stick. When she found a soda or beer can she crushed it underfoot then tossed it into a black plastic rubbish sack hanging from her shoulder. She looked about eighty and would probably be rooting about in rubbish bins like this for the rest of her life, because the pensions the government pays in Hong Kong are pathetically meagre. No one can survive on only a pension. The government relies on a traditional Chinese reverence for old age to solve the pensions' problem for them; it expects children and grandchildren to help to support their elderly relatives.

If you are unlucky enough to have no children or grandchildren then you either starve or do what this old woman was doing. Each flattened can would earn her a few cents when sold as scrap. When she had filled her sack, which would probably require a whole morning's back-breaking labour, she might have earned enough to buy a bowl of noodles. I gave her twenty dollars. She shot me a smile that showed she had five teeth left, and then went back to her job of poking about in the rubbish bin.

I passed though the park's exit gate and crossed the road. I was about fifty metres away from Kam Sau's apartment block when my mobile phone rang.

"Where the hell are you, dad?"

"What's wrong?"

"You've locked me out!"

"Don't you have a key?"

"Of course I do. I just had nothing better to do. So I thought I would stand outside the door looking a total idiot in my running gear while I called you."

"I said take a key, Kathy."

"The word key never passed your lips."

"You weren't listening as usual."

"I'm listening now — how do I get in?"

"Go downstairs to the lobby and see the caretaker. He keeps a spare for me. And if you go out again today, *make sure* to take the key. Are you going out?"

"I'm meeting some university friends in Sai Kung."

"Ah yes! I meant to ask last night about university."

"Ask what?"

"I'll explain later. The line's breaking up. You've forgotten to recharge your mobile again. I'll see you tonight and we'll …"

The line went dead.

THE LOBBY WAS empty. I could open Kam Sau's mailbox. I pulled out my Swiss knife, slid the blade into the gap between the sides of the mailbox and gave the knife a jerk. Bang! The sound of the flimsy lock snapping open was like that of a gun going off.

The box held a single manila envelope. I opened the envelope to find a phone bill inside. Was this what journalist Joe Chan had wanted so badly? No. Something this ordinary could not be Chan's package. The package must be inside the flat. I must have overlooked the hiding place yesterday.

I took the lift to the tenth floor. To my surprise, the old woman I had met yesterday was nowhere to be seen. Then I recalled that today was Saturday. She had said that she attended the hospital on Saturdays.

I walked down the corridor, brushing pearls of sweat from my brow. Jesus it was hot! There wasn't a gasp of breath in the air. It was so humid it felt like being inside a sauna. I halted outside Kam Sau's apartment and reached to my pocket for the key.

No need. The door lay open.

How? I had locked up last night. I was sure of it. I moved inside the flat and gasped — someone had turned it over. Furniture lay upended on the floor. The sofa and chair had been ripped apart, walls hacked away. I was puzzling over who could have done it when the bedroom door burst open and a man, probably aged about twenty-five or twenty-six, and wearing a red tee-shirt and faded jeans, emerged. He was two or three inches taller than me and a tough-looking character too. But it wasn't his height or tough appearance that made me freeze with fear.

It was the snub-nosed Colt automatic that he pointed at my chest.

9

I KNEW WHAT would happen if he fired. A bullet would rip through my chest, spinning me against the living room wall and shattering my lungs and God knows what other internal organs.

I would die slowly; people who are shot in the upper chest always do. Their faces turn blue as they struggle for breath — they choke on their own blood. Six years ago, at a shoot-out with robbers, I saw a constable get hit in the chest. Paramedics arrived quickly. They cut into his chest and inserted a plastic hose into his lungs, enabling him to breathe; the constable survived.

No paramedics would arrive for me.

People say that when you think your last moment has arrived, your past life flashes before you. It's true. As I stared down the blue-black barrel of that Colt, I thought about mother and her struggle to raise me after Paddy Duggan scuttled back to Ireland: and about the sacrifices she made to give me a happy childhood. Then about Suk Fan and the first time I saw her, and the blisteringly hot July day we married in Cotton Tree Drive registry office, and the many happy times we'd had until my bone-headed stupidity and selfishness had gone and wrecked everything: and about the daughter whom I loved most in this world: and I wondered what would become of Kathy when I was dead and gone and no longer able to protect her.

The man lowered his gun.

I breathed again.

"Who the fuck are you?" he snarled.

"I'm — I'm a friend. I — I work with Kam Sau."

"Why didn't you knock on the door?"

"I did. Only you mustn't have heard. Then I noticed … I mean the door was … So I came inside and—"

"Now you can piss off *outside!*"

He reached into his pocket and pulled out a piece of plastic the size of a bank credit card. He held the piece of plastic high in the air. "Ke Ge Bo," he announced, using the nickname for China's Secret Police. "If you're sensible, you'll leave now and forget you were here." He raised the gun. "Otherwise …"

I decided to be sensible.

I've never considered myself to be a man who scares easily. But if a scared man is someone whose heart beats hard enough to knock a three-inch hole in his chest, that was me. I was so shook up that I took a series of wrong turnings after leaving the apartment block and landed in the middle of a busy street market.

I struggled to get my bearings. The sign on the wall across the road told me I was in Ki Lung Street. Shops lined both sides of the street, which ran arrow-like straight for about a hundred metres. Shops on my left sold dried seafood, cheap clothing, CDs, electrical goods. Across the road was a butcher's, where large chunks of bleeding meat dangled from metal hooks, and a Chinese medicine shop that sold exotic stuff like dried bulls' penises and reindeer horns. You ground the bull's penis into a paste, and then added water and pieces of chicken to make a soup. The soup made you more sexually potent. At least that was the theory.

Above the shops were blocks of old houses, eight or nine storeys high, whose walls had been blackened by age. Some people had hung washing out to dry on poles which jutted from the windows of the houses.

A reek of dirty cooking oil, raw meat, chicken shit and petrol invaded my nostrils. The street resounded to the din of car horns, shop owners' sales pitches, the hits of pop star Gigi Leung. A crowd hovered by one of the shops which sold dried seafood. The crowd parted to reveal the shop's grinning owner, a balding fat man who clutched a cage containing a rat. He placed the cage on the pavement then gleefully poured a pan of boiling water over the trapped rat. It died squealing in agony, much to both his and the crowd's amusement. A lorry crammed with chickens bound for restaurant cooking pots lumbered past. I held my breath to avoid the exhaust fumes. The noises, smells, colours, confusion of the street; it all made me feel dizzy.

I staggered into the first noodles shop I came to and ordered a large cold beer, drained it in a few gulps, then instantly ordered another. I stared numbly on to the street as I drank the second bottle of *Tsingtao*, a bit more slowly this time. After about fifteen minutes the alcohol had worked its way into my blood stream. My brain returned to something like normal working order.

What role did the Ke Ge Bo play in this? Had the Secret Police ordered Alan Yip to sack me? Had that agent found Chan's package? What did the package contain? It must be something really important to get the Ke Ge Bo involved. What? I trawled my brain for answers. No good. I needed help. I phoned the man I always call when I'm in a tight spot, my friend and ex-colleague Sergeant Frank Ching.

"Are you still pals with that Ke Ge Bo guy, Frank?"

"Ah Yeung?"

"That's the one."

"We're on *fairly* good terms. Why?"

I outlined what had happened over at Kam Sau's apartment. Frank wasn't especially happy with what I told him. Anyone who has heard a bomb explode will have some idea of how he reacted.

"Calm down, Frank! You'll burst a blood vessel!"

"How can I calm down after what you said?"

"They say whisky works wonders."

"This isn't the time for your lousy jokes," Frank snapped. "Why are you mixing it with the Ke Ge Bo? You said you were looking for a girl. That this was a missing person's job."

"It is."

"Mess with those Secret Police jerks and—"

"Relax, everything is under control," I said easily. Two large cold beers had turned me once more into the fearless investigator: a man nothing and no one in this world could trouble: a super-sleuth who had conveniently forgotten that thirty minutes ago he had almost wet himself when staring down the barrel of a Colt.

"You have to quit this case, Pete."

"I can handle it."

"For your own sake and Kathy's — yes, I mean it. And for Suk Fan too. She still cares about you. And what's more …"

I sensed the start of another Frank lecture. In twenty years of working together, I'd received hundreds. It had never ceased to amaze me that although theoretically Frank's boss, I had constantly played meek husband to his nagging wife.

"I need to find out why the Ke Ge Bo are involved."

"You won't find out from me."

"I thought we were friends."

"It's *because* we're friends that I'm doing this — it's all for your own good."

"You sound just like my mother used to sound."

"And you talk just like my five-year-old son talks," Frank shot back. "Most people get a bit more sense as they grow older, but not you. Oh no! You're still as pigheaded as …"

I eased the phone a few inches away from my ear to reduce the volume level. I knew what he was like. He would go on for another half-minute, until he'd worked all of the anger out of his system. It was a waste of time trying to interrupt him. I signalled to the boss of the shop for the bill. Then I counted to ten before putting the phone back to my ear. Frank had almost finished his lecture.

"No way do I help. Not on the Ke Ge Bo."

"Forget the Ke Ge Bo," I said. "Tell me what you got from that murdered dishwasher's daughter."

"I gave you her number last night."

"I keep getting no reply."

"I still don't understand," Frank said. "How does that old woman getting strangled in the street connect with Alan Yip's missing secretary?"

The shop owner stood over me. I paid for my drinks and gave him a five-dollar tip. I said to Frank, "I'm not sure it does connect, but the two girls are good friends so the dead woman's daughter might know where Yip's secretary is holed up and … Will you help me or not?"

He uttered a weary sigh. "Doesn't matter what I say about dropping this case, does it? I could say half the Chinese army's waiting up the road to ambush you and you would still go charging on ahead."

"Finding people is what I do for a living."

He sighed again. "All right, all right, have it your way again. Just like you always do. But don't say I didn't try to warn you. I'll make some checks and see what I can dig up."

"I'll call back in an hour. Okay?"

"No," Frank said. "It's much better that we sort out something so important face to face. I'm due to finish my shift at two. Then I'm heading over to the Happy Valley track for this afternoon's race meeting. How about you drive over to see me at about three-fifteen?"

"I'll be there."

10

AN HOUR LATER, the beer-fuelled courage which had made me feel like Batman, Superman and the Incredible Hulk all rolled into one, had begun to fade.

Probably this was a good thing. Otherwise I might have been tempted to lay hands on the car of the selfish son of a bitch who had stolen my favourite parking spot, and then tried to fling the car into the harbour. Fortunately, I had sobered up sufficiently to realise my plan would fail. Not only would it make me look a jerk. It would also land me in hospital with a broken back.

I parked around the corner, about a hundred metres away from my office building. I work in a rundown part of Kennedy Town, where the tram line that runs up and down the length of Hong Kong Island grinds to a halt. It's a traditional working-class area, full of shops selling cheap fixtures and fittings for bathrooms and toilets, and places that do your laundry for you. It's almost one hundred percent Chinese. You don't see too many rich western stockbrokers wandering about there — not unless they have lost their way after a night's boozing in Wan Chai. Come to think of it, though, you don't see very many western stockbrokers wandering about anywhere in Hong Kong these days. Mind you, the place never was the great mixing pot of cultures and races that the guide books claimed it was. I remember reading one book that called it the most cosmopolitan place in the world. That's all garbage. Even fifteen years ago, when the British ran the show, there were only about a hundred thousand westerners, or *gweilos* as the locals disparagingly call them, working in Hong Kong, together with thirty-odd thousand Filipina maids and child minders and about forty thousand Indian tailors. Not really a big percentage. Not when you consider that six million Chinese were living in the place.

Foreigners are even thinner on the ground now. After China secured control of Hong Kong twelve years ago the big international banks and fund management groups relocated their Asian headquarters to Beijing or Shanghai, taking their *gweilo* staff with them. The only places where you're likely to rub up against a reasonable number of westerners these days are in the red-light bars of Wan Chai, or in the trendy restaurants of Mid Levels.

I tramped into my office block and asked Mei if I'd had any calls.

"*Aheya!* what's wrong?" she said, a concerned look on her face.

"I'm fine."

"Rubbish!" She waved her hand dismissively. "You look like you just went and saw Chairman Mao's ghost. What on earth happened to you out there?"

To those people who don't know her very well, my secretary can often seem a sarcastic soul. Appearances are deceptive, though. She might possess a look capable of turning a person to stone — she needs it when you consider some of the idiots she has to work with — but Mei isn't made of stone. While she owns a rough-and-ready tongue, you'll go a long way to find anyone with a warmer heart. In fact she is a mother hen — a female Frank Ching. I knew that the last thing I should do was tell her how that agent had pulled a gun. She would only fuss and fluster for twenty minutes.

I said, "I'm fine. What about those calls?"

"No one rang you. But the delivery men came and delivered the TV set."

"TV set?"

"You asked me to rent it for you last week," Mei said. "You told me you needed it so you could watch the all-day news channel — remember?"

It had totally slipped my mind. But I didn't want Mei to think me an even bigger fool than she already did. In the reassuring tones I use when trying to convince clients they haven't wasted their precious money hiring me, I said, "Yes, yes, of course I remember."

I could tell from her smile that she knew I was lying: she's one of those infuriating types who *always* seem to know when you're spouting rubbish. Still smiling broadly, she reached into the shopping bag on her desk and with that magical efficiency that never ceased to amaze me, pulled out a large jar of instant coffee.

"Here's another special delivery for you." She gave me the jar. "Pigs would start flying before you remembered to buy it yourself."

I leaned over and planted a noisy kiss on her fifty-six-year-old rouged cheek. "I don't know how I could survive without you. Miss Yeung! If I was only sixty years younger, and wasn't so crippled with arthritis, I would get down on one knee right here and now and ask you to marry me."

"You'd need to be at least sixty times richer before I ever accepted."

I went upstairs to the office.

The TV, complete with integrated video, rested on the desk beside my laptop — Mei must have used her spare key to let the delivery men in and then got them to unpack the TV and set it up for me.

I sat at my desk and soberly reflected on Frank's advice. He had been right to urge me to ditch the case. With the Secret Police now involved it had become dangerous. In theory, of course, the Ke Ge Bo were *not* involved because in theory no Ke Ge Bo agents operated in Hong Kong. When China took over twelve years ago, it promised Hong Kongers a large amount of autonomy and insisted that it would keep groups like the Secret Police out. But the Ke Ge Bo — the nickname derives from how Chinese people pronounce the name of another infamous Secret Police, Russia's KGB — have always been around in Hong Kong.

I had clashed with the Ke Ge Bo seven years ago, when I had investigated the shooting of a Party official in a Mongkok brothel. I'd had the backing of my department and had survived the bruising encounter, but this time would be different. I was now a private citizen, alone and defenceless, easy prey for the Secret Police. When you considered the situation logically, only someone with sawdust for brains would stick with this case.

Step forward Mister Sawdust Brain of the Year!

I tried to convince myself it was for noble reasons that I wanted to press ahead: a quest to discover the truth, a chivalrous desire to help Yip's secretary, a yearning for justice. The truth was I hate being pushed around. I was angry at the way Alan Yip had sacked me: angry at how that Ke Ge Bo agent had ordered me about: angry at myself for getting scared when he levelled his Colt at me. I wanted to show I wouldn't be pushed around. To prove no one could bully me. Frank had got it right: I was still the same pigheaded fool he had met twenty years ago.

I reached into my pocket and pulled out the phone bill I'd recovered from Kam Sau's mailbox. She had called twenty phone numbers during July. I would try them all. Hopefully, someone I called might give me a lead on her whereabouts.

One number stood out from all the rest: the only overseas connection — a UK number she had called seventeen days ago. I decided to try it first. I must have still been all shook up from that Ke Ge Bo incident because I let the phone ring for twenty seconds before realising it was pointless. Hong Kong is eight hours ahead of England. It was eleven-fifteen in the morning here. The Brits would still be sleeping.

I was about to put the phone in its cradle, when a woman said, "You have reached the constituency office of the Secretary of State for Business, Innovation and Skills, Ian Jeffries. The office is closed at the moment. It reopens on Monday at nine. To leave a message, please speak after the tone."

11

WHY PHONE IAN Jeffries?

Not on Alan Yip's behalf; she would have made a business call from the film studios. A wrong number? I examined the bill more closely. The call had lasted nine minutes. If she had phoned him by mistake she would have ended the call after only a few seconds.

No mistake on the number then. Was Jeffries linked to her disappearance? It would explain why that Ke Ge Bo agent had ransacked her flat; the Secret Police handled political matters. But if a link existed between her and Jeffries, what exactly was it?

Why not ask the man himself? If I waited for another six hours and then ... Hold on! It was now the weekend. Jeffries' secretary had said his office would be closed until Monday. Anyway, Jeffries wasn't in England. Had I not read somewhere that he was in Asia?

I dug my hands into the pile of newspapers on the floor and uncovered a copy of the *South China Morning Post*. Yes, Jeffries was in Thailand on a trade mission. He would arrive in Hong Kong the day after tomorrow, and then go to Beijing to sign a trade deal with China.

A picture of him rested beside the story. I stared at his face: a good-looking, square-jawed and masculine face. And according to what I'd read about him, Jeffries possessed charm as well as good looks and ... I jerked my gaze away. He had reminded me of someone I wanted to forget: the forty-something American lawyer who was my wife's boyfriend. The lousy, wife-stealing son of a ... I seized the newspaper, crumpled it into a ball and then hurled it into the bin by the wall.

Then I sat back, smirking. That had shown him! That had let Mister Lawyer Boyfriend know where he stood! I'd been unable to do everything I would have liked: I would have preferred it if he had been standing in front of me — that way I could have smashed his handsome, square-jawed face in. I'd still let him know the score, though. He knew now that he couldn't mess with Peter Duggan. No sir!

A car horn sounded outside to jerk me back to reality. I shook my head to rid it of insane thoughts. Carry on this way and the men in white coats would be measuring me for a strait-jacket. Throwing away my teddy bear would not bring Suk Fan back. I needed to forget her and focus on that missing secretary.

I walked over to the bin and retrieved the newspaper, smoothed out the crumpled pages and re-read the article. It didn't say which hotel Ian Jeffries was staying at in Bangkok, but most power-brokers bedded down at the Mandarin Oriental. I obtained the hotel's number from directory enquires and called it up.

"My name's Joe Chan," I told the young receptionist. "I'm a journalist covering the government minister's visit to ... Oh yes, he'll certainly take my call. He's one of my oldest and dearest friends."

After ten seconds, a man came on the line.

"I'm afraid the minister is going to be tied up in meetings for the rest of the day, Mister Chan," the man said in a warm and velvety-smooth voice. "Perhaps I can help you with your article. My name is Stephen Fung; I'm the minister's political adviser."

I decided to abandon the pretence of being Chan. Jeffries being unavailable meant that if I wanted to speak to him I would need to phone again. If Stephen Fung had discovered by then that I'd tricked him and had passed the word on to his boss, Jeffries would not be keen on helping me.

"My name isn't really Chan, it's Duggan," I said. "And I'm not a journalist, I'm a private detective."

There was a brief silence. Then Fung said, in voice that was at least five degrees cooler than it had been only a moment ago, "The receptionist assured me that you were a journalist."

"I thought you might not take my call if I told her the truth."

Another pause: followed by a loud, world-weary sigh of acceptance. "Well, I *have* taken the call, Mister Duggan. What is it that you think I can do for you?"

I explained about the call that Alan Yip's secretary had made to Jeffries' constituency office.

"I don't recognise her name," Fung said. "Are you sure you're not mistaken? What exactly is the number she rang?"

I told him.

"Strange," Fung mused.

"What is?"

"That phone number isn't for the general office. It's the ex-directory number for Ian's private line."

"You mean someone calling it would be bound to speak to Mister Jeffries?" I said. "Not to someone else in the office — someone like yourself for instance?"

"I'm not based in the constituency office," Fung said. "I work in Ian's House of Commons office."

"But you're telling me that it was definitely your boss she called?"

"No. All I'm saying is the number you've given me is for the minister's private line."

"How did she get it?"

I imagined him shrugging. "I'll check it out with Ian. If he knows anything that might be of use to you, I'll get in touch. How do I reach you?"

I gave him my number.

"I'll see what I can do for you," Fung said. "Goodbye, Mister Duggan."

I already knew basic details about Jeffries and Fung. But when you go into battle it's always wise to arm yourself with as many weapons as possible. I plugged in my computer and then did an Internet search on the minister and his young sidekick. I wanted to see if it threw up anything special on them.

It didn't. Google only offered mundane stuff. Jeffries had studied Chinese at university. Thirteen years ago he had entered politics and risen swiftly through the ranks. He was now the UK's Secretary of State for Business, Innovation and Skills. Before that he had served as the environment minister. During his stint in the environment job he had attended the global talks on climate change which had been staged three months ago in Hong Kong.

He had made the newspapers every day during the week-long conference. Yet even before then, he'd been no stranger to *Ming Pao* and the *South China Morning Post*. Partly this was because he was the UK government minister most friendly disposed to China — always urging improved trading links. However, it probably owed as much to the fact that Stephen Fung was his sidekick. Fung was a Hong Kong boy who had made good on the world stage. And Hong Kong's media loves to blow the trumpet for local boys made good. It didn't seem to matter that Fung was *no longer* a local boy. At the tender age of eleven he'd been packed off to boarding school in London and had remained in England for twenty years.

Fung's dad still lived here, though: Szeto Fung was a famous Hong Kong figure — or would *notorious* be a better description of him? Yes, it would be a much better description. Because he owned a large chain of jewellery stores, newspapers and magazines called him the 'Jeweller King'. According to his '*official*' biography, after arriving in Hong Kong as a penniless refugee forty-odd years ago, Szeto Fung had worked as a coolie on Kennedy Town's waterfront.

He had soon decided there was more to life than breaking your back lugging around sacks of rice and grain. Gathering his nine-hundred dollars in savings, he had headed for Happy Valley race track and staked the lot on a fifty-to-one no-hoper which romped home. He invested his winnings and one triumph led to another. Before you could say the words, 'diamond bracelet', he had been crowned Hong Kong's 'Jeweller King'.

According to rumours on the street, though, Szeto had joined the 14K Triad when a teenager. Extortion, armed robbery and the odd cold-blooded murder, not any great skills as a judge of horse flesh, had enabled him to grow as rich as Croesus. None of the rumours had been proved, of course. And you should never pass the sins of the father on to the son, I reminded myself. Just because some people say Szeto is a Triad boss it doesn't mean that his kid is a gangster. Sons are often very different from their fathers. Take yourself, for example. Paddy Duggan was a drunken waste of space: a total and utter jerk: whereas you …

Yes, well … Anyway, I should focus on Stephen Fung, not me. And while he might not be a Triad boss, he shared at least one of his father's characteristics. He was deadly ambitious — he'd said as much himself in one recent magazine interview. He was not content just to be a mere adviser to a government minister. He had a burning desire to become a minister himself.

How had that missing secretary obtained Jeffries' number? Had they met when he came to Hong Kong for the climate talks? Had Alan Yip given the number to her? Maybe I'd got it wrong before. I had assumed that because Kam Sau had phoned Jeffries' office from her home it must have been a personal call. But perhaps she had phoned from home on behalf of her boss. Maybe she was one of these eager-beavers who liked to take work home with them. There was an easy way to discover the truth. I got up and set off to see Alan Yip.

12

WHEN I GOT outside, I changed my mind.

It would be better to delay meeting Yip; at least for a few hours. My Internet search had only given me government minister Ian Jeffries' authorised biography. If a sinister reason existed for that phone call which Yip's secretary had made to Jeffries' office in Britain, then I would need the unauthorised version of his life story. The one that contained all of the half-truths and innuendo which the newspapers didn't dare print.

I pulled the mobile phone from my pocket and rang my journalist friend, Jack Spalding. If any unsavoury rumours about Jeffries existed, then Jack would have heard them. Surprise, surprise, Jack wasn't sitting at his desk in the *South China Morning Post*'s office, tapping out news stories for tomorrow's front page — he was propping up the bar in The Foreign Correspondents Club and knocking back ice-cold lager.

THE FOREIGN CORRESPONDENTS Club sits at the top of a hill a hundred metres or so from the banks and office towers of the Central business district.

I pushed open the swing doors and sighed with relief as I stepped into the club's air-conditioned comfort. I brushed beads of sweat from my brow, eased a sticking shirt from my skin; the past couple of hours had seen the humidity level soar. Despite only walking forty or fifty metres from where I had parked the Daihatsu, I was soaked.

Jack hailed me from his place by the bar in a loud, rasping voice that could have ripped open a can of his beloved Foster's at thirty-five paces.

"Over here, your highness! Over here!"

In case I was the only person in a five-mile radius who hadn't heard him, he waved his Chinese People's Liberation Army cap in the air, a general urging troops into battle. I shuffled across to the oval-shaped bar. Jack got up off his stool and made a little bow to me then threw out his arm in a courtly flourish.

"Park your arse, your majesty!"

He was so small that, stood up like this, he barely managed to peer over the top of the bar. Painfully skinny too: it never ceased to amaze me how, despite swallowing beer like a dehydrated fish and wolfing food enough for a man twenty times his size, Jack remained as light as a Happy Valley jockey.

"So how are we faring today, your lordship — a wee bit on the warm side out there in the street, wouldn't you agree?" He chucked his Chinese army cap on the bar and then ran a mottled hand through grey-ginger hair whose unruliness showed he still hadn't heard of the comb's invention. "Jeez! It must be four degrees hotter than the inside of a dingo's arse! Two of your biggest and coldest beers for me and my sweating comrade, Ah Yan," he instructed the elderly barman, "and another double Johnnie Walker chaser for your favourite uncle here."

He was dressed as elegantly as ever: tartan waistcoat, baggy khaki shorts, lime-green shirt, orange bow-tie. The clothing sent the loud-and-clear message: this man is different. Jack was now aged fifty-six, but a long love affair with the whisky bottle had ravaged his complexion so much that he looked more like seventy. His face, apart from a long and sharply pointed nose, was the colour of bruised apples and people who didn't know him well could have been forgiven for thinking he had a bad case of sunburn. Jack's nose gave the game away, though. It was a vivid purple — except on days when he'd been hitting the bottle extra hard. On those days the nose turned dark blue and swelled up so much at the tip that it would not have surprised me if it had suddenly exploded. Today was one of those days. Jack had probably been boozing all of last night then started again when he had woken up this morning.

We had first met twenty years ago. In fact our initial meeting had taken place in this very bar. In those days Jack had freelanced for the American magazines, *Time* and *Newsweek*. Now he wrote features for the local *South China Morning Post*.

"And make sure that both of those beers are *ice* cold, wing commander," Jack ordered our barman. "What's that? … No, you daft old bastard, of course I don't want any ice in the whisky. It spoils the bloody taste."

The barman poured my beer. I waited a moment for the creamy head to settle, then pressed the frosted glass against my face and let it cool me, before seizing a long, thirst-quenching gulp. Ah! that was good. The beer was so cold that it stung the back of my throat.

Jack raised his whisky glass high in a toast: "To all the world's drunkards!" He drained the glass and then wiped his lips with the back of one hand. He tilted his head slightly to one side and surveyed me with rheumy, sea-green eyes. "So, squire, how can Uncle Jack help this time?"

"I need the inside track on Ian Jeffries."

"*The* Ian Jeffries?"

"The same."

Jack contemplatively stroked stubble on his pointed chin. Either he had decided to start growing a beard, or more likely, he had forgotten to shave again.

"And why are we keen on digging up dirt on that particular joker, if you don't mind me humbly asking, your worship?"

I explained about Yip's secretary.

"I got the official line from newspapers on the Internet, but it's the unofficial version I want — what the papers won't print."

"Who says there *is* an unofficial version?"

"All these big-shots have some skeletons hiding in their closets." I reached over and clapped him encouragingly on his bony shoulder. "And if *anyone* knows where to find those skeletons, that man is my good and trusted friend, Jack Spalding — if scandalous rumours about Jeffries exist, Hong Kong's best journalist will be sure to know about them."

Jack has always adored flattery — the more outrageous the better — so he lapped all this up. Then he raised a finger to his lips and glanced furtively from side to side — he's always been keen on melodrama too. Satisfied no Secret Police officers lurked behind the beer taps ready to leap out and arrest us, he grabbed his cap and beer, and then ushered me to a table where we could talk without fear of us being overheard.

Not that such heavy security was necessary. Only two others sat in the club, a middle-aged westerner with a goatee and brick-red face, and his young Filipina girlfriend. Both of these looked so plastered that they would struggle even to remember their own names when they sobered up, never mind anything that Jack and I discussed.

"I *might* have something for you," Jack said in a teasing sort of voice after we had both sat down. "When the London hacks came over here for that big climate conference, I heard one particularly juicy story."

I waited in vain for him to tell me. He only tapped the side of his nose, the way he always does when showing you how amazingly clever he is. It's always the same gesture: tap, tap, tap; three times exactly. And it irritates me like crazy; I instinctively want to batter him senseless. But I would get no answers to my questions with Jack slumped half-dead over his beer. To succeed I needed to flatter him and make him think I wanted nothing more in life than to hear his tale.

I said earnestly, "I'm all ears."

He leaned closer, as though about to confide a vital state secret; his voice fell to a husky whisper.

"According to a journo on *The Times,* your mate Ian puts it about a fair bit — if you get my meaning." Jack tapped his pointed blue nose knowingly: "Goes for the classy-looking Asian birds too." Another tap of the nose: "Rumour has it that on one junket to Beijing he even screwed a high-up in China's Defence Ministry!" Jack gave his nose a third tap: "Got clean away too! But even if they'd found him with his pants around his ankles, those Chinese jokers would have done sod all about it — they love him on account of all the stuff he spouts about China being so wonderful and that trade deal he's going there to sign."

"Did Jeffries put it about much during that climate change conference?"

Jack shrugged: "Can't really say, your majesty, seeing as I wasn't in his bedroom at the time. Leopards don't usually change their spots, though, do they? I mean, take your uncle here. He still puts it about, doesn't he?"

I almost choked on my beer. Jack was such a crumbling physical wreck it was only his clothes that held the different parts of his body together: if he ever got undressed to 'put it about' he would fall apart.

"How about Jeffries' sidekick?"

"Young Master Fung?"

"What do you know about him?"

"I know he's a clever sod." Jack took a swig of beer then wiped foam from his lips. "I also know he's really close to Jeffries too — got a hell of a lot more clout than any adviser his age would normally have. A bit of a power behind the throne from what I hear; a Jekyll and Hyde too."

"Jekyll and Hyde?"

"One minute he was all lovey-dovey with me; next minute he wanted to break my bloody neck."

I said with some surprise, "You've interviewed him?"

Jack shook his head. "I interviewed his dad."

"When?"

"Six months ago when he was calling for a crackdown on street crime." Jack gave a snort of laughter. "Can you believe the bloody nerve of it? The 14K Triad boss demands *more* police action! But he was wearing

76

his other hat on the day I met him — he was playing the role of 'Mister Responsible Businessman'."

"Where does breaking your neck come into it?"

"Old man Fung always keeps hacks like me hanging around for half an hour just to put us in our place," Jack explained. "While I'm kicking my heels outside in the lobby, waiting for an audience with his Imperial Majesty, Fung junior comes waltzing out of his dad's office."

"What was he like?"

"Full of the joys of friendship at first. Said his old man would be busy for another half an hour, so why not wait in the VIP lounge? Junior's one of the new breed, see; likes to keep us hacks happy. Anyway, once we're in the lounge, he says to grab the crystal decanter and pour myself a whisky."

"And you did, of course?"

Jack grinned. "I tried to. The problem was that I'd already poured a few too many up here in the club, so my hands ... To cut a long story, I dropped the fucking decanter and it smashed into a zillion and one pieces."

"Fung wasn't happy?"

"If there'd been another decanter close by, he'd have brained me with it. Course, he had to *pretend* it was all right — like I say, he wants to be mates with ..."

Jack stopped talking as the door in the corner burst open and two men lugging beer crates stumbled into the club. They hauled the crates to the bar and left them for the barman to unstack. The sight of the new booze reminded Jack his own beer was unfinished. He drained his glass and was hollering out for refills, when he stopped suddenly and asked the time.

"Just gone twelve," I said.

"Jeez! I'm due to be meeting someone off the Star Ferry at five past."

"I'll drive you down," I said. "We can talk more about Jeffries in the car."

But the rumour he had told me in the club was the only one that he knew. Had Ian Jeffries 'put it about' with Alan Yip's secretary? It would explain her knowing his private phone number.

"Put the air con on," Jack said. "It's like a sauna."

"The air con's on."

"Well turn the bloody thing up higher, before I die of heat stroke."

I turned the air conditioning higher. I moved the Daihatsu off a traffic-packed Ice House Street and steered left on to an equally traffic-packed Des Voeux Road. We got stuck behind a double-decker bus. On the back of the bus was a huge picture of a young man who wore a snappy business suit and had spiky, jelled hair. The headline above him said his name was Alan Liu and assured students that he would get them all top grades in their exams — provided they gave him large wads of cash.

You saw these sorts of advertisements everywhere these days: on the backs of buses, on TV screens inside the buses; plastered all over the walls of MTR stations. There was no escape. Last week I'd seen a sixty-foot-long poster of one of Alan's friends hanging from the wall of the Langham Place shopping mall in Mongkok. It amazed me that people could be daft enough to surrender their hard-earned cash to Alan and his spiky-haired pals. Most so-called 'exam experts' looked like they hadn't even finished school let alone university. People did hand cash over, though. Massive amounts of it. A newspaper had recently revealed that characters like Alan could make *one million* dollars a month! I was in the wrong job.

I steered right on to Pedder Street. The bus carrying Alan continued down Des Voeux Road.

"Read about that dead journalist, Jack?"

"Joe Chan?"

"Know him?"

"I knew him."

"Friend of yours?"

Jack shook his head: "Just a joker who came into the newsroom every now and then to try and flog us some pictures. But he did most of his work for the Chinese-language rags."

I parked close to the International Finance Centre, which at four hundred and fifteen metres high is Hong Kong's tallest building. Big is not necessarily beautiful, though. The finance centre is the ugliest skyscraper on the waterfront.

"I'll have to love you and leave you," Jack said.

"Why the rush?"

"I need to wait over by the ferry exit. That's where I'm supposed to be meeting my mate."

"You'll melt. It's like the Sahara out there."

"It's not exactly the North Pole inside here," Jack complained. "Can't you turn that bloody air-con of yours any higher?"

I already had it running at a level cool enough to give an eskimo goose bumps. To keep Jack happy, I turned it up another notch. I said, "Do you know if Chan was working on anything special?"

Jack frowned. "Special?"

"Like a major investigative story?"

His look said my question was the daftest anyone had ever asked him.

"No bloody way!"

"Why so sure?"

"His sort never does *real* news stories."

"*Real* stories?"

"He was one of those jerks who did celebrity bullshit," Jack sneered; "soap-opera jokers getting pissed, or screwing a mate's bird — the same Peeping Tom garbage he shot before getting into newspapers."

"What do you mean, *before* getting into newspapers?"

"He worked for that dodgy surveillance agency," Jack said, "the one whose boss got three years for blackmail."

"Soong Corp?"

"The very same, your majesty."

Soong Corp had specialised in filming the amorous misdeeds of adulterous wives and husbands. Business had boomed until the firm's bosses had become too greedy. Why surrender videos to the aggrieved husbands and wives who had hired Soong Corp to spy on their partners? Surely it made better sense to hand over the evidence to the cheating partners themselves: providing, of course, that the cheating partners handed over large amounts of money in return.

"There he is!" Jack pointed through the windscreen at a short, squat figure in a pink tee-shirt: "My mate!"

I rested a hand on his shoulder. "Hold on, I've got a few more questions I need to ask you."

Jack pushed my hand away. "Relax, Lord Peter!" He yanked open the car door, ushering in air hot enough to fry eggs. "I'll be back in five minutes — scout's honour! But first your uncle has a bit of business to discuss."

His shoulders swaying like those of a bantamweight boxer he walked, or rather he swaggered, thirty metres over to where the man in the pink tee-shirt stood by the harbour wall. Jack had called the man a friend, although it didn't look that way to me. After Jack had offered a handshake which was sullenly rejected, the man began shouting and gesticulating. He shoved Jack in the chest. Then he shoved him again, more violently. If he was Jack's mate, I was the Queen of Sheba.

I turned off the car's ignition and pulled my keys from the lock. I opened the car door and got out. The man in the pink tee-shirt pushed Jack again: this was all starting to look very nasty. I began walking towards them. Jack held up his hands in surrender. This failed to stop the man in the pink tee-shirt.

The man threw a punch.

Jack tried to dodge it but was too slow. The punch caught him flush on the jaw and sent him sprawling. I quickened my stride. Jack's assailant thrust an empty hand into his hip pocket. When his hand re-emerged from the pocket it was no longer empty. Something squat, black and deadly was in it.

"Jack! Jack! He's got a gun!"

13

THE SOUND OF the shot came before the gun-flash. At least I think it did; it's hard to be sure when everything happens so quickly. In response to my warning, Jack had begun struggling to his feet. He was half-crouching, half-standing when the gunman fired. The shot slammed him to the pavement, where his body shook for a moment before going still.

Then the gunman turned on me, right hand extended in front of him. His snub-nosed, blue-black Makarov pistol pointed squarely at my chest. He stood only five metres away. He couldn't miss. Or so my brain said. Yet sometimes, even when your brain says it's the end, your body battles for survival. In an effort to ruin his aim, I used the only weapon I had — I threw my car keys at him.

Then dived for the floor.

Bang! Bang!

I hit the ground: rolled to my right: tried to get as far away from him as possible. The windows of a bus behind me shattered — had throwing my car keys spoilt his aim, or was he just a bad shot? A woman screamed. Maybe that was what made him run: before her scream alerted police.

Or perhaps he had no more bullets left.

Whatever the reason, when I glanced up he was sprinting to the ferry entrance. The gun lay by the harbour wall: he had tried to chuck it in the sea, but hadn't chucked it far enough. Should I dash to the wall and grab the gun — if the magazine still had bullets in it I could force him to stop. But supposing the magazine was empty? By the time I'd snatched up the gun he would have put another thirty metres between us.

I left the pistol and sprinted after him.

He shoved past an old couple, nearly bundling the woman to the ground, then charged up the passageway which led to the ferry. Yelling at bystanders to get out of my way, I dashed after him.

A hooter sounded to tell passengers that the ferry had docked.

The gunman vaulted over the ticket barrier.

He was about fifteen metres ahead of me.

I ran faster.

A bell rang to announce the ferry was ready to board.

I vaulted over the turnstile, sprinted for the ramp that led down to the boat. The ramp was steep and slippery. To negotiate it safely I needed to slow down. But if I did that I might never catch the gunman. I kept running. I lost my balance and fell. By the time I had picked myself up, the churning of the ferry's propeller blade told me it was leaving.

The gunman was on board. He would escape to Kowloon. Jack would be unavenged and … No! Hold on! I still had a chance. The ferry had only begun to pull away — the gap between pier and ferry was just a metre or so. If I jumped I could grab the passenger handrail that ran around the sides of the ferry. I could haul myself up and over the rail. Then drop safely onto the ferry's deck and tackle Jack's killer.

Yes. I could do it. One little jump, and then …

Looking back, I realise it was crazy. A sane person would have phoned the police. They would have been waiting for the ferry at Kowloon. When adrenaline surges through you, though, it's hard to act like a sane person. Rage over Jack's shooting had sent adrenaline roaring through me like a Niagara Falls torrent.

I jumped.

For one terrifying instant as I hung in the air, arms outstretched like a trapeze artist, ready to grab hold of the passenger rail, I thought I wouldn't make it; I would be crushed between the pier and boat, or plunge into the harbour and get churned into pulp by the propeller.

Then my hands gripped something cold and hard.

The handrail!

I seized a breath, summoned up my strength. My plan would work. In a moment, I would drop onto the deck. I had Jack's killer trapped. All I need do was to get over the passenger rail and …

I couldn't do it!

The handrail was too slippery — like a bar of well-lathered soap. I tried to grip it tighter for more leverage. No good. My grip grew weaker, my fingers slid away from the metal: one hold had gone entirely now, I clung on with only my right hand — the strain felt unbearable. In a moment I would lose my hold completely. I would plunge into the sea.

Then someone's hand gripped me by my left wrist. Another hand seized my right wrist. I was hauled up and over the rail like a sack of rice and dumped on the deck. I picked myself up and stared into the faces of my two rescuers. They were unimpressed by my exploits.

"What the fuck were you doing, pal?"

"You stupid bastard!"

Mumbling thanks and assuring them they would both forever be in my prayers, I pushed past them and scanned the boat for the man in the pink tee-shirt. I couldn't see him, but he must be here somewhere. People did not simply vanish into thin air. Then I realised what had happened. He had removed his tee-shirt. He was the man in the white vest. The one stood by the handrail at the front of the boat, pretending to admire the view. He stopped gazing at the waterfront, turned and shot a look at me: it was definitely him. I never forget a face. Especially when that face belongs to a man who has pointed a gun at my head.

I walked towards him. No need for me to rush. He was going nowhere. Or was he? The look he had just cast to the shore hinted that he might dive overboard and swim back to Hong Kong.

He didn't.

He rushed me.

I tried to give him a matador-type shuffle and to slip inside his charge. I was too slow. His shoulder bull-dozed into my chest, making me grunt as he knocked air out of me and drove me against a bin which crashed to the floor, spewing out its load of cans and bottles.

I heard the crunch of breaking glass as I stepped on a bottle. I tried to jam my fingers in his eyes, to knee him in the groin. No good. My stiffened fingers jabbed air, my knee hit his thigh. Then his leg was behind mine and he was shoving hard at my chest; and I was falling, landing painfully on my back; and groups of passengers were jumping up and down and screaming, but doing nothing to help me.

I tried to get up. But he jumped on top of my chest and I couldn't move. My shoulders were clamped to the deck; his oily hair was in my eyes; his hot, stinking breath gusting over me.

Where was the crew? Why didn't they stop him?

"Help! Help!"

Then I couldn't shout — I could only gasp for breath as strong hands seized me by the throat. I struggled to push him off. Impossible. No way could I break that iron grip. I began to choke. My hands flailed at the deck, searching desperately for a bit of extra leverage, for something that might help me push him off. No good. He was too powerful for me. The grip on my throat grew even stronger. I began to drift into unconsciousness.

Quick, quick! I screamed silently, as I continued to flail uselessly at the deck. Pull him off!

Then my hand no longer flailed the splintered wood of the ferry's deck. It hit something smooth and cold — something made of glass, something which even a brain half-starved of oxygen realised was a bottle — it must have spilled from the bin I had knocked over.

I seized hold of the bottle as eagerly as a drowning man clutching a lifebelt and then slammed it against the side of his skull. The bottle exploded like a grenade, sending glass splinters flying into the air. Blood spurted from a gash by his right ear. The grip on my throat vanished. I tried again to push him off. But although he was now unconscious, I still couldn't manage it; all of my reserves of strength had gone.

Then two crewmen were doing the job; now that there was no possibility of either of them getting injured, they had bravely galloped to my aid.

The crewmen helped me get up. My legs shook. I felt so light-headed that the boat started to spin: backwards, and then sideways, and then backwards again; all of the different colours: blues, greens and browns, merging into a white so pure and dazzling that it nearly blinded me. For a moment I thought I might faint.

The moment passed. I staggered to the handrail and vomited over the side.

FORTY MINUTES LATER I sat in the police station opposite Chief Inspector Ho, a man I knew from fifteen years back when we had both been sergeants with the Organised Crime and Triad Bureau.

Ho's chair looked ready to snap under the weight of his two hundred and thirty pound frame. Rolls of fat insulated his stomach. When he raised a flabby hand to scratch his right ear, I saw that his grey shirt had turned black with sweat underneath the armpits.

"You're *sure* about all this?" I eyed him doubtfully. "Jack's definitely going to be all right?"

Instead of answering me, Ho levered himself from the swivel chair, then reached over to the wall and straightened a framed photograph. It showed him shaking hands with China's deputy leader in Beijing's Great Hall of the People. Fifteen years ago, a different picture had held pride of place on the wall — Ho meeting Hong Kong's British Governor. Now that China ran the show here, though, Ho preferred not to broadcast how he had once sucked up to the colonial rulers. He liked to pretend all his *kowtowing* had been a masterful charade; he'd really been a secret Communist Party member.

I said, "Who told you he'll recover; the doctor?"

Ho finished rearranging the picture. With an effort that made him sweat more profusely, he squeezed back into the chair. He wiped his greasy face with a handkerchief. "Go to the top of the class, bright boy. Of course it was the doctor." He threw his crumpled blue handkerchief on the desk. "That bullet missed Spalding's heart — but only just. Five millimetres more to the left and your *gweilo* friend would be history."

"What about that character who shot him?"

"Eight stitches in his head — but he'll live."

"Are you going to tell me why he did it?"

I fully expected him to say no. During our days at the Organised Crime and Triad Bureau, Ho had never gone out of his way to help me. He had been as keen on doing me favours as he had been on being run over by a number nine bus. He had sneered about my mixed-race parentage: behind my back he had called me *jap jung*, a mixed-race bastard. So why help me now, when I was no longer a police officer?

To my amazement, he gave me the full story.

"Spalding was writing some articles about a teenage hooker racket and spoke to a kid who wanted out of the hooker business — her brother is that character whose head you split open. Spalding promised to get the kid out of Hong Kong but he didn't. The 14K learnt that she'd spilled the beans to him and … A bright boy like yourself can guess the rest."

"Dead?"

"Hauled from the harbour yesterday morning," Ho said matter of factly.

I frowned. I said slowly, "Why tell *me*?"

Ho leaned over and jabbed the intercom on his desk.

"The usual extra-large milky coffee with three large sugars for your favourite policeman, Ada my sweetheart," he cooed to his secretary like some love-struck teenager. "Although on second thoughts, hold that third sugar — I'm so naturally sweet I only need two."

As an afterthought, Ho asked me if I wanted anything. I shook my head. He told Ada sweetheart to be quick, and not to forget those two large sugars. Then he switched off the intercom and sat more upright in his swivel chair. He folded his flabby arms across his flabby guts and tried to look business-like.

"I've told you about Spalding for a reason," he said. "I don't want you getting fancy theories about him. I don't want you screwing around with stuff you should leave alone and causing us problems. We've got enough trouble with the 14K in Mongkok without you causing more: the brother blamed Spalding for his sister and shot him — end of story." Ho leaned forward. His bulk threw a shadow on the desk. The chair groaned under him. He eyed me in menacing silence for a moment. Then he said, "Unless, of course, you've *already* got a fancy theory you want to enlighten me with."

I had a hunch that he had not related the full story about Jack: sneaky types like Ho always hide *something*. But when you're sitting in a closed room with a sixteen-stone thug who's as fond of you as he is of a dose of gonorrhea, and who would love an excuse to rearrange your face, it pays to be diplomatic.

"I haven't got any fancy theories," I said. "I'm sure everything happened exactly how you say it did."

14

RUBBER BURNED AGAINST asphalt.

The town of Sha Tin flashed past. Apartment windows winked in soft pink-yellow moonlight. On the car radio, pop star Joey Yung crooned her new hit. The driver of the Mercedes shot another nervous glance in his rear-view mirror then pressed harder on the accelerator. The lights of Sha Tin became a distant silvery blur as the Mercedes sped faster down Tolo Highway.

Tolo Highway links Kowloon's teeming concrete jungle to the Chinese border some thirty kilometres away and cuts a swathe through what the local tourist guides, in an effort to create a mysterious aura for the place, have christened 'The Land Between'. This is the New Territories, a sprawl of farming villages, container terminal depots and towns crammed full of high-rise apartments, which all motorists must drive through before they reach China.

In the daytime, Tolo Highway is packed full of traffic. Lorries trundle up to the Chinese border laden down with cargo, some of it legal and some of it illegal; taxis ferry passengers between villages and new towns;

tour buses transport visitors to 'The Land Between'. Petrol fumes shimmer in the sticky air, horns blare as drivers become frustrated by long traffic jams in steamy heat. Curses are exchanged, fists shaken in anger.

At night, traffic jams disappear. On some stretches of Tolo Highway, far from the bright lights and high-rise apartments, swaddled by a thick, velvety blackness, you rarely encounter another car. At times like this, it is possible to feel you are the only person alive on the planet; which was how the driver of the Mercedes felt right now.

Alone and afraid.

He threw another anxious glance in his mirror. The long, straight road behind him remained empty. No one was following. What the hell had happened to the back-up unit? When he had contacted headquarters on the radio ten minutes ago they had assured him a back-up team was heading at full speed down the highway.

Where was it?

Should he pull over to the side of the road and wait? No. It might not be the back-up team which arrived first; it might be those Triad thugs. It would be safer to keep moving.

The Mercedes' speedometer needle moved to seventy-five as the driver pressed his foot even harder against the accelerator. Up above, the crescent-shaped moon nudged behind a cloud. The sky darkened.

Then the bomb exploded: everything went white.

The diver slammed on the brakes. The car screeched to a halt. The driver's door burst open and the driver jumped out, dragging a Colt .45 semi-automatic from his shoulder holster — he fired twice, his attackers who had exploded the bomb fired back at him. Bullets rattled the Mercedes' silver skin. The bullets ruptured the fuel tank. There was a reek of petrol. A dull click as though a cigarette lighter had failed to ignite.

The car burst into flames.

Before any of the flames could reach the driver he leaped high into the air, somersaulted over the blazing car and landed safely some five metres away.

The director yelled, "Cut!"

Workers armed with fire extinguishers jogged on to the film set. They sprayed foam over the burning car, killing the flames. Smells of burning rubber and plastic replaced that of leaking gasoline. The black-out curtains on the indoor set, which had been drawn to simulate night-time, were hauled back. Light flooded in.

"Wow!" exclaimed the tall and extremely excitable young man who was standing next to me. He was supposed to be escorting me to film producer Alan Yip's office, but had insisted on us pausing here to watch this new blockbuster being shot. "Totally terrific! Oh yes indeed! Wow! This film crew — they really know their job, Mister Duggan."

I noticed that my guide had attracted as much attention from the film crew as he was paying to them. He had the worst pock-marked face I've ever seen, but this wasn't the reason why crew members stared at him as though he had landed from another planet: it was his clothes. If ever there was a walking fashion disaster, then it was walking here beside me today. He wore baggy white pants, a shocking-pink shirt and a black-and-white spotted bow-tie. To say he cut something of a comic figure was putting it mildly: that bow-tie of his only had to start spinning and he would become Coco the Clown.

"Made you feel you were in the Mercedes yourself," enthused my guide. "Oh yes indeed! Then that explosion and somersault! Wow! We employ acrobats from China's circus to do all that leaping stuff, you know."

I struggled to feign interest: "Really?"

"Oh yes indeed!"

I glanced at my watch: almost two-thirty. I had planned to arrive here half an hour ago, but had made a detour to the library to check Chief Inspector Ho's story about Jack. Life is a complicated business, so I'm wary when something seems too neat. Ho's explanation about Jack's shooting had been as neat as a pressed suit. Then there was his reason for giving me the explanation. All that stuff he had told me about wanting to avoid trouble with Hong Kong's gangs didn't wash. Ho knew that I would never have caused problems with the 14K — I valued my health too much.

Why had he done it?

To find out, I had checked issues of the *South China Morning Post*. To my surprise, I had discovered that Ho *had* told the truth — Jack had written articles about child prostitution and fishermen had dragged a girl's body from the harbour yesterday. You're too suspicious, Peter, I told myself. Dislike of Ho shouldn't blind you to the fact he's a fellow professional who ...

"And once Mister Yip's gone and edited those shots, that driver won't just be jumping *two* metres in the air!" my guide announced. "Oh no! He'll go and jump twenty! Oh yes indeed — do eight or nine somersaults too! Mister Yip's a master of the production room, see. Mister—"

"I need to see your boss," I interrupted. "I need to see Mister Yip urgently."

He gazed at me, puzzled. "I thought ... Oh! You think Mister *Alan* Yip's my boss."

"He isn't?"

My guide shook his head. "I work for his son, John. Matter of fact, I'm not supposed to be guiding you today. But ... Well, I'm keen on learning all parts of the business ... When we're short-staffed at the studios ... Well I like to help out as much as possible."

"I need to get in touch with Mister Yip *urgently*," I told him. "Mister *Alan* Yip."

"No problems," my guide assured me, raising one hand in a gesture that told me to relax. "The office is just round the corner. But I knew you wouldn't want to miss seeing an Alan Yip film being made — it's what everyone who visits the studios wants to see."

Everyone but me: I've always found Yip's films as engaging as a trip to the dentist. I didn't tell my guide, though. I wanted to keep him sweet in case I needed his help later. Besides, it obviously made him happy to think that everyone shared his wild enthusiasm for Yip's junk. Why shatter his illusions?

"Of course, they're all surprised not to see characters from the Ming Dynasty wandering around here," my guide continued. "No heroes in long flowing silk robes battling evil landlords with swords, I mean — people kind of expect that ancient stuff from a *kung fu* film, huh? But Mister Yip — he's changing all those perceptions with his great special effects. Oh yes indeed! He's hauling *kung fu* films into the ... What did you think about the shot yourself?"

"Wonderful! Mister Yip is a true master of his art."

He clapped his hands in delight. "I knew you'd love it!" He pointed to a door. "We go in through here."

We climbed a stone staircase to the second floor and then tramped up a carpeted corridor that was lined on either side with large framed pictures. Not of actors and actresses, though. These walls were crammed with shot after shot of Alan Yip. There was Alan Yip the ace director, standing calm and masterful behind a camera; Alan Yip the genius producer, busy in the editing room; Alan Yip the victorious, belly straining against his dinner jacket as he swaggered forward to collect an award. I scanned the walls for pictures of him with the British government minister Ian Jeffries, but saw none.

My guide pointed to an oak-panelled door situated at the end of the corridor. "There's the office; that one over there. We …"

He stopped chatting as Yip's office door burst open and a thickset, middle-aged man barreled out into the corridor. He appeared so fast and suddenly it seemed that he must have been catapulted from the office.

"Yes, sir — it won't ever happen again," the man stammered as he stood in the doorway, his shaven brown head bobbing up and down like that of an out-of-control marionette. "And I'll handle that other thing now — yes, sir. I'll get with it immediately, Mister Yip."

He closed the door and heaved a huge sigh of relief. He wiped his sweating face with a handkerchief then tried to light a cigarette, but his hand shook so much he couldn't get his lighter working.

"So," my guide asked him cheerily. "How did your interview with the boss go?"

The man stiffened. "Are you being funny, pal?"

"No, no. I—"

"He's spitting blood! Some administrative prick who was supposed to be helping out Unit Four went and screwed up Monday's bank shoot-out scene. The whole thing needs to be re-shot. When the chief finds out who's responsible …"

The thickset man shuddered at the thought. He moved past us and headed down the corridor. I glanced over at my guide, whose boundless enthusiasm had vanished as suddenly and dramatically as yesterday's typhoon. He resembled someone who had just been told he had hours to live; his face had turned ghostly white, sweat stood out on his pimpled brow. You didn't need to be Sherlock Holmes to deduce who was the administrative prick who had screwed up with Unit Four.

I took pity on him. "No need to introduce me, I'll sort it all out myself." I winked conspiratorially. "Scoot back to work. Keep your head down and with luck it'll soon blow over."

He set off down the corridor.

I knocked on Yip's office door. No answer. I recalled how he had barged into my office uninvited. The least I could do was to return the compliment. I shoved the oak-panelled door open.

15

TO CALL THE office merely big would do it injustice;
it was roughly twice the size of China's Great Hall of
the People. At the far end someone I assumed was Yip
— the distance made it hard to be sure without binocu-
lars — sat at a desk.

I ploughed across what must have been about an
acre of deep-pile carpet, so lush that it felt like quick-
sand, until I drew close enough to see it was indeed the
great man. Behind him, a row of TV screens showed
the action that was taking place on different parts of the
film set: technicians tinkering with cameras and checking lighting and sound systems, actors rehearsing their
lines, stuntmen going over tricky martial arts moves. A
microphone stood to attention in front of Yip, who
spoke into it, oozing charm to the workforce.

"No, no, you dumb bastard, that's not it. How many
times must I say it, you totally useless piece of garbage?
If I've told you once, I've …"

I plonked myself down on a chair by his desk and
waited for the diatribe to end. I glanced around the
room. The pale yellow walls contained the same sort of

pictures that I'd glimpsed outside. On Yip's polished desk stood a bottle of cognac, wooden cigar box and silver ash-tray — so it was all right for him to dump ash on *my* carpet, but not on his own.

He finished haranguing his staff, switched off the microphone and turned to me.

"What do *you* want, Duggan?"

I said calmly, "To report to you on the state of the investigation, of course."

He leaned over the desk and hit me with a smell of after shave that was strong enough to sink a battleship. He leaned so close I thought for a moment he might be going to take a swing at me. But the wooden cigar box not my face was his target. He opened the box and pulled out a Havana. He sniffed at the Havana and stroked it, weighed it first in his left hand then his right, rolled it between his fingers, tapped it on the desk; about the only thing he didn't do was make love to it.

Then he growled, "You're no longer on the case."

I feigned surprise. "I don't understand. I've had a big breakthrough. I think I know where Kam Sau is. In fact, I'm sure of it. Spare me twenty minutes of your time and I'll explain everything."

This was his cue to dismiss me. If he had nothing to hide about his missing secretary, or anything to fear about her reappearance, he should kick me out. He was a busy man; show me the door and he could focus on his new film. Letting me stay here told me he *did* have something to conceal. Mention of a breakthrough had set alarm bells ringing in his head. He was worried I had discovered too much. He wouldn't eject me until he had found out what I knew. What would he do then? Report to the Ke Ge Bo? Go running to Ian Jeffries?

Yip struck a match and lit his cigar. "Kam Sau is no longer important." He tossed the spent match in the ash tray. "Since hiring you, I've discovered that those documents she stole from the office safe aren't the confidential ones I thought they were."

He snatched a puff from his Havana and blew smoke into the air. "But seeing as you're in here now …" He drew little circles in the air with his cigar while he considered the situation. "Yes, I suppose I might as well let you tell me about this so-called breakthrough you claim to have made."

He sat back in his executive chair. Cloth squeaked on leather as he made himself more comfortable. He gazed at me expectantly.

"Well, Duggan? I'm waiting."

I didn't know if he was waiting for me to applaud his generosity in allowing me to spend a few more minutes in his presence, or for me to start outlining my big breakthrough. Whatever it was, he was going to have to keep on waiting for a few more minutes.

I said, "What happens to the girl now?"

He shrugged. "She's unimportant."

"What happens to her?"

"She can screw herself for all I care."

"Will Ian Jeffries feel that way?"

Yip's eyes narrowed.

"The British minister," I said. "She rang him."

Yip frowned. "Phoned Ian Jeffries; why?"

"I was hoping you would tell me."

"How the fuck would I know?"

I gazed into his eyes. Forget all the stuff you read about trapping a guilty man through their sweaty palms; a skilled liar, or someone who is used to questioning

99

can control this. Or sometimes a person gets so nervous when you grill them that they seem guilty when they're actually innocent. Eyes are far and away the best indicator of guilt; eye movements are notoriously hard to control. You toss in a surprise question, like I just had about Jeffries, and then watch to see if the suspect's eyes narrow with tension, or if they blink more rapidly. Yip was doing both: he definitely had something to hide about Jeffries.

"She didn't call on your behalf?"

"No."

"Why would the Ke Ge Bo search her flat?"

"Ke Ge Bo?"

"I interrupted an agent ransacking the place. Was he after your missing documents?"

"There are no missing documents."

"Do you think the agent found them?"

"Are you deaf, Duggan? *There are no documents.* My staff misled me. The important papers are still locked in the safe. What Kam Sau took is worthless."

I shook my head. "I don't think so."

Then I sat back and waited for a storm to break. I had just called him a liar. I had done it deliberately because I wanted to make him furious not merely annoyed with me. Emotionally charged men can often make big mistakes. If Yip became outraged, then losing his temper might make him reveal things about his secretary which would otherwise remain hidden.

To my surprise, he never became outraged. He simply puffed at his cigar and then blew out smoke. Then he did something not only surprising but truly amazing — he smiled. What was happening? So far Yip had only played the part of Mister Surly. Why suddenly audition for Prince Charming? He had realised that he couldn't succeed by intimidating me, of course. He had decided he must change tactics.

He gestured to the bottle on his desk.

"Brandy, Pete?"

His voice had undergone a radical change. The growling old film producer had vanished like a puff of cigar smoke, replaced by this new and super-friendly character.

"You'll never taste a smoother or better drop than Alan Yip's private blend; a firm over in France makes it especially for me; or how about a nice fat Havana? Rolled between the silky thighs of Cuba's most beautiful and nubile virgins — heh, heh, heh! At least that's what my supplier says." Yip winked conspiratorially at me. "But then he's such a crook I wouldn't be surprised if he gets his own grandmother to do the job — heh, heh, heh!"

"I'll have brandy."

Yip poured me one.

"I'll join you," he said, pouring one for himself. "Always give myself the best. Know why? Alan Yip *deserves* the best! He's worked hard to get to the top. Sprang from nothing and look at him now! Runs the best film company in all Asia — and that includes those Indian jerks over in Bollywood."

I drank some brandy. It lived up to all of Yip's boasts. The sort of stuff which warms, rather than burns your throat as it slides down.

Yip said, "Anyway, Pete, although now I don't need you to find Kam Sau, I *can* use you on another job. I need to make sure an accountant I plan to hire isn't crooked." He jabbed a finger at me. "*You* are exactly the man to check him out. It should take about two weeks. At four hundred dollars a day you'll earn yourself a tidy sum."

So it had come to bribery. He was scared I'd dug up too much about his secretary and her possible links with Ian Jeffries and the Ke Ge Bo. He wanted to ensure that I unearthed nothing more. Bullying me had failed, so now he would buy me. Why the dramatic turnaround? Why would the man who only twenty-four hours ago been desperate for me to *find* his secretary suddenly beg me to quit the search?

He gazed at me expectantly. "Well? What do you say to my offer, Pete?"

I drank some more brandy then rested my glass on the desk. Then I said, "Why would that Ke Ge Bo agent ransack Kam Sau's flat?"

Yip's face turned purple. He thumped his glass so hard against the desk that the glass almost broke. He cursed me, threatened me with violence, vowed to make sure that I never worked again. He did everything but answer my question. The door opened and two burly characters swaggered into the room like gunslingers from a cowboy movie, revolvers slung low at their waists; Yip must have pressed a button on the desk to summon them.

"Throw him out," Yip ordered.

16

THE COWBOYS FROGMARCHED me downstairs. A man waited at the main door. He held up one hand like a traffic policeman.

"I want to speak to Mister Duggan."

My cowboy guards trooped back upstairs. The man introduced himself.

"I'm John Yip."

"I know," I said. "I've seen you on TV."

Yip's California-educated son was aged in his mid-twenties: well-groomed and slim, and at about five nine inches tall, slightly above average height for a Cantonese man. His steel-rimmed spectacles, smartly pressed navy blue suit and tasselled black loafers, gave him the look of an American corporate lawyer, but he was really his father's public relations chief. He appeared on TV whenever Yip had a new film to promote.

We went to his office.

You gain a useful insight into someone's character from their office. Just because a man jells his hair, wears an expensive suit and shines his shoes until you can see your face in them, it doesn't necessarily mean that he's a smart and business-like operator. Clothes are for public display. They reveal what someone is like when on their guard and eager to make a good impression. To learn about a person's *real* personality, examine their office. This is the private domain and they make it a home from home, a place where they can relax as well as work. That means you get an insight into how they act when they're not on their guard.

Exceptions to the rule exist, of course. Anyone viewing my HQ might fail to appreciate that the occupant is a super-efficient investigator, not some tramp squatting there. Nine times out of ten, though, the Duggan office test works effectively.

John Yip's place was about one-hundredth the size of his father's, and spotlessly clean and tidy, everything in its correct place. Two metal filing cabinets resided by the door. Three pictures of nudes, all tastefully done, decorated one whitewashed wall, while studded into another wall was a TV tuned to an American news channel. Once we got inside the office, my host politely switched the TV off. We occupied matching black leather chairs at either side of his desk. As with the rest of his office, the desk was pristine clean. Everything on it was in the right place: metal in- and out-trays, both of them clearly marked; newspapers and magazines, all of them neatly stacked; desk calendar, open at the correct date; leather pen holder complete with shiny silver pens; the most up-to-date laptop that money can buy.

Last but not least, he had one of those annoying ball-bearings pendulum contraptions; you set one metal ball swinging, it hits the other balls and puts them in a perpetual motion until you finish up with an endless and brain-destroying clack, clack, clack sound.

In other words John Yip was methodical, polite and modest; liked cleanliness and order; was an efficient organiser; maintained a keen interest in America; and had a geek-like fascination for the latest executive toys.

Someone knocked softly at the door. It opened just as softly and an elderly, grey-haired woman ghosted into the room, carrying a silver tray which had a silver teapot and two white porcelain cups on it. She put the tray down gently on the desk and then left as unobtrusively as she had entered. Yip junior reached over and picked up the teapot. His actions were all smooth and unhurried, a stark contrast to the aggressive finger-jabbing routine of his old man upstairs.

"Afraid I'm unable to offer you brandy like my father did." He poured a smooth stream of tea into one white porcelain cup and then handed the cup to me. "I never touch alcohol." He filled the other cup. "I can't permit you to smoke either. I like to guard my health, and the time I spent in California alerted me to the dangers of passive smoking."

It was a soft, cultured voice. Yet something else was mixed in there too, something that I couldn't quite put my finger on yet.

I said, "Jasmine tea is fine. And I stopped smoking months ago. But I don't think you showed me in here just to discuss the pros and cons of alcohol and cigarettes. What's really on your mind, Mister Yip?"

He drank some jasmine tea then dabbed his lips with a paper napkin. He said, "You talked about Kam Sau with my father, yes?"

"Did I?"

"He wants you to drop the case, yes?"

"Does he?"

105

John Yip smiled at me. A charming, boyish smile, it displayed teeth that were nice and white, though a little bit uneven; and revealed dimples in suntanned cheeks.

"Tell me," he said, still smiling broadly. "Is it your usual practice to always answer a question by asking one of your own?"

"I'm a detective. Asking questions is my job."

He drained his tea then poured himself a fresh cup. "Actually, I don't really need you to answer me," he said tonelessly. He leaned back in his chair. "I already know that what I've told you is true."

"Do you bug all your dad's meetings? Or was it just this one with me and him you were interested in?"

John Yip's wide-set dark brown eyes twinkled with amusement behind the square, steel-rimmed spectacles.

"Are you always this rude?"

"I occasionally take Sundays off. How come you know your father ordered me to quit the case?"

"*How* I know doesn't matter, Duggan."

I stiffened. The speed and unexpected sharpness of this last reply — so at odds with his good humour of just a moment ago — made me suddenly realise what it was about his voice that at first I'd been unable to put my finger on. Yes, it was a soft and cultured voice. There was something else in there too, though: the coldness and hardness of high-tensile steel. He might look a bookish lawyer type, a character whose face you could safely kick sand in. But appearances were deceptive. This was no geek-like pushover.

He sat up straight in the chair. "Want to hear why dad fired you?"

I nodded.

"They forced him to."

"They?"

"Let's just call them *influential* people for the moment. Some people in this world are *very* influential, Duggan. When they issue their commands then even the great Alan Yip must obey."

I gazed more closely at his face. It had grown much harder, making him look at least ten years older. And he had sneered rather than merely spoken those last few words about Alan Yip. Father and son obviously did not share an entirely loving relationship.

"Let me make my own position crystal clear to you," he continued brusquely. "I'm not interested in papers which may, or may not, be missing from the office safe — I want to find my father's secretary."

He paused to sip tea. He put the porcelain cup on the desk, leaned forward and steepled his fingers. He stared at me the same earnest way that he stared out from the TV screen, when in his role as his father's public relations' chief he tried to convince viewers that the latest Alan Yip movie was not the same blood-and-guts junk as the last five hundred Alan Yip offerings, but a not-to-be-missed cinematic masterpiece.

"An employer has certain duties," he said. "Oriental Pictures has a duty to ensure the well-being of all our staff. We owe it to Kam Sau to do everything possible to find her and make sure she's safe."

It all sounded plausible and sincere. But just as I've never bought all that junk about Alan Yip's films being cinematic masterpieces, so I didn't buy this concern about a missing secretary. Yip junior may have attended college in California, but he was still a Hong Kong big-shot. All the Hong Kong big-shots I've met over the years have only ever been concerned about the welfare of one person — themselves. There must be another reason for all of his concern.

"You wouldn't be romantically involved with Kam Sau by any chance?"

He stiffened. "I'm fond of her," he answered tersely. "How much did my father pay you?"

"Four hundred US dollars a day plus expenses."

"I'll pay five hundred for you to continue looking for her. Do we have a deal, Inspector Duggan?"

Inspector Duggan!

"Yes," I replied after a pause, "a deal."

We shook hands on it, and then I got up and left. He offered to show me out, but I told him I would find my own way. As I walked down the corridor towards the exit, I struggled to work out what sort of game he was playing with me. Why the sudden change of heart over his father's secretary? Yesterday he had threatened to break both my legs if I tried to find her. The longer my meeting with John Yip had gone on, the more convinced I'd become that I had heard his voice somewhere else recently.

Now I knew where. Calling me Inspector Duggan had clinched it. The man who had phoned yesterday to warn me off the case had also called me Inspector Duggan. Which was not really surprising: my caller and John Yip were the same man.

17

I PULLED UP in the car at Happy Valley race track twenty minutes later. Or rather I pulled up half a mile away; parking by the track on race days is like trying to walk on water; half a mile was as close as I would get. I locked the car and began walking — before going fifteen metres I was soaked. Typhoons normally eased the sauna-like humidity, but despite yesterday's storm today's air felt as sticky as treacle.

Why had John Yip warned me off Kam Sau then hired me to find her? Had I messed up over who had made that threatening call to my office? No, it had been him. Was he Kam Sau's lover? At first I'd thought so; I had assumed that was why he was desperate to find her. Now, though, I felt plagued by doubts. That picture of Kam Sau which Alan Yip had given me showed a happy-go-lucky kid. Yip junior did not seem her type; too serious and business-like. Opposites sometimes attracted, though. Who would have expected a sophisticated violinist like Suk Fan to marry me?

I took a short-cut through a side-street. Fifty metres away the two assassins lay in wait for me.

They were the strangest pair of assassins you might meet: the oldest hired killers in town. Aged almost eighty, they regularly disposed of more people in a year than I had arrested in my career. Yet they had never fired a shot, never stabbed or poisoned anyone: I don't think they had even struck anyone in anger.

They were the *man mai por*, friends of the dead.

They must be hoping to take advantage of the large crowds that had flocked to the Happy Valley area because it was a race day. Usually they hunkered down outside Wong Tai Sin Temple, on the other side of the harbour in Kowloon. Dressed from head to toe in black, they would wait patiently for temple visitors to approach them about enemies they wanted to dispose of. Some people wished to get rid of a rival at work, some people a love rival; others had lifelong enemies in the neighbourhood — the old women agreed to kill them all.

They had a simple technique. Clients handed over a picture of their enemy and the *man mai por* then muttered something, perhaps accompanying their remarks with a whiff of joss smoke before grabbing a *kung fu* shoe and beating the daylights out of the photograph. The enemy would then be pronounced 'dead'; he or she would spend the rest of their life in abject misery, clients were cheerfully assured. When not killing people the old women cleaned the police station, which was how I had come to know them.

They grinned.

"*Aheya!* It's lover boy!" one cried.

The other one brandished her shoe. "Want anyone taken care of? Give me your police commissioner's picture — I'll kill him now for you."

"And I used to think you were such a wise old woman, grandmother," I teased her. "Surely you must know by now that the police commissioner's one of my oldest and dearest friends."

They both cackled with glee.

My thoughts turned to Alan Yip. Should I have played him differently? If I had been less aggressive, would I have achieved more? No. Acting all meek and mild would have made him aware that I knew nothing to threaten him and …

My mobile phone rang.

"Why don't you pigs leave me alone!"

A young woman's voice: loud and full of anger. Full of something else too — fear. I had never heard the voice before yet I instinctively knew who it belonged to, though I can't explain exactly *how* I knew. It would be nice to say that it was because I'm telepathic — I've always dreamed of possessing special skills like that. But it probably owed more to the fact I had been thinking about her just a moment ago. So when my mobile phone rang, and I heard a young woman's voice, her name immediately flashed through my brain.

"Kam Sau?"

"I'll destroy him — I'm warning you."

"I want to help. Tell me where you are and I'll come to see you."

"He knows that I can do it and I will do it if I have to. Tell him."

"Tell who?"

"You know who."

"Trust me. I want to help."

"Liar! You work for him. He's hired you to kill me just like you killed Ah Chung."

111

"I've killed no one."

"Joe saw you break into my flat. Joe says you're evil."

"I've killed no one," I said. "I'm a private detective. You already know that, though, because you called my office to get this mobile number. Alan Yip hired me to recover papers he thought you stole."

"He's a liar! I stole nothing!"

"I know. Mister Yip made a mistake and he's sorry — he's told me to drop the case. There's no need to stay hiding. You can come back."

"You think I want to die?"

"They all want to help you, especially your friend John Yip."

"That bastard is no friend of mine."

"He wants to help."

"Tell him to leave us alone, or I'll destroy him."

"Tell who?"

"Your boss."

"Alan Yip?"

"You know who."

"Or do you mean John?"

"Make him stop. Or we'll release the stuff."

"If you're worried about trusting me, then call my secretary," I said. "You rang her for this number. Call her again. She'll …"

The line went dead. I tried to reconnect by pressing button three, but got an engaged signal. I checked the number she had called from. If she had used a residential line, the code would show whether she was still in Hong Kong. But she had called me from her mobile.

A COFFEE SHOP stood at the end of the street. I went inside and ordered double espresso, then sat back and tried to make sense of it all. Who did she think had paid me to kill her — Alan Yip? Why then, when I'd asked if it was him or son John, had she not said yes?

She had denied stealing documents from Alan Yip, and my instincts told me it was the truth. Yet at the same time she had claimed to possess '*stuff*' that could help to destroy her enemy. What was this stuff — documents stolen from someone else? Was Kam Sau a blackmailer? It would explain her avoiding the police — contact them and she risked being jailed for extortion. But if neither Alan Yip nor his son John were her blackmail targets, who was? I didn't know. I did know she had never been Yip junior's lover, though. She had even scorned the suggestion that they were friends.

Where was she? The fact she thought that Joe Chan was alive, even though local newspapers had reported his death, suggested she had fled from Hong Kong. Beijing seemed an obvious place for her to hide. She came from there and would have friends to help her. Or had she decided it was *too* obvious? That people would search there first? In that case she might avoid Beijing. She could be in Thailand, Singapore, Malaysia … Jesus! Why not just run through the atlas?

I needed to face facts: I didn't have a clue where she had gone. And I was wasting time drinking coffee here and waiting for a sign from God to fall from the ceiling. Perhaps I would fare better with Frank Ching. Maybe there would be a lead in that information I'd asked him to dig up for me. I got up and set off to see him.

18

THE RACE MEETING was in full swing when I arrived at the track. I climbed the steps of the packed grandstand and made for Frank's spot in the fourth from top row.

He sits there because it offers a panoramic view and he's superstitious; anywhere else will bring bad *feng shui*. Not that fourth from the top has ever brought much good luck; he loses more than he wins. But Frank is one of life's optimists, convinced the big win is waiting just around the corner. He didn't see me approach because he was too busy eating a barbecued pork bun, slurping coffee, chatting to the man beside him and studying *Sing Tao*'s racing form — all at the same time.

I slapped him on the shoulder. "How's it going?"

He glanced up from his newspaper: "Two hundred and fifty dollars down at the moment." He scrunched up the paper coffee cup and tried to chuck it in a bin two rows further down, but missed. "Play It Again Sam's a certainty for the next race, though, and I've put five hundred on him at odds of two to one — I should be a thousand up soon."

His husky voice made him sound as though he had a perpetual cold. Frank blamed it on the childhood asthma he had never fully shaken off. I reckoned it had more to do with him screaming himself hoarse at the Happy Valley and Sha Tin race tracks, as he tried to will home the no-hopers he backed.

"Make way there, Frank," said the man sitting next to him. He was a tall, skinny character in his mid-forties. His neatly pressed blue suit and blood-red tie would have been more at home in a company boardroom than a race track. "I'm off to the bar to drown my sorrows."

Frank moved aside to let the man pass.

"He just blew seven thousand on the last race," Frank explained, when the man was out of earshot.

"Friend?"

"Professional acquaintance; he runs a security firm in Mongkok — supplies bodyguards to big-shots who want protection from Chinese kidnapping gangs."

Frank chewed his pork bun. He took a tissue from his pocket and wiped his greasy mouth. As he dabbed his top lip dry, I suddenly realised what was so different about him from when we had last met for a drink three weeks ago. A slim moustache now adorned his moon-shaped face.

"What's with the face fungus?"

He shrugged. "I fancied a change. The wife thinks it makes me a lot more sophisticated. How about yourself? Do you reckon it suits me?"

It had turned him into a cross between Hercule Poirot and American funny-man Oliver Hardy, with a bit of the villainous Fu Manchu lobbed in for good measure. I didn't have the heart to tell him, though — he can be touchy about his appearance.

"It makes you very distinguished."

Frank's broad grin of thanks creased up his face and revealed a gap in his top front teeth.

"You really think so?" He beamed like a kid who had just heard he was to captain the school football team.

"I do."

He laid the newspaper flat on his lap. I spied the black circles he always drew around the names of horses he planned to back. Gambling is a passion with Frank, the same as it is with most people in Hong Kong. Personally, I've always found punting on horses only slightly more alluring than watching paint dry. Perhaps it's because I'm not full-blooded Chinese. Maybe my western side stops me blowing my cash like Frank. On second thoughts, my dad was a westerner. And according to those unlucky enough to have known him, Paddy Duggan was an even bigger gambler than he was a drunken bully.

"So?" I asked Frank eagerly. "Did you manage to dig up the stuff on that girl?"

Instead of answering me, he crammed the remains of the pork bun in his mouth. Eating is another of his passions. As a youngster he hoped to become a top chef; in fact he attended Hong Kong's top catering college. Not for long, though. Teachers soon discovered that far from being able to prepare nine-course banquets, he struggled to boil rice. The two sides had a nice long chat and Frank quit for a job as a baker's assistant. A problem also developed here, though; Frank's sweet tooth led him to munch too many pastries and cakes. The baker grew alarmed that if his assistant kept consuming the stocks at such a rate he would eat into his profits — so he fired him.

Luckily, Frank then met an ex-classmate who had joined the police and helped him to join them too. Frank should have been an inspector by now; he had the talent and he worked hard. Yet in the past, whenever I'd urged him to seek promotion, he had always insisted that he was happy enough as a sergeant.

I knew he hadn't meant it, though; he'd only said it because he thought he had no chance of making inspector; he wanted to avoid the hurt of rejection. So three years ago, without telling him, I'd confronted the top-floor bosses and urged them to promote him. They had responded by telling me he wasn't smart enough.

The bosses had got it wrong, though. They had made the mistake of judging on appearances, a department that Frank has never scored too highly in. For as long as I can remember, in twenty years of working with him, he's been at least twenty pounds overweight. Combine this with the fact that he's one of the shortest detectives on the force — he actually looks shorter than he really is because his legs are smaller than his upper body — and you understand how the office 'Fat Boy' taunts started.

Then there's the way that he slicks his hair back like some Nineteen Thirties' matinee idol, the dazzlingly bright shirts and bow-ties he wears (lovely wife Ah Yan thinks they make him look professional), the braces he uses to keep his trousers up; it all sometimes gives him the appearance of a comic opera performer — and this was before he sprouted that daft face fungus.

None of this should have mattered in terms of promotion, though: he was experienced and talented — a hell of a lot more talented than those who had been promoted as inspector ahead of him. While they might look the part in their smart suits and polished shoes, half of them wouldn't have spotted a criminal if he had jumped up and bit them on their bollocks.

People had been surprised at how I'd loyally stuck by Frank over the years. In my early days I'd won a bit of a reputation for ambition. Why waste my time supporting a plodder? But they didn't know Frank like me. I knew he had a lot of talent and I also knew that his talents complimented mine. I like to move things along quickly when I'm working, perhaps too quickly. Frank has always insisted on painstaking detail.

It's true that in our time together I often found his pedestrian methods maddening — more than once I came close to throttling Frank. At the same time, I appreciated the benefits of working with him; by forcing me to work at a pace similar to his, he made me take a closer look at things. I saw stuff that I would have missed had I been working alone, or with some-one who had a personality more in tune with mine.

Frank finished his pork bun.

"Well?" I asked eagerly. "Did you dig up the stuff?"

He nodded. "I talked with my Ke Ge Bo friend."

"And?"

Frank wiped his greasy lips: "Knows nothing about Secret Police agents searching that flat."

"Bullshit!"

"Ah Yeung's usually reliable, Pete."

"I saw that agent. He showed me his ID card."

"Did you examine the card?"

"He was pointing a gun at me," I said tonelessly. "So I had more pressing things on my mind."

"In other words, the answer's no?"

I had to admit it was.

"Then you can't prove he's Ke Ge Bo. He …"

Frank broke off as the track announcer's tinny voice cut through the air: *"Sallow Boy is in the stalls. Soon they'll be under starters' orders."*

I knew Frank was desperate to watch the action.

"Tell me after the race," I said. "I can wait."

The race was the Coronation Trophy Stakes: to be run over a distance of twelve hundred metres. Eight horses had entered for the race, although top newspaper tipster Captain Starlight reckoned seven of them had no chance of winning — Play It Again Sam was a certainty. Sam loved hard ground and had been superb in training. He was also ridden by the top jockey, Marcus Wong. With all of this going for him how could he possibly lose?

"They're off!"

The crowd roared as the eight horses shot from the stalls and thundered down the turf. Frank underwent a metamorphosis. My mild-mannered friend turned into a purple-faced, screaming fanatic.

"Go on, Sam, you can do it! Go on, you bastard!"

With four hundred metres left to race, the fifty-to-one outsider Sallow Boy was in front but had started to tire. Play It Again Sam, on the other hand, looked full of running and well placed to capture the lead. The river of noise surging through the grandstand swelled to a torrent as the huge crowd tried to will Sam home.

"Go on, boy!" Frank yelled. He punched my shoulder "He's going to do it, Pete, Sam's …"

"At the line, it's Sallow Boy!"

The winning horse galloped past. His jockey turned to the crowd and pumped his fist in triumph.

"In second place: Love's Pleasure. Third was Play …"

119

The rest of the announcement was drowned by a sea of groans, and by threats to disembowel a certain newspaper tipster — if Captain Starlight had sense he would lie low for a few days. Frank tore up his useless betting slip and then threw it into the air like wedding confetti. I gave him a moment to get over his loss.

Then I said, "I'm sure that gunman was Ke Ge Bo."

"What did he look like?"

I described him.

"I'll get back to Ah Yeung," Frank said. "I'll ask him to double check."

On the track below, a sweating Sallow Boy entered the winner's enclosure. Owner and trainer patted the horse. Both men looked delighted, particularly the fat trainer. He looked as though he was about to jump into the air and start clicking his heels.

I turned my attention back to Frank. I said, "Tell me all about the daughter of that murdered dishwasher. What did she say to you when you interviewed her?"

"Had to travel all the way over to China to do it you know," Frank said. "The interview with her, I mean. She never came back to Hong Kong."

I nodded. "Not even for her mother's funeral. Don't you find that a bit strange?"

He shrugged. "Not everyone gets on with parents. You should know that better than ..." He blushed. "Sorry, Pete, I didn't mean ..."

"Relax," I told him, "you don't have to worry about hurting my feelings. Paddy Duggan was a total bastard — I don't mind admitting it. Tell me about the girl. What's she like?"

"You can judge for yourself," Frank said. "I brought a picture of her with me to show you."

He picked up the black leather briefcase by his side and snapped open the twin locks, then reached into the case and pulled out a photograph the size of a small paperback novel. He handed me the photograph. It showed a pencil-slim, attractive girl in either her late teens or early twenties. She wore a pale blue tee-shirt and tight black leather trousers and was standing by a bookcase. The self-assured, almost arrogant stance — left hand on bookcase, right hand on hip, head tilted to one side — and the look on her face: lips apart, ebony eyes luring you closer; it all reminded me of other teenagers I've met over the years.

"Is she a hooker, Frank?"

He frowned. "What makes you ask?"

"Her looks remind me of the dancers in Wan Chai."

"She told me she's a photographer's model."

"Did she tell you anything else?"

He dragged a wad of paper from his briefcase.

"Interview transcript," he announced officiously. He handed me the wad. "Everything's written down there."

I think I've mentioned that Frank is keen on detail. This time he had excelled even his own exacting standards: this transcript seemed thicker than the Bible. He must have got that girl in China to relate her whole life story and then printed everything out in triplicate.

"The model stuff is near the back," Frank said.

"I'm more interested in whether she said anything to you about Alan Yip's missing secretary."

"The interview was about her mother's murder. Why would she mention Yip's secretary?"

I balanced the transcript in my hand. Judging from the weight of this hefty tome, she had mentioned every second person living in Hong Kong.

"I just thought that with her mother dying in Hong Kong and you being a police officer here … I thought the conversation might have turned to Hong Kong and … Well, I thought she might have mentioned having a few friends here."

"She did, but not your missing secretary."

"Who?"

"Her boyfriend lives here. She said that if I had to contact her again, but didn't want to go to Beijing and couldn't get her on the phone, then I should leave a message with him."

"What's his name?"

Frank gestured for me to hand back the transcript. "I can't remember offhand, but I know where I wrote it."

I returned the transcript. He licked his middle finger and began turning the pages slowly, one by one. I gritted my teeth. This sort of stuff had almost driven me crazy in our days together. Why must he always turn pages from the beginning, even when he probably already knew the name was two lines from the end?

"Yes, here it is," Frank said when he had found the page. "He lives on the fourth floor of Yee On Building; number twenty-eight. It's that old ten-storey apartment block near Mongkok MTR station, the one where all the hawkers hang around outside; or rather where they used to hang around outside. With the new trading laws the government's introduced, hawkers no longer—"

"Screw the bloody hawkers! Who's the boyfriend?"

"All in good time," Frank said, annoyed at my interruption. "If you rush things you risk making a mistake." He buried his nose in the transcript again. "Yes, here it is. He's a journalist. His name is Joe Chan."

19

MOSQUITOES HAD GONE on the warpath. One of them savaged me on the cheek as I turned left on to Johnstone Road. I swatted another two attackers away from my ear; sticky evenings like this one always brought the tiny bloodsuckers out in force.

A jet roared overhead. I looked up to see it slice through a purple-green sky. It was eight-fifteen. I was on my way to meet Giselle, the Filipina dancer who had left a message on Kam Sau's phone asking her if she wanted to play basketball.

My journey to Joe Chan's place had been a wasted one. A group of kids had been playing in the corridor outside Chan's apartment. I'd had to abandon my plan to break into the flat and had settled instead for talking to Chan's neighbours. None of them could tell me very much; he had only lived there a few months; he had kept himself to himself most of the time. Perhaps Giselle would know a bit more about him. Perhaps she would also know where Kam Sau was hiding.

I moved on to Lockhart Road. The US Fleet had arrived in port on a goodwill visit. Shaven-headed sailors in various stages of drunkenness crowded outside the bars, chatting up hookers in tight jeans and short skirts, who giggled obediently at jokes they'd heard a thousand times before.

It was fairly tame stuff, though, compared with many other Asian red-light areas. Wan Chai was a shadow of what it had once been during the Vietnam War, when American troops had packed Lockhart Road's bars. Compared to all of Manila and Bangkok's steamy goings-on, Wan Chai these days resembled a Buddhist nuns' convention.

A slim, long-legged Filipina lounged against the wall outside Popeye's Bar. She smiled sweetly. "Why don't you go inside with me for a drink, darling?" she purred. She ran her tongue slowly over her lips. Painted fingernails caressed the seams of her skin-tight jeans: "It's very nice, darling, very relaxing."

I smiled back at her. "I'm relaxed already, but thanks for the offer anyway."

She reminded me of my daughter, Kathy; she couldn't be more than eighteen. She smiled at me again. Would she smile as sweetly ten years on? I doubted it. She would be too worn out from booze and dope, and from servicing characters like the middle-aged western pair who had slouched up to her shoulder. Balding heads leaked sweat, beer guts bulged. They were both tourists, judging from their shorts and sandals. Probably respectable types at home, maybe even with teenage daughters of their own. Church-going pillars of the community, perhaps. Here, though, far away from the watchful eyes of families and neighbours, they mutated into sleaze-balls. The Aids' threat had scared away some sex tourists, but not nearly enough.

From the bar came silvery tinkling sounds of music and girlish laughter. The tourists decided not to waste any more time ogling the teenager; better lay on offer inside. They pushed past, almost knocking her to the floor. Another time, I would have dragged both the lecherous bastards back and forced them to apologise. Tonight I had no time for hassles. After making sure the girl was unhurt, I continued down the road to The Wild Cat Club.

Two drunken young sailors were throwing up by the door. I walked around them, pulled back the dark green velvet curtain which masked the bar's entrance and trooped inside. A thick fog of cigarette smoke made me gasp for breath. Swatting away the mist, I saw that the place was crammed with American sailors.

With difficulty I threaded my way past them and over to the bar. A Thai bargirl in an orange wet-look swim-suit and white, thigh-length PVC boots asked me what I wanted. As I had with her friend out on the street, I spoke English; the dancers in here had a limited grasp of Cantonese. I had to shout to make myself heard above the insanely loud music.

"I need to speak to Giselle."

With a flick of her jelled hair the bargirl indicated the small circular stage sited behind the bar. Two dancers, a Filipina and a Chinese girl, were grinding away on the stage to a brain-destroying disco beat. The Filipina, who wore white stockings, a suspender belt, G-string and stilettos, leaned over and touched the dance floor. At the same time she snaked out her tongue and then waggled it at a group of American sailors. One sailor tore off his tee-shirt and tried to clamber on to the dance floor to join the girls. His friends hauled him back. The second dancer, a pencil-slim Chinese girl whose sleek, bronzed body glistened with oil, grabbed the Filipina's hips. Then she thrust hard and rhythmically against the Filipina's raised buttocks, tossing back her long silken hair as she writhed in mock ecstasy.

The bargirl with the jelled hair touched my arm: "How about you buy me a drink, darling."

"If you promise to tell Giselle I want to talk to her."

"I promise; go on, darling, just a small drink."

Normally, I avoid Hong Kong's red-light bars like the plague. If you were allowed to just sit and sip your drink in peace and quiet then perhaps these types of bars might be tolerable. Although on second thoughts, considering their beer costs about four times what it does in ordinary bars, maybe even a bit of peace and quiet would not be enough.

Not that you ever do get peace and quiet. The dancers, mainly Thais and Filipinas with a few mainland Chinese girls thrown in for good measure, always want to talk to you so that they can try and squeeze more cash from your wallet. Their conversation would never win any Nobel prizes. It usually consists of asking you over and over again how old you are and where you live, and then telling you over and over again that you look much younger than you actually are and that you speak English really well ... Oh and how about you buy me another drink, darling?

I shouldn't be too hard on the girls, though. It's not really their fault. Many of them are from poor homes and support big families in Thailand, or the Philippines. They aren't all the hard-nosed gold-diggers they might appear to be either. In fact I know some bargirls so bashful that they've become tongue-tied when encountering me in the street. In the bars, though, it's different; it has to be. The girls make their money by persuading punters to buy drinks; the more drinks that a girl persuades a punter to buy, the more money she makes. And these girls are desperate for cash to send back home, to give their families a half-decent chance in life. So desperate even the shy ones force themselves to act like street-hardened pros.

I stumped up a sum that would be enough to buy me a decent meal in many local restaurants. In here all it bought my bargirl friend was a Coca Cola in a glass the size of an egg cup.

The two dancers began a new routine. They wrapped their legs around a long metal pole fixed between the floor and the ceiling, then slid their crotches up and down the pole and flicked their tongues across its shiny metal. It's an act that is staged every night in every Wan Chai red-light bar. On the occasions when I've seen it, all it has ever aroused is the thought that it must be really uncomfortable rubbing your bare buttocks against a piece of cold steel. The whooping sailors enjoyed it, though — they jumped up and down, beat their chests like gorillas and chucked ten-dollar bills on the dance floor.

My bargirl friend downed her egg cup-sized Coca-Cola in two seconds flat: "How about you buy me one more, darling?"

I pulled more bills from my wallet and handed them over. The dancers jabbed their tongues out for one last time, and then departed the stage to loud whistling and cheering. The sailor who had earlier taken off his shirt now tried to leap the bar to grab the Filipina in the suspender belt. His friends dragged him back again.

The bargirl with jelled hair called out to the Filipina dancer, and then pointed at me. The dancer scowled then sauntered over to me on her high heels, hips swaying catwalk-model style.

"I'm Giselle Maria Santiago," she announced in a firm, clear voice. She eyed me with a mixture of suspicion and insolence. "What's all this about, mister?"

"Can we go somewhere that's a little bit quieter? The music is killing me."

She continued to look me over. Satisfied that I was not a serial rapist, she gave me the briefest of nods. "You can buy me out of here for the night. It'll cost you, though. It'll cost you big money."

"How much?"

She named a sum that would have been enough to ransom a captive emperor. Never mind. John Yip was footing the bill. No way would I focus in here. I would only shout myself hoarse and burst both my eardrums. I paid the ransom and went outside to await the release of my captive.

20

SHE WORE A pale yellow tee-shirt, faded jeans and a grey baseball cap emblazoned with the name of the Chicago Cubs. Jogging shoes had replaced the stilettos, making her three inches smaller.

She seemed an entirely different person. A girl you could imagine living in the flat upstairs and working behind the counter of the local Hang Seng Bank; no longer the toughened professional who had strutted around stage, jabbing her crotch out at slobbering sailors. Perhaps she had sensed what I was thinking, because she suddenly grinned.

"It's only a job I do back in the bar, mister" — she pronounced it *meester* — "Just because I act that way it don't mean I *am* that way — Me, I'm going to be a photographic model."

"I didn't say you were that way," I said defensively.

Her dark eyes danced with amusement. "Your face did. It told me you're another one of those dinosaurs who ... Hey! Why are you smiling?"

"Because you sound just like my daughter."

We walked down Lockhart Road.

"How old's your daughter?"

"Eighteen."

"Married?"

"No."

"Must have a boyfriend — is he handsome? Tell her to dump him if he is. Take it from me: *all* good-looking guys are self-centred and … Hey! What's wrong? Why are you staring at your watch?"

"Can I borrow your mobile?"

"Mobile?"

"All this daughter stuff has reminded me I meant to call Kathy half an hour ago — but my own phone needs recharging."

She handed me the mobile. I quickly checked to see if Kam Sau's contact details were stored on it: find the phone number for the place where she had holed up and I might then be able to track her down. I found nothing. I rang my home, faked a brief conversation with Kathy, who was still out with university friends, and then returned the phone to Giselle.

"When did you last see Kam Sau?"

"Ten days ago, at basketball."

"Did she seem worried?"

"Nope."

"Act strange?"

"Nope."

"Where is she now?"

"How should I know? I'm not her keeper."

A sailor asked us for directions to the Country Club red-light bar. Giselle told him the way. She took off her cap and fanned her face. The glow of a street lamp turned her heart-shaped face the shade of milky coffee and made her mink-coloured eyes smoulder. She was pretty. If fate had not dealt her a bum hand, and if she'd been born in a big city rather than in a poor farming village, she might have become that photographer's model.

"Is she in China?" I suggested.

"Your guess is as good as mine."

"Does she have a boyfriend?"

"Don't know."

"So what's the boyfriend's name, Giselle?"

Her temper flared. "Jesus! I just told—"

"And I told you," I reminded her. "I told you I have a daughter. So don't try to con me. I know what girls discuss when they're out together — is her boyfriend John Yip?"

On the other side of the road, outside an Indonesian restaurant, four American navy policemen in crisp white uniforms were attempting to arrest two drunken sailors. A hooker in tight leather pants, who looked even drunker than the sailors, scratched the steamy air and screamed abuse at the navy cops.

"Well?" I asked.

"How old's this John?"

"Mid-twenties."

"It's not him."

"You're sure?"

"Kam Sau told me her boyfriend's much older."

"Is her boyfriend Alan Yip?"

Giselle gave a great squeal of laughter. "Are you *serious?*" She gazed at me, eyes wide in disbelief, amazed that I could have asked such a stupid question. "Do you *really* think she would ever date a guy like the Walking Eagle?"

"What?"

"We're talking her boss, huh — that asshole of a film-maker?" She shook her head. "Kam Sau hates him — she calls him Walking Eagle because he's so full of shit he can't fly."

She halted by Fortress electricals store and removed her Chicago Cubs baseball cap again. She wiped pearls of sweat from her brow, brushed strands of silken hair from one cheek.

I waited until she had put her cap back on. Then I said tonelessly, "What's the boyfriend's name?"

She threw up her arms in exasperation.

"Jesus! Don't you never give up?"

"Not when someone's lying."

"Screw you, mister! I'm going home."

She stalked off in the direction of Causeway Bay. I hurried after her and caught her up.

"What's his name, Giselle?"

She shook her head: "I don't know Kam Sau well — okay? She was in Victoria Park three months back, when my team played basketball — she joined in. Then she started playing every Saturday. But basketball's the only time we meet. We're not big friends — okay?"

"I heard the message you left on her phone," I said. "You called her 'Shooter'."

"So?"

"People only use nicknames if they're good friends."

We crossed Hennessy Road, avoiding crowded trams that clanked to Kennedy Town, Happy Valley and Shau Kei Wan.

"What's her boyfriend called?"

We were walking side by side at this moment, focused on the road ahead rather than looking closely at each other. She suddenly stopped walking and touched me on the shoulder, so that I stopped too. Then she turned around until she was staring into my face.

"Do you think I'm pretty, mister?"

"Is he Ian Jeffries?"

"There's a guy comes into my bar who thinks I'm pretty. He thinks I'm pretty enough to marry — asks me just about every other night. A rich guy too — got a big car and owns his own business. Yet I keep saying no — crazy, huh? Mama always said I was too soft to do well in this business, and I guess she was right about that too. Want to know why?"

"Is Kam Sau's boyfriend Ian Jeffries?"

"If I was a real hard-hearted bitch I'd marry this guy — then use this rich guy's money to put all my seven sisters through college." She shook her head. "Can't never do it, though," she sighed. "Too romantic, see — couldn't never marry someone I didn't really love. Not even if it means missing out on a chance to get rich. Besides, I'm a girl who likes her independence. Supposing I quit my job to marry this guy, then he suddenly goes off the idea and dumps me: what happens to poor little Giselle Maria Santiago then, huh?"

She would be in the same position as dozens of other girls like her have been in, I thought. No job, no money, no hope. In a few weeks she might even turn suicidal. I'd seen it happen. A businessman became besotted with a bargirl, told her he loved her and wanted to marry her. It was all rubbish, though. The only person these big-shots loved was themselves. You stood more chance of seeing Chairman Mao come back to life than you ever did of seeing a rich businessman marrying a bargirl.

We started walking again.

"I met this guy when he came to the bar last year with friends," she said. "Typical rich-kid pricks — all of them red-faced from beer; sure that because you're a Filipina you'll go down on them for a lousy fifty bucks." Her voice rose in a flash of anger. "Who do those bastards think they are? I'm every bit as smart as them — smarter even! I went to university and had a white-collar job back at home. But I make fifty times here what I do in Manila ... Yeah, I know, you've heard the same line before. Me, I'm different, though. Don't gamble or take dope — I'm just here for the cash. Another year and I'll have made enough to put my sisters through college. Then I'm off home to Manila. You reckon that's a good idea, huh?"

That had been no lie I'd told her earlier about how she reminded me of my daughter. She was doing what Kathy often did when eager to hide something: moving the conversation to other subjects, answering questions too quickly and briefly, bombarding me with questions of her own to try and seize control the situation.

I decided to get tough. I said: "I used to be a cop."

"Reckon I should marry this guy?"

"I still have some friends in the police force — in the Immigration Department too. In fact my *best* friend works in the Immigration Department's visa section. The next time that you go and apply to the Immigration Department for your work visa, you might find it's a little bit harder than usual."

I paused. Experience has taught me that when you put the boot into someone it always helps to pause before delivering that final crushing kick, it cranks up psychological pressure. When I had paused sufficiently, I said, "You *might* not get a visa at all."

She shot me a look that said she wanted to claw both my eyes out.

"Help me," I continued quickly, "And I *guarantee* that you'll have no problems — I'll even add a few hundred dollars to that money I've already paid you tonight."

"You're a son of a bitch," she hissed.

"What's the boyfriend's name?"

"I don't have it."

"You're lying."

"She only told me he's much older."

"Ian Jeffries?"

She shook her head. "Kam Sau don't like westerners. Had a western boyfriend once and he was a real bastard — turned her off westerners for good."

"What was the westerner's name?"

"Don't know."

"You're lying."

"No, honest, I ... Where are you going?"

"To the office," I said, "to telephone my visa section friend."

"No, please ... Okay, okay, I'll tell you."

"Well?"

"I swear she never told me her boyfriend's name. But I might be able to help on why she's disappeared."

"I'm listening."

"Our basketball team won a cup final three weeks ago and we all sank a few beers at Joe Banana's bar to celebrate. Kam Sau had a few beers too many and ... Well, she got pretty talkative that night. Said her and some friends had struck lucky and would make some really big money."

"How?"

"They had pictures of this big-shot."

"What pictures?"

"Didn't say, only this guy ... He would pay a lot for them. And if he didn't pay ... They'd sell the pictures to the newspapers. Then she called me up early the next morning and sounded real scared — made me promise not to tell anyone what she'd said."

"What's the big-shot's name?"

"She didn't tell me."

"You're lying, Giselle."

"It's true," she protested. "The only things she said are what I told you."

Had she spoken the truth? I was puzzling over the answer when a sleek, silver-coloured Mercedes pulled into the kerb about ten metres ahead of us. The front door on the passenger's side swung open and a man climbed out: the tough-looking Ke Ge Bo agent who had ransacked Kam Sau's apartment.

He jabbed a finger at me: "You! Wait there!"

I thought about waiting for him. He might arrest me this time rather than just scare me off like he had before. But once I had explained who I was, and then told him the name of the influential person I worked for, it would all turn out fine. Then I thought about journalist Joe Chan and the old dishwasher. Two people linked to this case were dead. Allow that agent to arrest me and it could soon be three. Even four — Giselle also had links with the case.

"Run!" I shouted. "Run!"

21

I GRABBED HER hand and ran.

At first she ran with me. Probably she was too stunned to do anything else. But when she had got over her initial shock she tried to pull away.

I gripped her hand tighter.

"Run!"

"No!"

"He's a killer!"

Bang! Bang!

Bullets exploded against the wall of the Shanghainese restaurant that stood in front of us. The bullets convinced Giselle that I had been speaking the truth. She stopped struggling against me. We started to run faster. As we ran, I shot a glance down the road. I searched desperately for an escape route.

A tram heading towards Happy Valley was pulling into the stop ahead of us, about twenty-five metres away. If we sprinted there and … No, it was crazy. Those two agents were only about fifteen metres behind, gaining on us quickly. No way could we use the tram. If we could get on board, then so could they.

So where did we go? Where did …

"That clothes shop!" I shouted; "on the other side of the road!"

We charged across the road. The driver of a cream-coloured minibus heading in the direction of Kennedy Town blasted his horn as he swerved to avoid us.

We made it safely to the pavement — the clothes shop stood five metres away from us. Once inside the shop we could bolt the door. We could lock the two Ke Ge Bo agents outside. Escape from them by using the back entrance.

An old woman emerged from the shop.

I had to jink sharply to my left to avoid hitting her. Too sharply — I lost my balance, stumbled and fell, pulling Giselle down to the ground with me. I struggled back to my feet — hauled Giselle up.

I wasn't quick enough. The agents were on top of us. A hand gripped my right shoulder.

"I told you to wait, you bastard."

I swung round, not stopping to think if his gun pointed at me, and instinctively shot out a fist. I felt my knuckles crunch against his skull. He grunted, staggered backwards. He lost his grip on my shoulder. I bundled Giselle into the shop, jumped in after her and banged the door shut.

Screw it! No lock!

Even if there had been a lock it would have done us no good. Both those agents were armed. They could easily blast open a lock. Too late, I realised that it had been madness to charge in here. I had led us straight into a trap.

"The back way," I snapped at the terrified shop owner; "quick, quick, where is it?"

He pointed to a door.

I grabbed Giselle's hand, pulled her over to the door. As we moved I knocked down racks of clothing behind us: shirts, hats, jackets, scarves — anything that might impede our two pursuers.

We reached the door.

"Get us out!" Giselle screamed. "Quick! Quick!"

I pulled at the door handle. Jammed. And now the agents were in the shop too. I could hear them behind us. Yelling at the shop owner to get the fuck out of their way. Pulling away those racks of clothing that I'd knocked down to create a barrier.

"I'll take them in here," one shouted. "You watch the street outside."

Giselle screamed louder: "They'll kill us!"

I kept pulling at the door handle.

Still jammed.

"Got them!" the agent in the shop cried triumphantly. "They're trapped!"

I pulled harder at the handle.

"Give it up," said the agent. "It's locked."

The door burst open.

We stumbled outside. I slammed the door behind us.

"Run, Giselle, run!"

A bus was pulling in; fifteen metres away.

"Over there!" I shouted; "the bus stop!"

We dashed for the bus. Not quickly enough. When we reached the stop, the bus was preparing to pull away. I pushed Giselle ahead of me.

"Go on! Get on board!"

I pushed her too hard — lost my balance and fell over again. She made it inside the bus. I didn't. By the time I had regained my footing the bus had begun to pull away. I lunged for the entrance door: managed to seize the door handle with my right hand: ran alongside the bus; tried to half-jump, half-pull myself on board.

I couldn't do it.

"Slow down!" I shouted.

It didn't slow down, it began to go faster. No way could I ever keep up. And now the entrance door was closing too. Unless I let go of the handle I was a goner. My arm would be torn from its socket.

Then, just as I was about to loosen my hold, the bus *did* slow. The door jerked open. I staggered breathlessly on board. With a loud hiss, the door slid shut behind me. Had the driver taken pity on me? Had Giselle made him stop? I neither knew nor cared. Being safe inside the bus was all that mattered.

"Daft bastard!" the tattooed young driver swore. "What the fuck did you …"

The fifty-dollar note that I shoved into his greasy hand, with an instruction to keep the change, halted him in mid-complaint. I half-sat, half-fell on the front seat next to Giselle. She was sweating and breathing heavily, shaking all over. Sweat poured from me too. My throat was dry. My heart pounded hard enough to punch a hole in my chest.

The old woman sitting behind us leaned over and tapped me on the shoulder. "You ought to act your age." She shook her head at what she viewed as my insanity. "You'll do yourself a serious injury if you ever try that sort of stupid thing again."

I smiled foolishly. "Urgent meeting," I gasped, "I can't afford to be late."

As I spoke, I scanned the street through the window. The two Ke Ge Bo agents were nowhere to be seen.

Had they been unable to open the back door of that clothes shop? I neither knew nor cared. We were both safe. That was the important thing.

Giselle clutched my hand for support, "Will those guys chase us again?" she asked in a timid, frightened voice. "I mean … Supposing …"

"It's all right," I said. "You're safe now. I promise I'll make sure that nothing happens."

"But just supposing those two—"

"They won't ever hurt you; I'll make sure of that. Trust me, Giselle; I'll keep you from harm."

My words did the trick. She began to relax. I must have sounded confident and reassuring. I wished I felt that way too.

22

WE GOT OFF the bus at the Star Ferry pier. I gazed across the oil-black harbour waters to Kowloon where the neon lights on waterfront skyscrapers glittered like huge pieces of gaudy jewellery.

Giselle lived near Kowloon's pier in Tsim Sha Tsui. The quickest way there was by ferry. After buying a cup of coffee at the Subway sandwiches stall by the ferry entrance, I shepherded her down the ramp, across the gangplank and on to the gently rocking boat.

No sooner had we sat down than she stood up again.

"I can't, mister, I need to go back to the bar."

"Sit down, Giselle."

"My bag's in the bar. I need to go get it."

"Sit the fuck down!" I was angry and frustrated by what had happened with the two gunmen. I vented my feelings on her. "Screw the bloody bag! Leave it in …" I seized a deep breath. This was unfair. Giselle wasn't to blame for what had happened tonight. She was an innocent victim. I grabbed another deep breath and calmed down. "Look," I went on as gently as I could, "those two were after you back there, not me — you're their link to Kam Sau. They heard the message you left on Kam Sau's phone, found out where you worked and came looking for you. And it wasn't to ask you to play basketball either."

"But why?" she pleaded with me to tell her. "Why do they want Kam Sau so badly?"

The full moon peeped out from a cloud and swept over her face. That swaggering bravado which had been on display back in her bar had vanished as completely as yesterday's dawn. She looked worried. In fact she looked frightened. Some of her fear might be due to the fact she knew nothing about what was happening. Fear of the unknown is one of the worst fears you can experience. Perhaps if I told her what this was about it might make her less scared.

I told her. Not everything, but as much as it was safe for her to know.

"If they're cops why can't I just tell them the truth?" she said, clutching at a vain hope that the solution to her troubles was simple. "They'll realise they've made a mistake and … Why are you shaking your head?"

"They aren't ordinary cops they work for the Secret Police. They won't say sorry then just walk away nice and polite. So I'm taking you home and then I'm …"

Take her home!

What sort of sawdust did I have for brains? No way could I take her home. Those agents might have twisted arms at the bar to discover her address. They could be on the street outside her apartment now, waiting for her to return.

"Do you live alone, Giselle?"

"A bargirl like me can't afford Hong Kong rents on her own. I share with two friends."

"Are they home?"

"One is. It's Davina's day off."

"Call her up," I said. "Tell her to bring a case full of clothes and your passport to Kam Chuen Lau restaurant in Cameron Road. Tell her that you're going to Thailand with a rich boyfriend."

She gaped at me in disbelief. "I can't fly over to Thailand."

"You're not. You're flying to the Philippines."

"Can't go over to Manila, neither; I don't have any money."

"I'm paying," I said. I pulled five thousand-dollar bills from my wallet and handed them to her. "It'll only be for a few days. I'll call you when it's safe to return."

She regarded me with dark probing eyes, wondering if it was a trick. Satisfied that everything was above board, she neatly folded the bills and then stowed them in a hip pocket of her faded jeans.

"Okay, mister. If you're *paying* me to go back home, then I'll go."

I shook my head. "I don't want to you to go home."

She frowned. "So why just say you did?"

"Those agents discovered where you work. They might also find out where your family lives. Ever been to Cebu?"

"Once."

"Make it twice," I said. "When you land in Manila, take another plane to Cebu and check into a hotel. You'll be safe, if you don't contact your family or friends until I tell you to. Can you do that?"

"I guess so."

The ferry pulled away from the pier with a jolt. A buzz of activity came from tourists on board. Cameras clicked, whirred and flashed. I knew why the tourists were eager to grab pictures. It was a spectacular view: the skyscrapers and their dazzling lights, the purple-black hills, the fiery glow from rich people's homes on the hill-top enclave known as the Peak. If only the smell was as impressive. The days when fragrant harbour — what the words 'Hong Kong' mean — had been an apt name for this stretch of water had long gone. Tonight, just as it does every other night, the harbour stank like an open sewer.

Giselle dragged a mobile phone from her pocket and rang her friend Davina. I drank my coffee and tried to work things out. A method of working I have is to sometimes throw up theories, no matter how wild they seem, and then test them till I prove they're unworkable. I call it using imagination. Others describe it as me jumping to mad conclusions.

How about this imaginative theory/mad conclusion? Kam Sau and British government minister Ian Jeffries are ex-lovers who met in China when he was there on a visit. She has damaging goods on him — all politicians hide skeletons in their closet — but keeps quiet while they're lovers. The affair turns sour and she attempts to cash in. Her and some friends try to blackmail Jeffries. But China is eager to sign a trade deal with Britain. Screw Jeffries and you screw the deal. Ke Ge Bo agents are despatched to silence the trouble-makers.

A plot from an Alan Yip film? I didn't think so. To me it seemed a realistic scenario. Politicians are ruthless types who will justify anything to protect themselves. They would firebomb a city to save their skins.

Giselle finished her call. "Davina says that she'll meet us at the restaurant in an hour."

I drained my coffee, scrunched up the paper cup and chucked it into a rubbish bin. 'Keep Hong Kong clean', said a sticker on the bin. When would the authorities target real pollution, like all the pig shit pumped into the harbour by New Territories' farmers and the chemicals churned out by Kwai Chung's factories?

My binning one paper cup wouldn't help to win the war on global warming. In a moment a crew member would do his bit for the environment by picking up the bin and then cheerfully emptying its contents into the harbour. It was easier than waiting for the ferry to dock then dumping the rubbish in an incinerator.

"What'll you do?" Giselle asked. "Fly to Manila too?"

"I'll be safe here. They don't know who I am."

"Might find out, mister, might come for you and your family."

The back of the seat was digging into my spine. I stood up to ease the discomfort. "My wife and daughter don't live with me."

"Divorced, huh?"

"Separated."

"Why?"

"I don't really …"

The ferry docked with a jolt that put an abrupt end to our talk. It almost put an end to me. The pilot missed the landing marker and had to slow suddenly to compensate for his error. I was flung against the rail and almost sent splashing into the water; with fifty tonnes of raw sewage bobbing about in the harbour death from typhoid would probably have followed.

Safely back on dry land, I pulled a paper handkerchief from my pocket and wiped sweat from my face. Even worse than the sticky heat were the mosquitoes

146

which dive-bombed my face and neck. I swatted one tiny attacker away then another. Then I stood and weighed up our options. It would be pleasant to travel in the mosquito-free, air-conditioned comfort of a taxi. But the queue snaked for about thirty metres. It might take us an hour to reach the restaurant.

"Let's walk," I said. "We'll get there quicker."

We set off down Salisbury Road. We moved past the exclusive Peninsula Hotel, where a silver Rolls Royce was depositing a rich-and-famous guest, then past the YMCA next door. A tout approached and asked me if I wanted to buy a fake Rolex. These sorts of watches look amazingly like the real thing and are a lot cheaper too. But the plastic parts inside them ensure they break down after only a few months. I told the tout I wasn't interested and we kept walking.

A left turn brought us on to Nathan Road, Kowloon's biggest shopping area, which was bursting at the seams with bargain-hunters. Near Chungking Mansions, a tower block full of curry houses and budget hotels, a squad of Indian tailors patrolled the pavement. They smiled alligator-like smiles, pushed price lists into the hands of passers-by and tried to drag the more prosperous-looking tourists into their shops to buy suits, shirts and ties. The tailors ignored me. These characters know a true pauper when they see one.

At the Holiday Inn Golden Mile Hotel, I gestured for Giselle to take a right turn. "Down there," I told her, pointing out the way. "The restaurant's a few minutes walk down that way."

Sichuan is my favourite Chinese food. This is heresy as far as most Hong Kongers are concerned because Cantonese folk are the worlds' biggest food snobs. For them, no food even comes remotely close to matching the glories of Cantonese cuisine. Personally, I've always found Cantonese food to be either stir-fried blandness or the sort of exotic garbage — sea-slugs, snake bile, fried ducks' bollocks and the like— that I wouldn't put in my hand let alone my stomach. I prefer my food spliced with chillies, which is why I like Sichuan. It's not quite as hot as Indian food, but almost.

Giselle asked me to choose the dishes. I asked for spicy soup noodles, fried green beans with chilli, cold pork with chilli sauce, a plate of onion cakes and two *Tsingtao* beers. The waiter brought the beers almost immediately. Beads of perspiration coated the sides of the chunky green bottles. Good. The beer would be icy cold. I filled my glass, waited until foam at the top of the glass had thinned out, and then took a long, thirst-quenching gulp. Ah! that was good. The beer was so cold that it stung the back of my throat.

"What does your daughter do?" Giselle asked

"She's at university."

"What's she studying?"

"Good question," I said. "She signed up for Chinese history, but whether she studies any is debatable. She seems to spend all her time listening to rock music and chatting with friends."

I drained my beer in about two minutes flat — the sauna-like conditions outside had left me with a raging thirst — then signalled to the waiter for another. He brought this one as quickly as he had brought the first.

"You said you were at university in Manila," I said to Giselle as I poured the new beer into my glass. "What did you study?"

She didn't answer.

148

"Let me guess. Art? Music?"

"What the hell's it to you?" she snapped.

I held up my hands in surrender. "Hey, hey, relax. If you don't want to talk about it, fine."

We sipped our beers in uncomfortable silence for a few moments. Then she said, "I shouldn't have done that — shouted at you, I mean. The truth is ..." She flushed with embarrassment. "Well, I lied to you about going to college. Our family's real poor, see. Mama didn't make very much cleaning floors so ... Well, I had to work to support the family." She shrugged and made a helpless gesture. "You know how it is."

I nodded. "You had seven sisters to look after."

She perked up. "You remember, huh?" She seemed pleasantly surprised by my last words. "Remember about my seven sisters, I mean?"

"I've got a good memory."

"Most guys aren't interested in stuff like that. The ones who come into my bar only want one thing." She shot me a knowing look. "Get my meaning, huh?"

The waiter arrived with the wafer-thin slices of pork and a silver jug of chilli sauce. He placed the food on the table then left as unobtrusively as he had arrived.

"Not you, though, huh?" she said.

"Not me what?"

She picked up a slice of the pork with her chopsticks. "Working in a bar like mine you see so many guys that you know right off what they're about." She chewed the pork. "I knew when you walked in that you weren't interested in us girls." She swallowed some beer then wiped froth from her lips: "Didn't think you'd turn out to be a cop, though. You don't look very much like other Hong Kong cops I've run into."

"I'm not a police officer, I'm a private investigator."

The waiter returned with the rest of our food: green beans, onion cakes and spicy soup noodles. The green beans looked fresh and crunchy. The soup noodles were loaded with so much chilli that the tangy aroma made the small hairs inside my nostrils curl.

Giselle eagerly filled her bowl. "Used to be a cop once," she pointed out. "What made you join?"

I grinned. "I've asked myself that question for twenty years and still haven't found a satisfactory answer. It couldn't be the pay, because it's lousy. Maybe I was born crazy. Or maybe it's Ah Sung's fault."

"Who?"

"In my early teens I went off the rails for a while," I explained. "I hung around with a bad crowd and got caught robbing a shop. The police officer who caught me was Ah Sung. He knew my mother well — the two of them had gone to school together in Lamma. In fact I think he'd had a crush on her. Maybe that's why he decided to give me a second chance."

"Let you go, huh?"

"He did more than that," I said, remembering with affection and gratitude the man who had given me such an important break in life. "He took a fatherly interest. He came home and explained how mother needed me and how I was letting her down by doing what I was doing. Then, when I was old enough, he suggested I join the police. He got all the papers I needed, arranged references for me, put in some words with his bosses. After all of the effort he'd made I didn't have the heart to hurt his feelings by saying no."

Giselle piled noodles into her bowl. I was surprised that someone so small and slim could eat so much.

"You're not a cop now. Why quit?"

I shrugged. "Some people say I jumped before being pushed. Personally, I like to think it's because I enjoy working alone." I filled my bowl with noodles and then added chilli sauce. "It makes life easier. When you mess things up you've only got yourself to blame." I added crunchy green beans to my bowl. "The money's just as lousy, though."

Giselle grinned: "You should have stuck to robbing stores. You'd be rich now."

"Or doing twenty years hard labour in prison … I think that's your mobile ringing."

She pulled the phone from her pocket. "Yeah, this is Giselle … Okay I'll come see you." She put the phone on the table. "Davina's waiting outside. I'd better get … Hey! What's wrong? What are you staring at?"

"Your phone," I said dully.

"What the hell's wrong with my phone?"

"It's different." I rested my chopsticks on the table. I no longer felt even slightly hungry. "Different from the one you gave me outside the bar. And different from the one you used to call your friend Davina when we were on the boat."

"That's because I've got two," she said quickly. "Lots of us girls in the bars do. You give the boss at your bar the number for one phone and give the other number to friends. That way, you always know who's calling you; if I'm tired and don't want to talk to my boss, I don't answer."

I didn't know whether to be angry, or applaud her skill. Here was the great Peter Duggan, smugly thinking himself the world's greatest detective: Philip Marlowe, Sam Spade and Charlie Chan rolled into one. This girl

151

had exposed him as an amateur. That trick of checking if Kam Sau's contact details were stored on her mobile phone — a trick I thought I'd played with such masterful aplomb — had not fooled her for a minute. She had seen the punch-line coming three blocks away.

"You conned me," I said.

She pretended to be confused. "Huh?"

"When I borrowed your mobile outside the bar — you gave me the phone that you use to take calls from your boss." I pointed at the phone lying on the table. You couldn't give me that one there, could you? It's got the number for the place where Kam Sau's hiding stored on it. You were scared I might use that phone number to track her down."

This time she made no attempt to act puzzled. "I made her a *promise*, mister." She gazed levelly at me with a mixture of stubborn pride and defiance. "Giselle Maria Santiago — she's a girl who don't *never* break her word to her friends."

I sighed wearily. "She's also a foolish girl."

Her chin jutted forward. "So what are you gonna do about it then, huh?" She eyed me challengingly. "Steal my mobile phone in front of everyone in here and download Kam Sau's details, huh?"

"Look," I said reasonably. "I'm not asking you to betray your friend — I'm not asking for the address of where Kam Sau's hiding. Just for you to tell me if she's crossed the border and gone to China. That wouldn't be breaking your promise to her, would it? She comes from Beijing, right? Has she gone back there? Is she in Beijing now?"

My instincts told me if Kam Sau was in Beijing she would be holed up with her friend, the daughter of the murdered dishwasher — the woman who had been Kam Sau's neighbour in Hong Kong. My friend Frank Ching had interviewed the dishwasher's daughter in Beijing. He had told me where she lived.

"You said working in a bar taught you all about men, Giselle," I reminded her. "You said you could easily tell what kind of person someone is."

She nodded. "I can."

"Then you must know I won't harm Kam Sau."

She stared intently at me. Maybe she was making sure those first impressions she had formed about me had been the correct ones. After a few seconds she nodded again. "I guess you're okay."

"Where is she?"

She shook her head. "A promise is a promise."

I seized a deep breath, counted to five to try and keep my temper. Then I said as slowly and as persuasively as possible, "This isn't a game we're playing here, Giselle. You saw tonight the danger your friend's in. I can help her. But first you're going to have to help me. Where is she?"

For a moment, I thought she would continue to rebuff me; it looked like I would have no alternative but to reach over and grab that mobile phone from her. I didn't think she would be foolish enough to scream rape in a crowded restaurant. But if she did … Well, they reckon prison cells are much more comfortable places these days. Fortunately, it never came to that. After a silence which seemed to last minutes, though it was probably only seconds, she spoke.

"Kam Sau is in Beijing."

23

SHE WAS IN Beijing with her friend. But not at the friend's flat: Kam Sau had decided that they would be safer elsewhere. They had rented an apartment in another part of the city. Giselle gave me the address then phoned Kam Sau to say I would be coming to see her tomorrow and could be trusted.

No one answered the call.

"I'll phone her again when I'm back in the Philippines," Giselle said. "I know now you're okay — I'll tell Kam Sau she can count on you."

I gave her another fifteen hundred dollars of John Yip's cash — if she didn't need it herself then she could send it to her family — saw her safely on the plane and then went home.

It was ten-thirty when I reached the flat. I had two phone messages. One was from Kathy who wanted us to have lunch tomorrow to discuss something 'ultra' important. The other message was from Stephen Fung in Bangkok. He had checked things out with Ian Jeffries. His boss knew nothing about any missing secretary called Kam Sau.

I thought about calling Fung at his hotel but decided against it. He would only repeat that line about Jeffries not knowing Kam Sau. It would be better to wait until Jeffries touched down in Hong Kong tomorrow and then tackle him face to face.

I phoned Kathy to say I would be away most of tomorrow. She told me to have a good trip and to make sure I turned the fridge cold enough to keep her lobster nice and fresh. I warned her that if she ever mentioned lobsters again I would strangle her. Then I set the alarm for six-thirty and crawled into bed. I slept fitfully: Paddy Duggan was trying to kill mother. His hands were around her neck when the nightmare was halted by what I thought was the alarm clock ringing, but which turned out to be the phone. Perhaps Giselle was calling to say she had contacted Kam Sau.

"Yes," I said sleepily.

"Sorry, Peter, I didn't mean to wake you." It wasn't Giselle; it was my wife, Suk Fan. "I thought you would be already up — Kathy said you're taking the early flight to Beijing."

I glanced at the clock: six-fifteen.

"I have to be at the airport by eight-thirty."

"You sound strange," Suk Fan said in a concerned tone. "Are you all right?"

"I'm fine."

I was lying: I felt apprehensive. Why had she rung me? She had not phoned for weeks. Was she calling to say she wanted a divorce? It would explain the concern for my health. She wanted to ensure I could cope with such a massive boot in the balls before she delivered it.

"I just wondered, because I ..." Suk Fan paused. I tensed for the inevitable; she was going to marry her

American lawyer boyfriend: "I know the anniversary's approaching and … Well, I wondered if you were managing to cope." I relaxed: she didn't want a divorce; at least not today. "I know how much those dreams of your father can affect you. I wanted to make sure you're all right."

Of course I'm not all right, was what I should have said. It's not only nightmares of Paddy which keep me awake. I've slept terribly since you left. Come back and it will all be different this time. I promise I'll change.

Instead I said, "I've found a new method of coping with Paddy. A sleeping draught called whisky. A bottle of that and you forget him — forget everything."

"You shouldn't drink so much," Suk Fan said. "It's bad for your liver and—"

"Kidney, heart and every other internal organ," I interrupted tersely. "I know — you've told me before. Nine hundred times if memory serves me right, or is it a straight thousand?"

I knew as soon as I had opened my big mouth that I should have kept it shut. Yet whenever Suk Fan has a go at me I can never resist hitting back; it's instinctive; I don't mean half of what I say. Over the years we'd had hundreds of these sorts of tiffs and quickly shrugged them off. When you're standing next to someone, such minor disagreements are easily sorted out: a smile, a contrite look, a grovelling Duggan apology — they can all put things right. At least they used to be able to.

This morning, linked only by a phone line, our tiff seemed much worse than a minor disagreement. Maybe it was because I couldn't see Suk Fan and smile an apology. Or was the polar-like atmosphere due to the fact that our marriage had well and truly burned out?

"Don't let's argue," Suk Fan pleaded. "I didn't call you up for a row."

"I'm sorry," I said. "I shouldn't have snapped at you like that. You know how like a pig with a sore head I am this early in the morning. I'll be better after I've swallowed half a gallon of coffee."

"Kathy's been acting strangely," Suk Fan said. She paused, before adding in the hushed tones of someone confiding a state secret, "I think ... In fact I *know* she's got a boyfriend."

A boyfriend!

Call out the Lord Executioner! Give her the death of a thousand cuts! Off to the killing fields with her! Why shouldn't Kathy have a boyfriend, I felt like saying; her mother has one. But I couldn't bear to mention Suk Fan's American lawyer: I wanted to pretend that he didn't exist.

I said reasonably, "It's hardly a hanging offence."

"I don't want to see her hurt. She's not as tough as she makes out."

"Get her to bring the boyfriend home." To me, the solution seemed simple. "I'm sure you'll find that he's a decent kid."

"She won't even tell me his name! If I ask her she goes crazy and ... So I thought ... Well, maybe you can talk to her — you might learn more than me."

"It'll cost you," I said, "two hundred dollars a day plus expenses."

I had meant it as a joke, and in the old days she would have laughed. True, she wouldn't have split her sides — a lot of my jokes are as funny as a kick in the groin — but at least she would have smiled if only from a sense of duty, or pity. And she would also have known that I was *trying* to be light-hearted. Evidence of how far apart we had drifted was that today she thought I was jeering at her.

"No need to be sarcastic," she said, in a tone warning me to get serious.

"I'll even chuck in a free surveillance camera," I said, ignoring her warnings and making matters worse.

"Oh shut up!" she shouted. "Shut up!"

"What the hell have I done now?"

"Never grown up!" she snapped. "I mean, here I am worrying myself sick about our only daughter, and all you can do is to make stupid juvenile jokes."

The conversation had begun to mirror our married life. Not life in the first sixteen years, when we had been happy, but when rot had set in during the last year, before Suk Fan had decided to leave. When the only things that had bound us together had been our love for Kathy, and memories of the past and how good it had once been — and a belief that it could never be as good again. And all of it interspersed with frequent misunderstandings and apologies — nearly all of them mine — and a tension I would try to ease with a lousy joke, only to fail miserably; and then get angry at Suk Fan, as though the failure had been all hers.

"Why *shouldn't* Kathy have a boyfriend?" I said.

My wife did not reply. I knew she was there, though, because I could hear her breathing.

"She's eighteen," I pointed out. "You can't wrap her in cotton wool forever."

"You know what a worrier I am, Peter. I just …"

I could tell from the quiver in her voice that she was on the verge of tears. Suk Fan has always been incredibly protective of Kathy. In that respect she's no differ-

158

ent from other Chinese mothers. They all fret endlessly about a child's health, education and job prospects; the suitability of boyfriends and girlfriends. Often their concerns come close to being paranoia.

But it wasn't her fear that Kathy's boyfriend might prove to be a modern-day Genghis Khan which had got my wife into such a state: Kathy's betrayal had caused the pain. Suk Fan has always regarded Kathy as a best friend, as well as her daughter; until now they had kept no secrets from each other. She saw Kathy's refusal to discuss her boyfriend as a betrayal of trust.

"I'll chat to her," I promised. "And I'll also check out the boyfriend to make sure he's all right. Will that put your mind at rest?"

"About Kathy, yes," Suk Fan replied, after a pause. "Although …"

"Something else?" I probed gently.

Another pause, and then a hesitant, "I wondered … When are you going to the temple?"

"Same day as always: the day after tomorrow. Why?"

"I thought we could go together."

"The temple?"

"Us two living apart doesn't alter the fact I loved your mother. She would want us there as a family. She'll be watching from the after-life and it would hurt her not to see us together. So I'll come if that's all right?"

I should have realised Suk Fan would feel this way. She may *seem* westernised, but scratch at the surface and you will find someone as Chinese as the Great Wall. A mistake many Americans and Europeans make about educated Hong Kongers like my wife is to assume that because they speak English and like American music, and can tell the difference between John Wayne and

Joanna Lumley, they're westernised. It's not true. It would take more than Big John and the US Cavalry to shake my wife's sense of being Chinese.

"Of course it's all right," I said.

I wanted to add that anything she said was all right; whatever she asked me to do I would do, any promises she wanted me to make I would make — and keep my promises this time. Instead, I just said I would phone her after I returned from Beijing and fix a time for visiting the temple. Then I hung up and cursed myself for being a fool. I had missed a golden opportunity to ask for one last chance to save our marriage.

I shuffled over to the window and stared out. The sky was tombstone grey. It had been the same drab colour this time last year when we had travelled to Tsuen Wan's Buddhist temple. It was strange how the weather had changed so dramatically; when we left home the blue sky had been cloudless, sun melting the pavement.

An hour later, as I placed pork and rice wine beneath mother's cremated remains to ensure she never went hungry or thirsty in the after-life, clouds scudded over. When Kathy laid her smouldering joss sticks in front of mother's framed picture, then bowed three times and said a prayer, the rain fell.

We sloshed to the temple's furnace; it lay knee-deep in ashes. I drew so close that heat from the furnace drew plumes of steam from my wet shirt, crinkled my hair. I threw ghost money into the curling blue-yellow flames; mother would need it in the after-life. Kathy and Suk Fan hurled in packets full of paper clothes and shoes; she could swap them for the real things in the after-life. It was when Kathy tossed in her last parcel of

160

clothes that the wind really got up, blowing hot ashes into my eyes.

I began to weep.

"The ashes! They sting like chillies!"

Suk Fan draped her arm around me, held me close. "Go ahead and cry, Peter. Go on, it's not a weakness to cry. Not for someone you loved. Let it all flow out."

Yet after she said that, I couldn't cry for mother. I still tasted the ashes, though. The taste of them had stayed with me for days: hot, dry and coppery. It had taken days to escape the smell of Kathy's burning joss sticks, too; a sickly-sweet odour, a bit like the smell of rotting apples. But I'd been unable to cry again. Not that day or any other. Until the day my wife left me.

24

I BOARDED THE plane with all the cheerfulness of a man facing a firing squad.

Cathay Pacific's flight to Beijing was full; I'd had to settle for Air China. While no misfortunes had befallen me on the previous two occasions that I'd used it, I knew the horror tales about China's state-owned airline. On one flight a passenger had wanted a bowl of fried rice, so the crew had trundled a wok into the aisle and begun cooking. On another trip a cabin attendant in need of fresh air had tried to open the emergency window — at 25,000 feet.

To take my mind off such scare stories, I read the newspapers. I scanned the *South China Morning Post* for news about my friend, Jack Spalding. I found a two-paragraph report on page three — there had been a slight improvement in his condition.

I flipped through China's *People's Daily*. Its front page was dominated by an editorial attacking the 'renegade province' of Taiwan, and warning of 'tough action' if Taiwan's government failed to do everything China told it to do. Page one also carried a report about British government minister Ian Jeffries and his visit to Beijing. There was a picture of him and his young political adviser, Stephen Fung. Jeffries' hand rested paternally on Fung's shoulder. He gazed at his adviser fondly. In fact it was more than that. He looked at Fung the way that a proud parent looks at a favourite son.

I put the *People's Daily* down and grabbed a copy of the Hong Kong gossip magazine, *Next*. A feature on film producer Alan Yip began on page six, the usual rubbish about how a boy from Mongkok's slums had grown up to become the king of Asia's movie scene.

A joke picture accompanied the article. The magazine's photographer had skillfully superimposed the heads of Yip and his rivals from India's 'Bollywood' on the bodies of a group of studio models. The Bollywood boys all paid homage to Yip, who wore a king's purple robes and cradled a sceptre. One of the Bollywood team members seemed distinctly unhappy about bending the knee to King Al. He looked like he wanted to grab the sceptre and beat his majesty to death with it.

The magazine also contained an article on Yip's son, John. It focused on changes he might make to the film-making empire when he inherited it. Two pictures of John Yip accompanied the article; one showed him stood beside the Bollywood figure who had wanted to batter Alan Yip with his sceptre.

According to the caption, this picture had been taken in Hong Kong at a party held in the Mandarin Hotel to mark the end of the global conference on climate change. The Bollywood figure's name was Henry Parwani, owner of Parwani Cinema Corporation, one of India's biggest and most profitable film-making outfits. In that joke picture, Parwani had scowled at

163

Alan Yip. The party one with Yip Junior showed him flashing the grin of a man having the time of his life. But it was the second picture of John Yip which really grabbed my attention. It had also been taken at the climate change party. In this shot, Yip Junior chatted to a pock-faced young man who wore a shocking pink shirt and a black-and-white spotted bow-tie: the same pock-faced young man who had guided me around the film studios yesterday.

You should know better, Peter, I told myself. You should know by now never to judge people only by appearances. It was the spotted bow-tie and pink shirt which had thrown me. Surely someone who dressed like that couldn't be taken seriously — I had assumed that he was just an office gopher. But John Yip would not have taken a mere gopher to a major event like that climate change party.

Had the crazy clothes and yesterday's over-the-top enthusiasm all been a clever act staged by my pock-faced guide; an attempt to get dim-witted private detectives to underestimate him? The attempt had succeeded brilliantly. I realised now how John Yip had known about my discussions with his father. There had been no need to bug dad's office. An ear pressed to the door by his faithful young lieutenant had sufficed.

I put the magazine down and tried to grab half an hour's rest. I must have been exhausted because I woke up three hours later to hear a cabin attendant announcing on the speaker system that we were about to land and telling me to fasten my seat belt.

AFTER CLEARING CUSTOMS and passport control, I called the number Giselle had given me for Kam

164

Sau. No answer. I hailed a cab outside the airport terminal and instructed the driver to head for Chang'an Jiem, the main highway that runs beside Tiananmen Square. When we were about four hundred metres away from the Great Hall of the People, I told my driver to stop.

As if on cue, the moment I stepped out on the pavement, it rained. Photographers and artists touting for trade on the edges of Tiananmen Square scurried for cover. Some of them opened golf umbrellas which they then sheltered under. A group of tourists standing by the Monument to the Heroes of the People pulled on raincoats. I had brought no raincoat or umbrella with me — before walking ten metres I was soaked.

The air resounded to the roar of motorbike engines. Thirty years ago it would have been hard to have glimpsed even a single motorcycle on Chang'an Jiem — pedal power had been the name of the game back then. But in recent years Hondas and Yamahas had become increasingly popular with China's middle-class. The real royalty, though, was the four-wheel stuff: gleaming new Mercedes and Rolls Royce models whose chauffeur-driven owners jabbered on mobile phones, or glanced at jewelled watches to check they weren't running late for important business appointments. These characters, with their slicked-back hair and smart Armani suits, were the new 'super rich'. Living symbols of an all-thrusting, all-dynamic China.

They had listened carefully, seventeen years ago, when the country's former leader Deng Xiaoping had told them that 'to get rich is glorious'. Yet not everyone had heard, or been able to heed Deng's message. Parts of old China still remained, even in a metropolis like

165

Beijing. A skeletal-like pensioner, pushing a bike so loaded with bulging striped bags that it looked in danger of collapsing, showed that not all of the country's one billion-plus citizens had yet become paid-up members of the super-rich club.

I tramped for five minutes down Chang'an Jiem then turned left on to a street where the old and new Beijing existed side by side. Teens wearing the latest European fashions flounced past old crones clad in the dowdy Mao pyjama suits that, until thirty-five years ago, every Chinese female, both young and old, had worn. I walked for about fifty metres down this street, almost choking on the petrol and diesel fumes that poisoned the air. China's rocket-like economic progress had come at a cost. Beijing was now one of the most heavily polluted cities in the world.

I wiped rain from my face and turned right. Fifty metres ahead of me a row of ugly grey-black apartment blocks rose sullenly into a leaden sky. The developers who were responsible for all these architectural monstrosities had made sure to get their money's worth. They had crammed as many apartment blocks into the area as possible. Only a few feet or so of space seemed to exist between each block. Stand on the roof of one building and you would be able to step over to the next one in the row.

I moved into the lobby of the first block. Apart from a blue-uniformed security guard-caretaker, who sat at a desk, the place was empty. In another example of how capitalism had boomed in China, the caretaker shouted down the phone at his stockbroker, angrily accusing him of buying the wrong share options. He was so focused on giving the stockbroker a dressing-down that he failed to notice the stranger who had entered the lobby. I pressed the lift button to open the double steel doors, stepped inside the lift and jabbed the button for the eighth floor. I got out here and turned left. The third door from the lift shaft was the door I wanted. I rang the bell. No answer. I knocked but still got no reply.

I glanced up and down the corridor. Empty. No one would be likely to turn up and disturb me either because this apartment block was mainly inhabited by young people. They would be out working, trying to become 'super rich'. Good. That gave me a chance to break in.

I bent down and examined the metal grille which guarded the wooden entrance door. The grille's lock was an old type; it shouldn't prove too hard to crack. I reached into my jacket pocket and pulled out the ten-centimetre strip of wire that I had brought specially for this purpose. I put the wire in the grille's lock then moved the wire around until I heard a dull click. Those days of hanging about with teenage gangsters had not been entirely wasted.

With my free hand, I slid the grille open.

I removed the wire from the lock and replaced it in my jacket. Then I examined the lock on the wooden door. It was an even older and more flimsy type than the lock on the grille.

I took a credit card from the pocket of my trousers, slipped the card into the gap between door and door frame, and then slid the card down until it rested against the door's flimsy bolt. With a firm twist of the card, I snapped the bolt back and opened the door. I entered the flat to discover I was not the only housebreaker in town — it had been ransacked. Furniture had been tipped on the wooden floor, clothing dragged from a wardrobe, the sofa torn apart, the phone pulled to pieces.

"Hello! Anyone there?" I called out.

Then I realised how crazy it was: I had just broken in. What did I say if someone emerged from the bedroom — go back to sleep, it's only your friendly burglar Peter Duggan come to pay a call? Not that anyone would be sleeping: if Kam Sau or her friend had been snoozing they would have woken up as soon as that other burglar began to trash the apartment.

Other burglar!

Was he still here? Hiding in one of the other rooms?

Apart from the entrance door, four doors led from the living room. I opened these doors one by one, to discover what lay behind. The two doors that stood furthest away from the flat's entrance opened on to bedrooms. No one was hiding inside them. The first bedroom was hardly big enough for a person to sleep in, let alone hide in. The main bedroom was three times bigger. A window in the main bedroom gave access to a metal fire escape, which led from the roof on the twelfth floor all the way down to the ground.

Both bedrooms had been ransacked.

It was after I had checked the main bedroom that the madness of my actions hit me. Apart from a Swiss Army penknife I had come unarmed. Supposing that burglar *was* still around and had a gun? What did I do when he pointed the gun at me? There wouldn't be much I could do. Apart from thrust my hands in the air and hope he was feeling merciful. Too late for me to change plans now, though. I continued searching.

168

The third door opened on to a tiny kitchen where broken cups and dishes littered the floor. This meant that the fourth and final door must lead to the bathroom. I nudged this door open, moved inside the bathroom and encountered the smell that always sends a shiver coursing down my spine.

It seemed to come from the shower unit. I couldn't see inside the unit because someone had dragged the blue plastic shower curtain across the entrance. I reached over and yanked back the curtain to reveal a sight, which even after twenty years as a police officer and private investigator, never fails to turn my stomach. A girl stood in front of me. She was naked. Her eyes had the faint stale glitter of death.

25

HER HANDS WERE stretched above her head, palms pressed together in a praying position. The killer had roped her wrists to the shower rail. The rope had cut through her skin, probably as she thrashed around to try and free herself.

She was warm, suggesting she'd been dead less than three hours. The stink of cordite was strong enough to make me think she had been killed even more recently, perhaps within the last hour. The killer had shot her in the head. A hole the size of a ten cent coin, hardly big enough to probe with my smallest finger, marked where the bullet had entered the front of the skull. Where it had exited at the back of her head lay a crater large enough for my fist. Scorch marks on her brow revealed the killer had fired from almost point-blank range: a victim's skin always becomes tattooed with gunpowder burns when the killing distance is so close.

The killer had tortured her first. Purplish-red burn marks, probably caused by a lit cigarette, scarred the area around her left breast. Two of her fingernails had been ripped out from ...

Jesus Christ!

Revulsion swamped me. What animal could do this? Bile surged to my throat. I leaned over the sink, turned on the tap and thrust my head under it. The shock of icy water exploding against my skull kept me from vomiting; but only just.

I dragged a pack of tissues from my pocket and used some to dry my face. I seized deep breaths to calm myself. The girl wasn't Alan Yip's missing secretary, Kam Sau. She was Joe Chan's lover. The girl in the snapshot my friend Frank Ching had shown me; the girl whom I had assumed was a prostitute. So where was Yip's secretary — had the killer abducted Kam Sau?

I played out a scenario in my mind. The gunman bursts into the flat and demands those pictures Giselle had told me about, the blackmail weapons Kam Sau had claimed could destroy her enemy. When the girls refuse, he tortures one of them until they give up the pictures, and then leaves, dragging Kam Sau with him, and ... Hold on! It couldn't have happened that way. If they had surrendered the photographs, he would never have ripped the flat apart hunting for them, would he? And why burn this girl so badly? She looked a type who would scare easily. There would have been no need to burn her. The mere threat would have set her talking. And why only one body; why not silence both the witnesses?

I gazed more intently at the girl, as if doing so would answer all of my questions. It only sent a fresh wave of nausea rushing over me. It was the smell of her body, as much as the sight of it, that made me feel sick. Or rather the smell I imagined to be coming from her body. It probably sounds strange, considering I was a policeman for two decades, but I've never got used to the scent of death. It's a problem that dates back to the first post-mortem I attended twenty-two years ago. It wasn't so much the sight of the bloated blue-grey corpse hauled from Victoria Harbour which so unnerved me, but its smell; stale raw flesh, stale blood, stale piss — stale everything. The smell had invaded my hair, saturated my skin pores, penetrated my sinuses — taken a month of hot showers and scrubbing myself with strong carbolic soap to escape it.

The corpse had been so decomposed that the police surgeon had worn a gas mask. There had been no spare mask for me, so I had sat cross-legged on the floor, afraid that the moment I tried to stand up I would keel over. This girl may have only been dead an hour, but the sight of her resurrected all the memories and smells of that first post-mortem. If I stared at her any longer, I might throw up.

I went into the living room and considered my next move. Being an ex-policeman, I suppose I should have felt duty-bound to report everything to the Beijing Public Security Bureau. However, I've never felt duty-bound to behave like a fool. China might have undergone huge economic changes in recent years, but things on the bureaucracy front had not changed all that much. The local cops would detain me to 'help with inquiries'. Knowing their crazy bureaucracy it could be weeks before I got home, perhaps years — someone eager for an arrest and conviction might fit me up for the girl's murder.

I decided to return to the airport. But not before removing all signs of my presence. I took the remaining tissues from my pocket and walked around the flat, wiping away my prints; then returned to the bathroom, intending to flush the tissues down the toilet. Once I was back inside the bathroom, though, I forgot about disposing of tissues — I was too busy focusing on the sink where I had washed my face. Water had still not flowed away from the sink. There must be a blockage in the pipe.

If it had been an older apartment, I wouldn't have been surprised; plumbing systems in old houses are forever breaking down — mine seems to need fixing every week. But this flat was virtually brand new, less than one year old. That made me curious about what had caused the blockage.

I knelt by the sink and unscrewed the U-bend of the discharge pipe, jumping aside as icy water gushed out. I fumbled inside the pipe and located the object that had caused the blockage. It was wedged in there tightly, but after a few minutes of effort I managed to drag it free: a small, hard object wrapped in layers of black plastic to make it waterproof. I peeled away the plastic layers and gazed at two tiny video cassettes.

A strange person this murderer, I mused, stowing the tapes in my pocket. He ransacks every other room. Yet here in the bathroom, where the tapes are hidden, he leaves things untouched. Why? And why didn't the dead girl give up the tapes? Why not avoid that torture by surrendering the cassettes? Had she not known where they were hidden? Maybe Kam Sau had chosen the hiding place. For some reason — perhaps she had thought it would be safer — Kam Sau had kept the hiding place a secret from her friend. So why hadn't she ended her friend's agony? Why had Kam Sau not told the killer where the tapes were hidden?

I played out a new scenario. When the killer bursts in only one girl is home — Kam Sau is out. Joe Chan's lover protests she doesn't know where the tapes are. But the killer refuses to believe her and burns her to get her to reveal the hiding place. Eventually, though, he realises she's telling the truth about not knowing. He rips the furniture apart, hunting for the tapes, kills the girl to prevent her identifying him, then leaves.

But why not ransack the bathroom? And why not wait here for Kam Sau? That dead girl must have told him who had hidden the tapes. Why not stay in the flat until Kam Sau returned and then force her to reveal the hiding place? Had that girl told him Kam Sau wouldn't be returning? Supposing her and Kam Sau had decided to split up for a few days, thinking it might be safer that way. In that case the killer would have forced the girl to reveal Kam Sau's new address, and then headed off to that address to find Kam Sau.

And kill her!

I yanked the phone from my pocket and punched the Manila number for Giselle. Her phone rang for ten seconds. Ten became fifteen, then twenty and thirty.

"Come on," I hissed. "Pick it up."

I had almost given up on her answering, when I heard a click, followed by the sound of Giselle's voice.

"Yeah?" she drawled sleepily.

"This is Peter Duggan. You need to warn Kam Sau."

"Huh?"

"Someone's on his way to her flat to kill her."

"*Kill her!*" Giselle was suddenly wide awake.

"If I warn her she'll know when she sees the phone number that it's me. She won't answer me — the call must come from you."

174

"What do I tell her?"

"To head for the airport immediately; when she gets there she goes to Cathay Pacific's departures desk and waits for me." I described what I was wearing, so that Kam Sau would recognise me. "You have to keep trying to persuade her to trust me, Giselle. To make her understand I want to help. Can you do that?"

"I'll try, mister."

She hung up. Would she succeed? I hoped so. Or Kam Sau would suffer the same fate as her friend. Or was it already too late? More than an hour had passed since the gunman had murdered Joe Chan's girlfriend. Perhaps he had already killed Kam Sau too. Maybe he had … The murmur of sirens broke my thoughts. I strained my ears and tensed for the sound to grow louder; I had a sickening feeling that the police were coming this way.

The sound remained faint. Then it vanished and I decided that they had gone somewhere else. Then the murmur returned, faint at first but steadily growing louder until it became a harsh, ear-splitting wail. Now there could be no doubt. The police were heading here.

26

I RUSHED TO the window at the end of the corridor and stared down at the street. Three patrol vehicles roared to a halt. Car doors were flung open. Armed Security Bureau officers leaped out. But perhaps their target was another apartment block.

And perhaps pigs might fly.

It was definitely this block, because two officers were charging into the lobby. In fact it wasn't only this block, *but this floor* — another uniformed officer running to the main entrance jabbed a finger up in my direction. Or perhaps he had pointed at another flat on my floor: it was possible, wasn't it? About as possible as those pigs suddenly growing wings: the officers had come here for me, I needed to get out fast.

How? No way could I take the lift. Or go down the stairs then walk casually through the lobby — officers would be stationed there. They wouldn't be talking stock markets, or commodities contracts, like that security guard had been doing when I arrived. They would be on red alert for a killer. They would grab me the instant I emerged from the lift: strangers draw attention. I would stand out like a bruised finger here. I don't look Chinese; I take after my Irish father Paddy Duggan for looks.

Then I remembered the fire escape fixed to the wall outside the main bedroom: it led from the twelfth floor all the way to street level. It ran down the back of the building, hidden from the officers out front: use it and they would be unable to see me. Open the window and get on that fire escape, then climb down and … Yes, it would be easy.

I dashed back to the flat, had the bedroom window levered half-open and was debating whether I should hail a taxi when I reached street level, or simply walk away to safety, when I glimpsed something below: the peaked cap of a Security Bureau officer.

Screw it! No way could I use the fire escape now.

Then I remembered how, walking along the street to get here, I had noticed the blocks in this row were all packed close together: I had cursed the greedy developers for leaving only a few feet of space between each building; for jamming them so close together that you could get on top of one of the buildings then step over to the next.

Which is exactly what you will do, Peter.

I drew up my plan. Take the lift to the twelfth floor and open the doors leading to the roof. Then step or jump over to the roof of the next block in the row — repeating this manoeuvre six times until I stood on top of the block furthest away from the Security Bureau officers — shove open the roof doors here, enter this new building, head down to the ground floor — no police would be waiting in this lobby to grab me — stroll out on to the street, take a cab to the airport …

177

Yes, it would work. I shoved open the door of the flat and strode towards the lift. But there was no need to rush. Stay cool, I told myself. Remember that stuff you learned at school about more haste bringing you less speed — it will happen if you lose your coolness. You have a good plan. The plan will work if you stay relaxed. Take it easy and you'll avoid screw-ups. You have no reason to panic because ...

Bullshit!

I had every reason to panic. The lift was on its way up here. According to the flashing red light above the metal doors, it had already reached the sixth floor — only two floors below me. The lift was full of armed police who would shoot first and ask questions later.

I sprinted to the staircase.

I kicked open double doors and charged up four flights of stairs, taking the stairs two at a time. I made it to the twelfth floor, staggered out on to the roof. I snatched deep breaths — the mad dash up here had almost given me a heart attack. The pain had been worth it, though, because now I would be safe. All I had to do was to step over to the next building, and then the next and ...

Dream on!

Rushing up here had been insanity. I had charged straight into a twelfth-floor prison cell. At the moment no officers could see me: they were searching Kam Sau's flat, or in the lobby, or checking the back of the building. Only one of them needed to leave the lobby, though — he would be bound to look up here. What did I shout down — that I'd stepped out on to the roof for fresh air? I might as well hold a sign with the words 'murder suspect' written on it.

The cops were not my main worry, though — it was all those gaps between the seven apartment blocks. Viewed from street level, the gaps had seemed so ridiculously small that a child could step from one roof to the next. When you're more than a hundred feet up and facing the prospect of scrambling your brains on the pavement, things look different. Back there in the bedroom, my plan had been inspired genius. Now it seemed crass stupidity. Only the long jump world record holder could leap from one block to another.

Stay here, though, and the Security Bureau officers would grab me. It might take them a while before they puzzled things out, but eventually they would check the roof. Unless I plucked up courage and jumped, I would spend tonight and perhaps every night for the next thirty years, in a Chinese prison cell.

I jumped.

Fear had made me overestimate the distance — I jumped too far and lost my balance when I landed; I pitched forward on my hands and knees, shaved the skin from my palms. Better that, though, than mashing my head on the pavement below.

I stood up and prepared to jump to the next block.

Then I threw myself face down against the roof. Had that officer seen me — the one who had just emerged from the apartment block? No. He would have shouted out. I crawled to the edge of the roof and peered down. He opened the door of his car, reached into the car and dragged out a black briefcase. I expected him to take the briefcase to the lobby. To my horror, he stored the case on the car's roof then lit a cigarette. I cursed. The longer he stayed there smoking, the more chance there was of one of his friends coming out of the building

179

and spotting me. Two minutes droned by — would he ever finish that lousy cigarette?

Finally, he did. He returned to the apartment block. I stood up, took a deep breath and then jumped to the next roof. It was easier this time. I kept my balance on landing. But this was no time to stand around praising my technique. The longer I stayed up here the more I risked someone spotting me.

I repeated my long jump routine another five times, until I stood on the last block in the row. I opened double doors leading into the building, made my way down to the lobby. The security guard was reading the newspaper. I strolled out on to the street unchallenged, turned left, walked about fifty metres then swung left again. For once in my life, a taxi happened to be passing when I needed it. I flagged it down and told the driver to head for the airport.

In any different circumstances I would have felt euphoric about my escape. But how could I feel elated when a girl lay dead in that flat? I should still have felt some relief, though: I would soon reach the airport — in six short hours I would be home. Yet I remained tense. Supposing some alert Beijing citizen had spied me on the roof? Supposing he or she had also seen me hail this taxi, jotted down the registration number then phoned the Security Bureau headquarters? I had a vision of flashing lights, wailing sirens; a patrol car pulling alongside; police officers pointing guns and ordering us to stop. But when I glanced through the cab's rear window I saw nothing suspicious.

My mobile phone rang.

"I did it, mister! I did it!" Giselle cried.

"You spoke to Kam Sau?"

"I did well, huh? Made her see sense; got her to make for the airport — just like you wanted. Told her to trust you too; I did well, huh?"

"When does she arrive at the airport?"

"She's there already. I did well, huh?"

"You did brilliant, Giselle."

I put the phone in my pocket. Tension began to fade from my body. I would be safe; Kam Sau too. We would meet at the airport, return to Hong Kong … Yes, everything would be fine. No one had witnessed my Spiderman antics on the roof. I had evaded the Security Bureau officers.

"We're here," my driver said, "Beijing airport."

I paid and tipped him, climbed out of the car and strode over to the terminal. Its air-conditioned coolness made me even more relaxed: I was safe and so was Kam Sau. I only had to find her in this crowd and then catch the first available plane to Hong Kong. Everything would be fine. My phone call to Giselle and then Giselle's persuasiveness had saved Kam Sau. If only we could have also saved that other girl from … I broke away from my thoughts as someone seized me by the shoulder. I swung round angrily, wondering who could have dared grab me. I glimpsed a peaked cap, black leather holster. The man who had me in his grip was a Public Security Bureau officer. One of those I thought I had escaped from. I was trapped.

27

IN A MOMENT he would shout for help from other officers: I could see it in his eyes. I couldn't allow him that moment. I had to strike now while he was alone. One hard blow to the ribs to break his grip on my shoulder — that was all it would take. Then get out of here fast. No one would stop me. Passengers would be too scared to intervene. The police would never shoot at me in a crowded terminal. They would be scared of hitting the wrong person.

I clenched my fist.

Felt muscles in my arm grow taut.

Now! Do it now!

Before I could throw a punch the officer did something which stopped me in my tracks — he released his grip on my shoulder. Then he did something even more amazing: he smiled; a bashful, apologetic smile. As politely as if he was asking me the time, he said, "Excuse me, sir, but would you by any chance be called Mister Peter Duggan?"

I nodded dumbly at him He pointed in the direction of a row of seats in front of the flight departures' board, about ten metres away. Someone sitting in one of the seats held up her hand — Kam Sau.

"She was calling your name and pointing at you," explained the officer. "But you didn't seem to hear her — you looked like you were in your own dream world."

I unclenched my fist. There would be no need to deliver that blow to the officer's ribcage. My assault on the world record for fastest dash from an airport terminal could take place another day.

"So I thought that I'd better draw your attention to the young lady," the officer continued. "I hope I didn't startle you too much — grabbing you like I did."

"No," I said, hoping he couldn't hear the noise my heart made as it gouged an eight-inch hole in my chest. "You didn't startle me, officer. Thanks for your help."

"No problems, sir."

He snapped out a salute and strode off.

I walked over to Kam Sau who sat hunched up on the chair, arms folded tightly across her chest. Perhaps she was afraid that if she unfolded her arms she would be unable to stop them from shaking. She wore a dark red sweatshirt with Nike written on the front in white capital letters and faded jeans tucked into knee-length, black suede boots. Her long, shiny black hair was tied back in a ponytail with a dark red ribbon.

A ponytail is a hairstyle that I've always thought makes women look much younger. Not her, though. She looked at least ten years older than she had looked in the photograph film-maker Alan Yip had showed me. The cheery, girl-next-door grin which had been captured by the camera had vanished like yesterday's dawn. Her pale face bore a tight, pinched look.

"Are you Duggan?"

183

"Yes."

"Prove it."

"But you *know* I'm Peter Duggan," I protested. "You spoke to Giselle. She told you what I looked like and what I was wearing."

She shook her head. "I want definite proof. Or I start screaming my head off and bring that police officer running back here."

I stared more closely at her. I'd known she would be scared, of course. But I had not expected to glimpse pure unmitigated terror in her face. People as frightened as she was often did the craziest things. Unless I gave her exactly what she wanted, she might carry out her threat about that cop. I spoke quickly about Giselle and the phone call I had made to Manila. Then about that call Kam Sau herself had made to me in Hong Kong. I breathed a sigh of relief as suspicion started to fade from her face.

"Giselle says you'll protect me."

"I will," I promised her. "First, though, we need to talk somewhere quiet." I pointed to a bar at the end of the terminal. "We can go there."

The bar proved to be a pseudo-minimalist affair: chrome seats, lacquered tables; whitewashed walls. There was nothing minimal about its prices, though. Drinks cost double what they cost at other places in the terminal; which probably explained why apart from two young business types who had slicked-back hair and wore snappy blue Armani suits, the bar was empty.

As soon as we had sat down, Kam Sau dragged a pack of cigarettes and box of matches from her pocket. I was shocked at how much her olive-coloured hands shook, and by how badly she had chewed her painted fingernails. She had almost bitten some of the red nails down to the quick. An elderly, silver-haired waiter arrived at our table. He asked me what we wanted to drink. I ordered two large glasses of brandy.

"You'll have to drink both," Kam Sau said, after the waiter had gone away. "I never touch strong alcohol."

I was about to say she would need to touch it today: it would help her to cope with the shock. I stopped myself just in time. It would be best to keep silent for a while longer: to wait until she had fortified herself with a slug of brandy before breaking the news about her friend. In fact it might be wiser to pretend that the girl was still alive. Kam Sau seemed on the verge of cracking up. Revealing what had happened in that flat might cause her to lose it completely.

She had already guessed the truth about her friend, though. She nervously licked her chapped lips. She said, "Ah Fah ... She — she's dead, isn't she?"

"I'm sorry."

Her hands shook as she tried and failed three times to light a cigarette; she finally made it at the fourth attempt. "It should really have been me," she said in a quavering voice. "I'm the person who really should be dead." She snatched a shaky pull from her Marlboro then blew out smoke. She said, "And Joe? ... Is he ..."

"I'm sorry."

The silver-haired waiter arrived with our drinks. He put the glasses down on the table then went away as quietly as he had arrived. I picked up one of the glasses and pressed it into Kam Sau's hand.

"Drink it," I told her. "It'll help you cope."

She did as I said and drank half of it in one go, gasping as it scorched her throat.

"What did you mean a moment ago?" I asked her. "When you said you're the one who should be dead?"

She darted nervous glances around the bar.

"It's all right," I said. "No one knows we're here."

She took a hurried pull from her cigarette then just as hurriedly crushed it out.

"It was Ah Fah's turn to shop for dinner, but she'd just washed her hair." Kam Sau nervously flicked strands of her own dark hair from her brow. "So I went instead. Ah Fah wanted me to buy tuna, but the market was sold out so I called to tell her. We had a safety system with the phone. I let the phone in the flat ring three times then hung up and called her back. Ah Fah never answered, so then I tried her mobile. When she didn't answer me this time I knew something was wrong. But I thought ... I mean ... Well I was scared that the police might make things even worse. So at first, I never rang them up for help because ..." She made a helpless gesture. "You don't understand! I was so confused!"

"But finally you managed to calm down enough to think straight," I said. "You realised you had no other choice — you called the Security Bureau."

She nodded. "That's what I did."

So it was her I had to thank for forcing me up on the rooftops: she had phoned the Beijing police and they had rushed over to her block.

I said, "How did that gunman find your flat?"

She snatched up her glass, drained the remains of the brandy. I signalled to the waiter for another. She lit a new cigarette. She said, "Guys all went nuts about Ah Fah." She sucked hungrily at her Marlboro. "Ah Fah was pretty, you know — I mean *really* pretty."

186

"I know. Someone showed me her picture in Hong Kong. How did the gunman track you down?"

"I don't know. Joe and Giselle were the only people who had the address of the flat."

"How did you call Joe? Did you use the telephone in your flat?"

She shook her head. "Always mobiles; Joe said it was safer that way because … No, that's wrong. On Friday morning, Ah Fah used the phone in the flat."

"You're sure?"

"She had to. Her mobile's battery was low."

So that was it. Ah Fah had pronounced her own death sentence. According to eyewitnesses, journalist Joe Chan had been killed in a hit-and-run accident. Had the witnesses been bribed? Intimidated? Chan's death had been no accident. After running him down, the killer had climbed from his car to make sure Chan was dead. He had searched Chan's pockets, found his phone and seen the stored number for the Beijing flat — the number Ah Fah had left when she'd called Chan on Friday. If the killer had been an ordinary member of the public, he would have found it hard to trace an address from that number, probably impossible. Not if he worked for China's Secret Police, though. Not with the power of the state behind him.

"Giselle said I can trust you," Kam said. "She promised me you'll protect me."

"I will," I said. "But you have to promise to do something for me too."

"What?"

I leaned forward, gazed levelly into her eyes: "To tell me the truth. I need to know exactly why Joe and Ah Fah and her mother were killed."

"It's a long story."
"I'm a patient listener."
"Where do I start?"
"Begin at the beginning."

28

"IT ALL STARTED three months ago when all the big-shots were in town for that big conference — you know the one I mean, huh?"

She meant the global conference on climate change that had taken place in Hong Kong. Power-brokers from around the world had attended. The conference had hijacked the television screens for days.

"I know the one."

Kam Sau took a deep pull from her cigarette. I noticed that her hands now shook a lot less than before. Colour continued to ebb back to her cheeks. Her voice had become steadier too.

"Joe asked me to help him gate-crash a party at the Mandarin Hotel after the conference finished. Parties were going on at all the top hotels — the big-shots needed to unwind, see."

The waiter arrived with Kam Sau's second brandy. I didn't need to tell her to drink this one. She snatched up the glass, took a gulp and then licked her lips. Then she said, "The guest of honour at the Mandarin's party was China's foreign minister."

"Wu Zheng?"

"Joe wanted me to get him and Ah Fah in there. Those organising the Mandarin's party were my boss and his son, see — John Yip gave me two tickets."

"John Yip?"

"Yes, he … What's wrong?"

I frowned. "It makes no sense."

"What doesn't?"

"You told me about John Yip yesterday," I reminded her. "You said you weren't friends."

She shifted in her chair. "So?"

"Joe wouldn't have got you to ask Yip for tickets," I pointed out. "Not unless he thought you were friendly enough to have special influence."

"That bastard John Yip didn't do it for me. He did it all for Ah Fah."

Her voice had changed. She no longer sounded scared, now she was bitter and angry. She leaned over and stubbed out her cigarette. Unlike last time she had waited until she had smoked this one before using the ashtray. Her hands no longer shook. Had the nicotine in those Marlboros calmed her, or the brandy?

"He was nuts about Ah Fah! Practically drooled when I told him she wanted to go to his lousy party! The son of a bitch was so busy wetting his pants he didn't even bother asking me *why* she wanted to go."

"So why did she?"

Kam Sau shifted in her chair again. "It was all Joe's idea. She just went along with him same way she always did — Joe had a lot of control over her."

"Why was Joe so keen?"

Instead of answering me, she picked up her brandy glass then played with it in her hand, slowly swirling

190

around the dregs of golden-brown liquid the balloon-shaped glass contained.

"You promised me the truth," I reminded her.

She drained her glass. Although she had claimed not to like alcohol, she was giving a good impression of being unable to live without it. Displaying amazingly good resistance to its effects too: that made two doubles in fifteen minutes and she still sat upright. When you knock it back as quickly as she'd been doing, booze rushes to your head. Someone as unused to the stuff as she had claimed to be would probably be lying on the floor by now.

"Joe didn't give any details. He just said it was a chance to make big money."

"How?"

"Didn't say."

"You were in that flat with Ah Fah."

"So?"

"She must have explained."

"Joe kept her in the dark too."

I didn't believe her. Chan must have told either her or Ah Fah why he had wanted to gate-crash that party. Had he been chasing an exclusive? Was that why he had wanted to mix with Foreign Minister Wu Zheng and those big-shots? I had read no exposés in the papers, though, certainly none with Chan's by-line.

"At first Joe was fine," Kam Sau went on. "He said we'd made big money and I'd get my share. Then, ten days ago, he suddenly calls up real scared and orders me to leave town."

"Why?"

"Didn't say."

"If I'm going to help I need the full story."

"I'm telling you the full story."

The elderly waiter came over and asked if we wanted more brandy. I said we were fine. I told him to bring us the bill.

"How did John Yip and Ah Fah first meet?" I asked after the waiter had gone away.

"She visited me in my office one day," Kam Sau said. "He was walking through on the way to see his father."

"Was she as crazy about him as he was about her?"

She shook her head. "Ah Fah loved Joe."

"But Joe never told her why he was desperate to get into that party?"

She stiffened. "Are you calling me a liar?"

"I want to help," I said. "But I can't if you keep feeding me half a story."

She shot me the sort of look a petulant schoolgirl might give a teacher who had accused her of copying.

"It's the truth! Joe never said why he wanted those party tickets."

"What did Ah Fah say happened at the hotel? Did she enjoy the party?"

"She never spoke about it much."

"Was Ian Jeffries a guest?"

"Who?"

"The British government minister; the man you phoned in England two weeks ago."

She stared at me blankly.

"Why did you call him?"

"I didn't."

"I've seen your phone bill. You spent nine minutes talking to him."

She shook her head. "It was Joe who called him. But he used the phone in my flat."

"What did Joe and Jeffries talk about?"

"Joe never said."

"You're lying."

"No, I swear it's true. He called while I was in the bathroom. And Joe was a really secretive guy. He never … Why are you sighing?"

"Tell me," I asked tonelessly. "Is the sign above my head written in red or blue ink?"

"Sign?"

"The one saying 'Duggan is a jerk'. Do I look gullible enough to swallow this stuff? It's like the plot from an Alan Yip film."

The waiter brought our bill. I paid and tipped him and he went back to the kitchen.

I leaned forward in my chair. I said to Kam Sau, "What was in that package you left for Joe?"

She shot me another blank stare.

"Joe came to my home," I said. "For a package he said I'd stolen from your flat. What was in it?"

"I don't know."

"Sure it wasn't videos?"

"Videos?"

I reached into my jacket pocket and pulled out the two tapes I had recovered from the bathroom of the Beijing apartment. For a moment, I thought she was going to deny knowing anything about them. Eventually, though, she came clean. "All right, so I hid them for Joe. But he never said what was on them."

"And you never checked to find out?"

"No."

"Why?"

"Joe said not to; Joe said … You … You don't think I'm telling the truth, do you?"

"Your story has more holes than Swiss cheese," I said. "Do you seriously expect me to believe you never took even a quick peek at those tapes?"

"I didn't."

"Why?"

"Joe told me not to."

"Was that before he disappeared in a puff of smoke? Or did the wolf gobble him up?"

"What do you mean?"

"I mean this is bullshit you're giving me."

She shook her head. "I never checked those tapes."

I got up from my chair: "Now's your chance."

"Where are you going?"

"To buy a video camera; we're having a film show."

29

WHEN THE AIRPORT was situated in Kowloon, surrounded by a forest of high-rise apartment blocks, arriving home used to be a scary experience: a white-knuckle ride every bit as nerve-jangling as those on offer at the world's best amusement parks. As the pilot forced the plane's nose down and then banked sharply to avoid the skyscrapers, I always used to wonder if today would be the day he screwed up and sent us plunging into the harbour.

But ten years ago the government moved the airport from Kai Tak to Lantau Island. Arriving home had become as thrilling as watching a pan of rice cook. That you no longer spent all your time worrying if this day might be your last did have compensations, though. It allowed you to focus on other things. Like why a girl you wanted to help could behave so foolishly.

Kam Sau had lied through her teeth. Why?

As my plane emerged from clouds and began its descent into Lantau I gazed through the cabin window, hoping to see something below which would produce a flash of inspiration that might help answer my question.

Tiny ships moved slowly across a blue-grey sea which seemed made of polished glass. I stared long and hard at these ships, but no inspiration came.

I had hoped that buying a camera in Beijing — one with a TV screen attached which would let me watch videos — might persuade Kam Sau to tell the truth. After viewing the tapes I'd seized from her Beijing flat, surely she would see sense. To my dismay, the airport shops had not had any cameras in stock; which had placed me in a dilemma. Bringing her back to Hong Kong would give me more time to squeeze the truth from her, but it might also put her in greater danger. Supposing those Ke Ge Bo thugs discovered she had returned? I couldn't be her bodyguard twenty-four hours a day, could I?

I had sent her to the Philippines to stay with Giselle.

Should I inform John Yip that I'd sent her there? Surely professional ethics required me to tell him — he was paying my wages after all. But he was only paying to make sure Kam Sau was safe. I reminded myself. Kam Sau wasn't the only liar in town; Yip junior had told his share of whoppers. My instincts told me I could trust him as much as I could trust a King Cobra. So I would tell him nothing about Kam Sau being in the Philippines, I would merely say that she was safe. And that would be my job done.

Wake up Duggan!

My job would only be done when I had found out why that old dishwasher, her daughter Ah Fah and journalist Joe Chan had been murdered; and when I had discovered the identity of the murderer. Sending Kam Sau to the Philippines wouldn't help me much on that score, would it? Should I have risked it and brought her to Hong Kong? Or pushed harder for the truth before putting her on the plane to Manila? On second thoughts, I had pushed as hard as I could: I had stressed the dangers over and over again, warned her that unless she told me everything I couldn't help.

I had hoped to spare her the truth about the way her friend had died. Yet it had seemed the only way to make her realise the danger she faced. So I gave her all the details. She turned deathly pale and for a moment I thought she would be sick. The moment passed, though, and I realised my shock tactics had failed. She continued to insist she had never viewed the tapes.

"Why not tell Ah Fah where you hid them?"

"I did."

"You're lying."

"I told her everything."

"That killer ripped the flat apart because she couldn't tell him where the tapes were hidden. Because you never told her, did you? You never—"

"All right, all right — so last night I took them from the kitchen."

"And never told Ah Fah?"

"No."

"Why?"

"I thought it would be safer to hide them in the bathroom."

"Why not tell Ah Fah?"

"I was going to, but I forgot ... I ... It's the truth, Mister Detective — I just plain forgot."

I could tell from the way she averted her eyes from my gaze that she had lied to me. She had deliberately kept the new hiding place a secret. Why? Perhaps the answer lay on the tapes themselves.

"Cabin crew get ready," a male voice said over the intercom; "get ready for landing, please."

There was a loud rumbling as the pilot lowered the undercarriage. I gazed from my economy class window and watched the runway loom closer. The plane gave a jolt as its wheels bumped the tarmac. Four Rolls-Royce engines screamed as the pilot shoved them into reverse thrust to slow the plane. The seat belts' light went out.

"Ladies and gentlemen, we have now arrived in Hong Kong," said the voice on the intercom. "We hope you had a pleasant flight with us. Local time is twelve minutes past seven in the evening."

AFTER MAKING MY way through crowded passport control and customs channels, I boarded a crowded MTR train and travelled to Causeway Bay.

I left Causeway Bay's MTR station at the Pearl City Mansions exit, emerging on to a busy street. I brushed beads of sweat from my face; the sun might be fading from a salmon-pink sky, but the humidity level remained excruciatingly high. A crowd queued outside Pearl City Plaza cinema, where Alan Yip's new *kung fu* epic was showing. I moved past the crowd and headed for an electronics shop by the Excelsior Hotel. I bought a video-cassette adapter from the shop. It would allow me to use the TV in my Kennedy Town office to view the action on Kam Sau's tapes.

No underground trains serve Kennedy Town: the MTR only runs as far as Sheung Wan, a mile or so from my workplace. I took a cab. I reached my office block at a quarter to nine, paid my driver, stepped on to the street, took a deep breath — then instantly regretted it. Because there was not even the slightest breeze to disperse it, the harbour's rotten-eggs smell seemed worse than usual tonight, almost nauseating.

Holding my breath to avoid the smell, I strode to my office block and unlocked the main door. The lobby was deserted. Even my secretary Mei, almost always the last person to leave, had packed up and gone home. I took the lift to the eighth floor, got out and tramped down the corridor until I stood about four metres from my office door.

Then froze.

Something had just crashed to the floor inside my office. It had sounded like a piece of crockery breaking: a stray cat knocking a coffee cup or saucer off the desk? Don't be stupid! How could a stray cat get inside a locked office? I listened more intently. Had I got it wrong about that noise? No. Now I could hear the office drawers being yanked open, papers being shuffled about.

My instinct was to rush in and confront the intruder. Then I remembered the two Ke Ge Bo thugs shooting at me in Wan Chai, remembered the dead girl in the flat in Beijing. Unless I was careful about how I tackled this intruder, I might wind up as dead as she was. I didn't need to tackle him at all, though, I told myself. I could back off down the corridor, phone the police and hand the job of tackling him over to them.

The trouble was that the police would arrive with their sirens blaring. A door at the back of my office opened on to a fire escape. Alerted by the sound of the sirens, my intruder could use this fire escape to escape. I didn't want him to escape. I wanted to trap him here, and then grill him and learn who had sent him and why. I edged down the corridor until I was standing beside the office door. I reached tentatively for the handle with my right hand. Silently praying that the hinges wouldn't squeak, I pushed gently down on the handle and nudged the door open a few centimetres.

My luck with the hinges held.

I nudged the door open a few centimetres more. Peered into the office through the slim crack I had created. One man stood inside. He had his back to me, so I couldn't be sure, but I didn't think he was one of those Secret Police thugs. Judging from his build, he was much weaker than either of the two Ke Ge Bo agents. Good. That made him easier to tackle. Unless he had come armed. It didn't matter how puny you were. Not if you had a gun and were ruthless enough to use it. Supposing that he was the same ruthless bastard who had killed that girl in China? Supposing he …

Stop worrying! You can take him!

Yes — I could handle him. The longer that I gazed at him the punier he seemed to become. I also had the weapon of surprise on my side. He didn't know I was here. He would stay unaware too. He was so focused on those papers that he wouldn't swing round — not if I kept quiet. You can be quiet, Peter, I told myself, at least for a short while. A short while is all you will need; it's only four steps to the desk — you'll reach him in a few seconds. Even if he does swing round, it'll be too late for him to do anything. You'll be on him before he can react.

I nudged the door open wider, slipped silently into the room. I took one step forward, and then two — he was nearly within touching distance now, head bent low over the desk, still oblivious to my presence. In a moment I would have him. Two more steps; that was all I needed to take. I clenched my fist, felt the muscles in my right arm go taut. I took another step forward. There was a loud crack as I stood on a piece of broken crockery. The intruder swung round. His hand moved to the gun in his shoulder holster.

30

I DIVED FOR his legs.

Bring him down and he might lose his grip on that gun. Once we both lay sprawling on the floor, I could overpower him. You can do it, Peter, I told myself. He hasn't snatched up the pistol yet. His hand hasn't reached the holster. His hand reactions are too slow.

There was nothing slow about his footwork.

I clutched thin air as he performed a side-shuffle worthy of boxing champ Muhammed Ali. I grunted with pain as my shoulder missed his legs and crashed into the desk. I looked up, expecting a gun to be trained on me, to hear a bang and then see blackness.

He didn't shoot. He hurdled over me and ran for the door; either he was feeling merciful tonight or I had got it wrong about that gun. Jogging shoes pounded the corridor floor as he sprinted for the lift.

I hauled myself up, yanked open the office door and lurched out on to the corridor. My intruder stood by the lift, about thirty feet away. He was having problems making the lift work. He jabbed repeatedly at the call button, thumped the metal doors in frustration. I got within about twenty feet of him. The lift doors remained shut; I would trap him, if my luck with those doors held. It did. He kept jabbing at the button, but the doors refused to open; only ten feet separated us now. He turned his head and I seized a good look at his face. It was a face I recognised.

"Snakefingers!"

The lift doors jerked open.

He jumped inside.

I lunged forward, but too slowly; the lift doors closed, the lift descended without me.

I sprinted to the stairwell: if I was quick enough I might still catch him. I grabbed a deep breath, shoved open double doors and charged down the stairs. I kicked open more double doors at the bottom of the stairs and dashed out on to the street.

Snakefingers was about twenty-five metres away. I didn't waste time ordering him to stop: he would take no notice and I was too exhausted to shout.

But Snakefingers was tired too: gasping for breath: walking not running now: almost staggering. He shot a glance over his shoulder and I glimpsed panic in his face as he realised I was gaining — only about fifteen metres separated us. I knew he could never outrun me. He knew it too. So instead of heading down the road, he ducked into a *mahjong* parlour: make it out the back and he might lose me in the streets which ran behind the building.

I followed him inside, swatting away a dense tobacco mist that stung my eyes. From behind the grey-brown fog came the sounds of burping, spitting, cursing, and the clack, clack, clack of hundreds of *mahjong* tiles being shuffled. At a table by the wall, some fifteen feet away, a shadowy figure panted so much that I could hear him even above the other noises.

Playing *mahjong* is a tense business for Hong Kong gamblers — they often sweat and feel short of breath when making big-money moves. But the game isn't so tense or physically exhausting that it leaves the players gasping like racehorses who have just finished a five-mile gallop. Unless one of the Happy Valley or Sha Tin thoroughbreds had trotted in here on its way back to the stables, that shadowy figure over there by the wall was Snakefingers.

I moved towards his table.

"Be sensible, Snakefingers, we can talk this out."

The table was overturned. Glasses and *mahjong* tiles crashed to the floor. I felt a rush of warm air by my ear as a bottle hurtled past — my safe-breaker friend was obviously not in a talkative mood tonight. He broke from his place by the wall. I tried to stop him, but he did another Ali shuffle and left me grabbing at air again.

He yanked open the door and lurched out on to the street. I dashed after him. When I got outside he was about fifteen metres away and heading for a houseboat moored at Kennedy Town's waterfront. If his plan was to seize the boat and then escape by sea, it was a bad one: it would take him at least thirty minutes to haul up the boat's anchor.

He never got as far as pulling up the anchor because when he boarded the houseboat the captain's wife confronted him. Angry that he had interrupted the family's dinner, she clouted him on the head with her metal chef's ladle. As he ducked to avoid a second stinging blow from the ladle, Snakefingers lost his balance. He splashed into the harbour.

FIVE MINUTES LATER he was drying himself with a towel which the captain's wife had given him after she had fished him out of the water with a boathook.

I gazed at the man regarded as the best safe-breaker in Hong Kong. Forty-six years of animal-like cunning dripped from a greasy, pointed face. A pink-yellow tongue flickered over thin, pink-yellow lips. Beady black eyes moved furtively from side to side. He looked much the same as he had looked at our last meeting six months ago: as much like a jackal as a person can look.

He brimmed with apologies, of course — he always does after you've caught him red-handed. It had all been the most terrible mistake. He would never knowingly have hurt his good pal, Mister Duggan. It was just that he was a bit hard up at the moment because of bad luck with the horses, so when a kindly figure had come along and offered ten grand for an easy job ... Well, he knew I would understand the difficulties of him being put in so tempting a position. Me happening to be the most understanding police officer it had ever been his good fortune to meet.

"But on my dead wife's ashes, I never knew it was your office," he protested in the lying voice I knew well. "Or I swear to Lord Buddha I wouldn't never have done it!" He shook his head so adamantly that I thought it might fly off and go splashing into the harbour. "I wouldn't never screw you around, chief. Not after how you helped out my kid."

A year ago I had helped to keep his junkie daughter out of jail, by appearing as a character witness at her trial. She had been a first offender and I've always believed everyone deserves a second chance. To say that Snakefingers had been grateful for my intervention was putting it mildly: he would take a bullet in the chest for me, walk barefoot over hot iron; Duggan only had to command and Snakefingers would instantly obey.

I had known it was rubbish, of course — I've never swallowed any of the stuff about crooks like Snakefingers being honourable types. The character sat hunched up in front of me was aptly named. Not only was he snake-fingered, he was also snake-minded. Perhaps he possessed a touch more morality than a King Cobra; though on second thoughts, probably not.

"Why did you run away from me when I told you to stop, Snakefingers?"

He coughed to clear his throat then leaned over and spat on the deck. "I'd just burgled your fucking office," he replied, as though the answer was obvious. He grinned, showing uneven, dirty yellow teeth. "Punters usually aren't in the mood to buy you a beer when they see you stealing the family silver."

"Why pretend you had a gun?"

He grinned again. Did he think he had the sort of disarming smile that would make me forgive him everything? He was sorely mistaken. His grin was the sort that a hyena might give its mate — seconds before biting the mate's head off.

"Just my little joke, chief; I thought if I made you think I was all tooled up then you'd leave off grabbing me. And you did too — heh, heh, heh!"

"Were you having a laugh back there in the *mahjong* parlour too?"

"Come again, chief?"

"Oh, nothing important," I said lightly, "just the small matter of you almost breaking my skull when you chucked that bottle."

206

He shook his head: "Not me."

"Bullshit!"

"On my dead wife's ashes! I swear I never … Come on, chief, you know you can trust me."

Trust him! He should stop cracking safes and get a job cracking jokes as a stand-up comedian. I trusted him as much as I trusted putting my hand in the mouth of a starving crocodile.

He finished drying himself. He tossed the wet towel on the deck then stood up. "Anyways, I need to be getting off home. See you around town, huh? Buy you a beer sometime, huh?"

I said tonelessly, "Do I really look as stupid as that?"

He frowned. "I don't get you, chief."

I stood up, grabbed both his shoulders. I forced him to sit down again. "Then allow me to explain," I said. "You've got as much chance of leaving here before I get answers as you have of sleeping with Gong Li tonight."

His eyes narrowed: "Answers?"

"Who got you to ransack my office?"

"Come on, chief," he pleaded. "I can't—"

"I want a name."

"It's more than my life's worth. You know what these bastards are like. If they ever …"

He shuddered and left the sentence unfinished. I knew why he had begun to sweat with fear. Two years ago Frank Ching and I had discovered a police informant in a Shau Kei Wan flat. His feet had been nailed to the floor, his hands and prick hacked off — he would have bled to death if the torturers hadn't already choked him by stuffing his balls down his mouth. But I was in no mood to feel squeamish about Snakefingers.

"A name," I snapped. I pulled my mobile phone from my pocket. "Or I call my friends at the station and get you two years for burglary."

"Give me a break, Mister Duggan," he pleaded with me pathetically. "Think about my poor kid. Think what'll happen to her if—"

"You've got five seconds."

"But we're friends," Snakefingers whined. "We're … All right, all right — put your phone away."

I replaced the mobile in my pocket.

"Who hired you?"

"He reckoned you might have all the stuff stashed in your safe," Snakefingers said. "That's why he needed to use a top cracksman like me."

"Who is *he*, and what stuff am I supposed to have?"

"He wanted me to find stuff about a girl."

"Called Kam Sau, yes?"

Snakefingers stared at me in amazement. "How the fuck did—"

"I'm psychic. Who hired you?"

"Don't know his name."

"You're lying."

"On my wife's ashes! He … I *swear* it's the truth, chief. All I can do is to tell you how he looked."

"So tell me."

"It won't help."

"What do you mean?"

"I mean the joker I met isn't the joker who hired me. The joker I met looks like a college punk, the sort who piss themselves when you just look tough at them." Snakefingers shook his head. "No way could a punk like that be boss." He leaned over and spat on the deck. "This punk was just a messenger boy."

"What did he look like?"

"Already told you; a snot-nosed college kid."

"I need details."

"About your height and weight," Snakefingers said; "maybe a little bit taller and a bit skinnier. Had a really screwed-up pock-marked face and glasses with some wire frames. Was wearing a bright pink shirt, a black-and-white spotted …"

I no longer heard him. Instead I heard the voice of the pock-faced young man who had guided me around Alan Yip's film studios. He was telling me that he didn't actually work for Alan Yip. He was aide to the film producer's son, John. The guide had been roughly my height and weight. And he had worn a pink shirt with a black-and-white spotted tie. John Yip's aide had hired Snakefingers to burgle my office.

31

"I GOT NO problems with that first part of your plan," Snakefingers said. "He's a college punk. Getting him to swallow your story should be easy as spitting."

He coughed to clear his throat then spat on the road. We were walking down Kennedy Town's waterfront in the direction of my office block. The sky had grown darker. Out at sea, orange and yellow lights winked on container ships which lay at anchor. We had left the houseboat five minutes ago. I had just finished outlining my plan: Snakefingers would tell John Yip's aide he had discovered nothing about Kam Sau in my office, and then follow the aide and report his movements back to me.

"As far as the second part goes ..." Snakefingers licked grey-brown spittle from his lips then glanced up slyly at me. His mean little eyes moved slowly over my face, searching for clues as to how far he could push his luck. He must have glimpsed something there that told him he could push it all the way, because in the airy tone of a man who thought he could pick and choose which parts of my plan he went along with, he said,

"For what it's worth, I'm not sure I'm happy about this second part of the job."

I stared more closely at him. I was surprised to see he had grown more confident, even cocky. He seemed to have forgotten that my catching him burgling my office meant I had him by the balls. It was time to give him a reminder.

I said tonelessly, "For what it's worth, I don't give a flying fuck if you're happy about it."

The Adam's apple in his scrawny throat bulged so much that I thought it would burst the skin. "Have a heart, chief," he pleaded in a pathetic, whining voice. "I can't waste my time tailing punks around town — I've got a life to live."

"You'll be living it in jail," I warned him. "Unless you do exactly as I say."

He raised his hands in surrender. "Okay, okay, take it easy. There's no need for cops. That stuff back there in your office ... Just a little mistake, huh? Me and you are still friends, huh?"

"Providing you do as you're told," I said. "And that means reporting back to me on *everything* our friend does. Nod if you understand me, Snakefingers."

He nodded. We split up; he set off in the direction of the Central business district, I headed for my office. Would he do as he had promised and follow my instructions? Or double-cross me like he had double-crossed half of Hong Kong over the years? The more that I thought about it, the more likely it seemed that Snakefingers would play me for a sucker. Yip's aide had paid him ten thousand dollars to burgle my office; Snakefingers probably anticipated ten thousand more for selling me out.

211

Why pay him so much in the first place? Snakefingers said he'd been told to recover papers I had on Kam Sau. What made the papers worth ten thousand dollars? Who had them? Not me. Perhaps the answer lay on the tapes I had found in that dead girl's apartment. I patted my jacket pocket. The two videos were still there.

I entered my office block.

I took the lift to the eighth floor, got out and walked down the corridor which led to my office. When I was about halfway to the office, I reached down and scooped up the video adapter from the floor; I'd dropped it when I had tackled Snakefingers.

A light on the office phone told me I had messages. I listened to Kathy ask what time we were going to Tsuen Wan's temple to pay respects to my mother, then heard my wife ask if I'd solved the problems with Kathy's boyfriend. Then Kathy was back, demanding to know why I hadn't responded to her earlier call. Typical, I thought, she takes four days to answer my messages — and that's in a good week — yet I'm expected to reply to her in minutes. My last message was from Frank Ching. He had spoken again to his Ke Ge Bo friend, who still insisted China's Secret Police had nothing to with my case. Frank also wanted me to call back and confirm our weekend dinner date. He would have to wait. I was returning no calls until after my film show.

I switched on the TV. I snapped a cassette tape into the video adapter and pushed the adapter into the video slot on the television. Then I sat back and watched the action. Either the cameraman had forgotten to adjust the volume, or the tape was faulty, because there was no sound. A man and woman occupied a bedroom. I couldn't see his face, but she was Ah Fah; he sat on the bed and she leaned casually against the wall. She wore a jade-coloured dress. The clock on the wall behind her showed a time of nine-fifteen.

They chatted for a while. At least he chatted; she merely nodded and smiled weakly. You could tell from her eyes that his talk bored her. They had the glazed look a woman's eyes have when a man is relating his life story, particularly the part about his wife no longer understanding. He chatted and she nodded and smiled for thirty minutes, until the tape rolled to a halt; hardly Oscar-winning stuff. Perhaps the second tape would be better.

The action on the second tape began as excitingly as that on the first one had ended. In fact for two minutes there was no action at all, only grey fuzziness. I had begun to think the second tape must be a dud, when the man came into view. He no longer sat on the bed, he was leaving the room; a quick tug at the door and he had gone — and I still hadn't seen his face. Pillows and blankets on the bed were now crumpled. Had that chat ended with Ah Fah joining him between the sheets? Where *was* Ah Fah? I could no longer see her on the screen.

The bedroom door swung open to reveal journalist Joe Chan; was he the same man who had left the room a moment ago? No. Chan was smaller, his clothes different. He gesticulated — shouted. I rewound the tape and then played it again, but in slow motion this time. I examined Chan's face closely, tried to puzzle out what he was saying. No good. Even skilled lip-readers would have found it almost impossible. I still couldn't see Ah Fah, but she must be there in the room because Chan was yelling at her. He moved out of sight and for the next twenty minutes all I saw was an empty bed-room, then greyness as the tape spooled to a close. Where had all the missing action gone? The two tapes did not immediately follow each other: that crumpled bed suggested a sex scene had taken place before the man left the room and Ah Fah disappeared from view.

What had happened to this romantic action?

I got up and brewed some coffee; a strong shot of caffeine might help my brain work better. I downed half the double-strength Nescafé in a few gulps, sat down again and rewound the tape to the place where the man had left the bedroom. As he passed the clock on the wall, it showed a time of ten forty-five. When the first tape had ended, the clock had shown a time of nine forty-five. One hour was missing between the end of the first tape and start of the second.

I drank the rest of my instant coffee. What had happened to those missing sixty minutes of action? Had the camera broken down and the camera operator been unable to fix it for an hour? No. It seemed too much of a coincidence that the camera had been broken for exactly an hour. Or that it should have stopped working at precisely the moment when a sex scene had taken place. So if the camera had not broken down, what would have happened? The camera operator would have continued filming, of course. He would have filmed that hour of missing bedroom action. Which meant the sex scene must be on other tapes.

So where were these tapes? Who had them?

My mind flashed back to Ah Fah's flat in Beijing. To the bathroom where I had found the two videos I had just watched. Back in China, I had wondered why the killer had ransacked the rest of the flat but left the

214

bathroom untouched. Now I thought I knew. There had been no need for him to rip the bathroom apart. He had already found what he wanted in another part of the apartment — videos containing the missing bedroom action. And that girl Kam Sau knew exactly what had happened too. Yet she had stayed silent about it. She had told me nothing.

The fool! The stupid little fool!

I rang the safe-house in Cebu where Kam Sau and my bargirl friend Giselle were staying. I wanted Giselle to pick up the phone. To my dismay, Kam Sau answered. In a bright and cheerful voice, she asked if I'd had a pleasant flight home. I was in no mood to exchange pleasantries.

"What's on the other tapes?" I asked roughly.

She acted puzzled: "Other tapes?"

"Don't play games."

"What games?"

"Each video lasts thirty minutes," I said. "The action on the first tape ends at a quarter to ten and the action on the next one starts at quarter to eleven. That means that there's an hour-long gap between the two tapes. It also means two thirty-minute tapes are missing. What's on them?"

"I don't know."

"They show Ah Fah and that man in bed, don't they?"

"I — I don't know. Joe said—"

"Joe Chan is dead," I snapped. "He can't help you any more. And unless you start telling me the truth, I can't help you either. You've got exactly ten seconds to answer my next question. And you had better answer it truthfully. Because if I decide you're lying to me, then you're on your own." I paused to allow my words to sink in. To give her enough time to realise what being alone would mean. Then I said, "Who's the man in that video?"

"He's Ian Jeffries."

"How did he finish up in bed with Ah Fah?"

"You're so clever, Mister Private Detective, why don't you tell me?"

"All right, I will," I said. "Joe Chan was doing what he did when he used to work for a company called Soong Corp — filming men in bed with women who aren't their wives. He played a 'honey trap' at Alan Yip's party. He got Ah Fah to lure Jeffries into bed and then filmed them — then blackmailed Jeffries. How am I doing so far?"

Her lack of protests told me I was doing fine.

"You said Chan and Ah Fah were lovers," I reminded her, unable to hide my distaste, not only for Chan but for her too; she was supposed to have been that dead girl's friend — how could she have let Chan use a friend like that?

Perhaps she had guessed what I was thinking about her. Because in a voice that was half-angry, half-defiant she said, "Joe and Ah Fah weren't normal lovers, they were more like business partners.

"That bastard sold her down the river!"

"Ah Fah was no sweet little innocent, Duggan. She knew what she was getting into. She agreed on the plan — she knew it was a way to make big money."

"What made Chan sure Jeffries would pay? Politicians have brazened out sex scandals before. Jeffries could have done the same."

"You just don't get it, do you?"

"Get what?"

216

"You're not as smart as you think, Mister Private Detective."

"What do you mean?"

"Jeffries didn't just screw Ah Fah. He raped her."

32

I WAS STUNNED. Not only by what she had said, but also by how she had said it: she had spat out those last few words. My mind flashed back to when film producer Alan Yip had shown me her photograph. I had known instantly what type of person she was. I'm like that, you see; amazingly perceptive; able to work a person out just by viewing their picture — that's how I had known she was soft hearted. The warmth in her chestnut-brown eyes had done it; that and her smile. The smile of a friendly girl next-door type; a girl who was good-natured and ...

Wake up!

If I possessed even an ounce of perception, then my dad Paddy Duggan had been the most sober man in Hong Kong. Good natured and warm hearted? Dream on! This girl was as warm as a bowl of liquid nitrogen.

"And that bastard Chan kept filming — even when she was being raped?" I couldn't believe it. "Why didn't he rush in and stop it?"

"He tried, but he was too late."

"Bullshit!"

"You don't understand," she said. "Joe — he wasn't there in the hotel. The camera worked automatically — he was sitting in his car watching it all on a screen. When he knew what had happened he ran to stop it. But he got there too late."

"You had all the evidence on film. Why not go to the police with it?"

"Ah Fah wanted us to. She wanted Jeffries arrested."

"What stopped you?"

"Joe said to keep the police out of it."

"Even after his girlfriend had been raped?"

"Joe said we could get big money from Jeffries."

"And what did Ah Fah say?"

"In the end she came round to Joe's way of doing things — same as she always did." Kam Sau paused. With barely disguised contempt, she said, "Ah Fah was stupid — Joe could twist her round his little finger."

The lousy son of a bitch, I thought, his girlfriend is raped and all he thinks of is getting rich. And this girl I'm speaking to is as bad. She went along with the plan, full-speed ahead.

"At first Jeffries promised to pay," Kam Sau went on; "then he started to threaten us. But I thought his threats were a bluff; that in the end he'd see sense."

"What changed your thinking?"

"Ah Fah's mother; I thought she was a mistake — that it was me they really wanted dead."

"How much did you want from Jeffries?"

"Half a million dollars."

"Hong Kong dollars?"

"American."

"Not all politicians are millionaires. What made you think he could pay so much?"

219

"Joe said Jeffries was rich and had more than enough money to pay us. And I trusted Joe because he was always so clever, see. Joe was *really* clever."

Had she been in love with Chan? It would help to explain the dreamlike voice she used whenever she uttered his name; and her and Ah Fah being love rivals might also explain the bitter tone she used when talking about Ah Fah.

"Where does John Yip come into this?"

"I told you already — he got me tickets for the Mandarin's party."

"Why did he get someone to burgle my office?"

"I don't know."

"The burglar wanted information about you. Why?"

"I don't know."

"Why did John Yip want Ah Fah at that party?"

"I told you — he was cracked about her."

"But it's Ian Jeffries in those videos?"

"That's right."

"You're sure?"

"Yes."

"Why didn't you tell me there were four tapes?"

"Because when we met at the airport, I didn't know if I could really trust you ... I — I was scared of you ... I even thought you might kill me and ... I — I wasn't thinking very clearly."

A day ago, I might have swallowed it; she was good at acting the scared little secretary. But I had learned too much about Kam Sau in the past twenty-four hours to let her sucker-punch me again. A fear of big bad Duggan had not kept her quiet; I may not have been gentleness personified back there in Beijing, but I hadn't auditioned for mad axe-man either.

Why had she stayed silent?

For the same reason she did everything, of course — to get rich. But how would her staying silent about those tapes make her rich? The only way to get half a million would have been by blackmailing Ian Jeffries. She couldn't do that now. She no longer had those tapes. The tapes that showed Jeffries raping … Hold on! My mind flashed back to Beijing airport. Had she been carrying a bag? A bag where she could have stored copies of the two tapes? No, she had not been carrying a bag. Those tapes were small, though. She could have stuffed them in her pockets, or in the tops of her boots.

But why refuse to tell me about them?

She still hoped to cut a deal with Jeffries, of course. Yes, she had been scared of me when we had met in Beijing. But not scared that I would kill her. She had been afraid I would make her take those tapes to the police. Terrified I would destroy her chances of screwing a cool half million from Ian Jeffries.

"You've got copies, haven't you?" I said.

"Copies?"

"Of those tapes," I snapped; "the tapes that show Ian Jeffries raping Ah Fah."

"No."

My instincts told me she was lying: I cursed myself for not acting tougher at the airport. I had spent too much time playing noble Sir Peter of Hong Kong, protecting the damsel in distress. I should have concentrated more on being the Bastard of Beijing. I should have strip-searched her to find those tapes.

"Don't lie."

"I've got no video tapes." She paused. "But I *have* got a letter that Ah Fah wrote."

It wasn't an admission, more of a boast. Her coming clean had nothing to do with my tough questioning: she wanted to show me how smart she was.

"I told you before," she went on, "Ah Fah was stupid. I got her to write her story — to write all about what happened with Jeffries. The stupid bitch wrote it and signed it and I've got it — I've got the letter!" There was a leer of triumph in her voice; she wasn't only boasting now, she was gloating.

"Let me speak to Giselle."

"Why? So you can tell her to grab the letter?"

"Put Giselle on the phone."

"She's out shopping. And don't bother trying to call her on her mobile, because she forgot it — it's here with me. There's *nothing* you can do, Mister Private Detective."

"You can't mess about with these people," I said. "They'll—"

The line went dead.

I felt sick. Greed! The things it did to people. Turned them into heartless idiots, blinded them to danger; made them think they were invincible. Did the greedy fool still not realise, despite the evidence of three corpses, that the letter would only bring her a bullet in the head? I wanted her to be standing beside me. Then I might be able to shake some sense into her. She wasn't standing beside me, though. And getting angry wouldn't help either her or me; it would only stop me from thinking straight. I needed to calm down.

I brewed fresh coffee.

So the man in the bedroom was Jeffries. Or was it — could I trust Kam Sau to tell the truth? Why lay a honey trap for Jeffries? Other guests at that party had been much richer. Why not target one of them? Perhaps Ah Fah *had* targeted one of them; only it hadn't worked out, so she had switched her focus to Jeffries.

I plugged in my laptop and did an Internet search for spy cameras. I found a site which sold what it claimed was the world's smallest video surveillance unit, a snip at only five hundred US dollars. The camera was no bigger than a finger-end and could be easily fixed on a wall, or attached to a shirt button. It was linked by wireless to a video recorder and could be operated at a distance. So Kam Sau probably *had* told the truth about Chan sitting in his car when the rape took place. If that part of her story rang true, the bit about Jeffries as rapist might also be accurate.

I drained my coffee then poured another cup.

If Ian Jeffries was the rapist, it would explain the phone call Chan had made to Jeffries' UK office: Chan had been making blackmail threats. It would also explain why I kept running up against China's Secret Police — they handled politically sensitive cases. Why had Jeffries embarked on a trail of death rather than yield to blackmail? Had he decided that Chan could not be trusted — that even if he paid him this time Chan would keep returning for more? Had he felt it would be safer to silence Chan and his blackmailing friends?

Or had matters been taken out of Jeffries' hands?

I played a scenario over in my mind. China's Secret Police discover what has happened: perhaps they are tapping Jeffries' phone. The Ke Ge Bo can't arrest Jeffries. He's a powerful foreign politician. What's more, Jeffries is due to sign a major trade deal with China. If he goes under, the deal might collapse. China's leaders are desperate to keep their economy booming; they'll never let that trade deal fail. If a few insignificant blackmailers have to die, so be it. Ke Ge Bo agents strangle that old dishwasher, in case her daughter Ah Fah has told her too much. Then they kill Joe Chan and Ah Fah, and then …

A knock at the door jerked me from my thoughts. My watch showed ten-thirty. Who could be calling at this late hour? How had they entered the building? — I had locked the main doors. I swallowed to dislodge the lump in my throat. Was it those Ke Ge Bo thugs who had shot at me in Wan Chai? I moved to the door, bent down and peered through the spy hole. Two men stood outside. I relaxed; neither man posed a threat. One was the building's elderly caretaker. Who had dragged him from his home? That man standing there beside him, of course. I had never met this other man but had seen his picture often enough in the newspapers.

Why had he come here?

There was an easy way for me to find out. I opened the door. The caretaker stepped aside and allowed his companion to speak. The companion looked to be in his early thirties: about five feet six inches tall: slim and clean-shaven. His jet-black hair had been jelled then combed back severely in a style favoured by tango-dancers eighty-odd years ago and now popular with corporate wheeler-dealers. A diamond stud glittered in his right ear. He wore groin-crushing white pants and a garish purple shirt.

"Evening, Pete," he said brightly. "We spoke on the telephone two days ago." He thrust out his right hand. "Stephen Fung, political adviser to Ian Jeffries."

33

"YOU SEEM SURPRISED to see me, Pete."

Whatever gave him that idea? Had no one told him a foreign government official called here every night? On Wednesday it had been the ambassador to Togo; tomorrow, the Emperor of Japan was due to pop in and say hello. Why should I be surprised if the political adviser to a British government minister knocked on my door?

The caretaker coughed to attract attention, and then muttered something about having to go home. With no small amount of difficulty — those virginal white trousers fitted so tightly that they seemed glued to his skin — Fung pulled a wad of American hundred-dollar bills from his hip pocket. He peeled off two bills and gave them to the caretaker. To say the old man expressed gratitude for a handout the size of his weekly wage would do him injustice. He didn't kiss Fung's feet, but only because I cut short his grovelling display. I spun him around and propelled him to the elevator.

"I arrived from Bangkok barely an hour ago," Fung announced after the lift's steel doors had closed behind the caretaker. "I rushed here from the airport."

His voice was different from when we had spoken on the phone. Then he had been serious and business-like; had sounded a lot older than thirty-one. Tonight he had abandoned boring bureaucrat-speak; he sounded breezy and bouncy.

He looked hugely different too. Different from how he looked in newspapers that is. When the local media ran pictures of Fung they always gave you the air-brushed version; he wore a formal shirt and tie — a typical power-broker in a suit. The boardroom aura was missing from him tonight. In fact he had something of the air of the street about him; he would have looked at home hustling alongside Mongkok's pimps.

Those clothes, probably; his garish purple shirt and ball-crushing white pants were your typical pimp-style gear. Or maybe it was the jelled hair; or that diamond stud which glittered in his right ear. The stud was always air-brushed out by editors, in case it made him appear non-statesmanlike. Did all budding prime ministers wear them these days? Or was it Fung's way of telling everyone he was different — a new breed of trendy politician?

He jabbed a thumb at the lift. "What say we head downstairs too, Pete?" he suggested breezily. "My old banger's parked outside and I've booked us a restaurant in Mid-Levels — a great little place in Soho. I thought it would be more comfortable us talking there."

I would rather have talked in my office; it might be a dump to others, but it's home sweet home to me. But I like to think that I'm an amenable soul. If Fung would feel more relaxed in his Soho restaurant, then Soho restaurant it would be. Not before I discovered why he'd turned up out of the blue like this, though. Had he

226

found out that I knew about Ian Jeffries raping Ah Fah, and dashed over here to protect his boss?

"Come on, Pete!" Fung tapped his gold Rolex in mock irritation; he was really throwing himself into the part of the informal politician tonight. "Get your skates on. Unless we hurry we'll—"

I interrupted.

"Before we hurry off anywhere, how about you first explain why you're here?"

He looked at me as though the answer was obvious.

"I realised I made a mistake that last time we spoke, of course. So I thought I'd clear …" He threw another glance at his watch. "What say we skip the boring details till we're in the car, Pete?" He gestured again to the elevator. "Shall we leave?"

As we went down in the elevator Fung leaned closer, swamping me with Ralph Lauren aftershave. He rested a hand on my shoulder.

"I hope you don't mind me calling you Pete."

"People have called me worse."

The lift shuddered to a halt at the ground floor. We tramped across the deserted lobby, our shoes making loud clack, clack sounds on the tiles.

"I don't mean disrespect." Fung pushed open the building's main door and we stepped out on to a sweaty, mosquito-infested street. "It's just … Well I find all of the Mister-this-Mister-that stuff so dreary and … There we go!" He pointed to the opposite side of the road: "My old banger!"

The description was hardly accurate: if his sleek, silver Rolls-Royce was an 'old banger', then I was Chairman Mao's mother-in-law. It looked ridiculously out of place beside the decrepit pick-up trucks that were parked alongside it, a Ming emperor disdainfully surveying lesser mortals.

Fung yanked open the car door and ushered me onto a seat that was almost as big as a four-poster bed. He followed me inside then tapped his driver smartly on the shoulder. The Rolls purred like a cat sitting beside the fire as the driver started the engine. We turned right on to Shing Sai Road, then moved on to Connaught Road.

"Beautiful, isn't it?" Fung said in a dreamy voice. He pointed through the window to the harbour. "I've lived in England twenty years now, but I've never seen anything even half as spectacular."

I gazed across the two miles of crow-coloured water which separated Hong Kong Island from Kowloon. Neon signs on Tsim Sha Tsui's skyscrapers blazed in a purple-black night. A cruise liner berthed at Ocean Terminal gleamed pearly white. Further out in the harbour, lights twinkled Christmas tree-like on ships that were waiting to unload cargo into Kwai Chung's port: it was certainly beautiful. But I hadn't accompanied Fung to admire the view.

I said, "Has your boss remembered that he spoke to my missing girl?"

"Afraid not, Pete."

"She rang him about a party he attended."

Fung fished a pack of Marlboro and box of matches from his pocket. He lit a cigarette, took a leisurely pull and then blew out a smooth stream of smoke. He said, "I want you to know, Pete, and I speak here for Ian too, that I'm going to do my best to help all I can." He nodded slowly to confirm the sincerity of his words. "I know that you're worried about this girl and Ian and I both share your concerns." He leaned closer, swamping me with aftershave again. "And I can also assure you of this — we'll leave absolutely no stone unturned. We'll both do everything we possibly can to help find her."

He sat back, took another pull from his Marlboro. I had got it all wrong about him burying the bureaucrat-speak for tonight — it was alive and kicking. Only a born politician could deliver such a reply. Prattle on and on about how you'll help, but make sure to give no specifics about what form your help will take; and never, but never, answer the question you were asked.

"The party took place at the Mandarin Hotel," I said.

Fung flicked ash from the tip of his cigarette into the ashtray by his seat. He turned his head away from me and stared out of the window. He said so softly that it was almost a whisper, "There was no phone call, Pete."

"After the global warming conference had finished," I pressed on.

He turned his head away from the window. "Didn't you hear?" A slight testiness had crept into his voice. "There was *no* call."

"You're sure?"

"I'm *positive,* my friend."

Until now his face had borne the relaxed look of a man on a night out with his best pal. No more. The mask of friendship had slipped: no longer was I the bosom buddy he wanted to treat to a slap-up dinner — I had become the annoying character he would like to shove out of the door. His dark, intelligent eyes probed mine, daring me to contradict him. I resisted the urge. Nothing could be gained from angering him. Not yet.

"I've checked and re-checked," he told me, suddenly best friends again. "The phone company screwed up.

Someone there got Ian's number confused with another number when they made out that girl's bill."

We motored past Shun Tak Centre, where crowds of gamblers board high-speed jet cats which whiz them off to the glitzy casinos of Macau, sixty kilometres away across the South China Sea.

"Attend that party yourself, Steve?"

He nodded.

"Meet a girl called Ah Fah?"

"Her name rings no bells."

"Did Mister Jeffries meet her?"

"He didn't mention it, but that's not to say he never met her — I'm Ian's adviser, not his mother."

"She was at the party."

"As were six hundred other people, Pete; you can't speak to everyone."

"What was that party like?"

He frowned: "Why all this interest in the party, and why the questions about this Ah Fah? I thought your missing girl's name is Kam Sau."

"They're friends. Find one and I may find the other."

Fung pressed a button on his seat rest to wind down the window. He leaned over and flicked his cigarette into the oily-black night.

"The party was lousy, Pete, but don't just take my word. Ask your boss — Johnny Yip was there."

We turned on to Des Voeux Road. Through my window I could see Jardine House, whose hundreds of porthole-type windows have inspired locals to call it *ba gung yau*, the building of a thousand arseholes. The view disappeared as our driver steered right and we began the steep climb to Mid-Levels and the trendy restaurant area of Soho.

"How do you know I work for John Yip?"

"You told me on the phone, of course."

I shook my head. "I said I was hired by *Alan* Yip."

Fung shrugged. "Maybe Johnny told me."

"You've spoken to him?"

"This afternoon, when … No need to look amazed, there's nothing strange in me calling Johnny — we're old friends. We went to school together in …" He pointed over my shoulder. "Feast your eyes! It's even better than the last view!"

We had reached roughly half-way between the Peak and the harbour, which lies five hundred and fifty metres below. A panoramic view of the waterfront unfolded: skyscrapers swarmed in aubergine-coloured air like fireflies, harbour waters gleaned the colour of sheet metal.

"John Yip must have mentioned Ah Fah," I said.

Fung frowned. "Why?"

"He was in love with her."

Fung gasped with surprise: "Johnny?"

"That's right. He invited her to that party, so …"

I stopped speaking when I saw Fung grinning. I was surprised at how badly his teeth were decayed; this was something else that local editors air-brushed from their pictures.

"Johnny couldn't be besotted with this girl, Pete."

"Why?"

"Johnny's gay."

34

I SAW NO sudden tension in his face, which would have warned me he had lied. But you never do see it when the person you're staring at is a good confidence trickster. Fung would be well-skilled in deceit: most politicians are expert liars. Although not this time, I decided; my instincts told me his surprise had been genuine this time. I'd stunned him with that John Yip-Ah Fah lovers' stuff.

So if he had told me the truth about John Yip being gay, what had Kam Sau been up to insisting that John Yip had been crazy about Ah Fah? The same as she had been up to all along, of course: lying through her teeth in the hope that it would make her rich; insane greed causing her to ignore all the dangers and spurn my efforts to help her.

"Not much longer to go now, Pete," Fung said. We turned right on to Old Bailey Street and began moving down a steep hill. "The restaurant we want is in one of the streets running off Hollywood Road."

So why had we come this longer, roundabout way? Why not take a short-cut to the Soho restaurant area from my office? Had Fung chosen the scenic route because he wanted to admire the harbour view? It was possible; about as possible as me winning fifty million dollars on the Mark Six lottery. He hadn't decided to take this longer route to give himself time to correct his mistakes, either: in the twenty minutes since leaving my office he had corrected precisely nothing.

If he was desperate to put me right about mistakes he'd made in Bangkok, why had he not simply picked up the phone in Thailand and rang my office? Because then we would never have met, of course; and he needed to meet up, then whisk me off on this magical mystery tour to give himself time to work me out; to discover how hard, or easy, I would be to keep quiet.

Fung smacked his lips. "It's a *brilliant* place, Pete! Serves genuine Cantonese food: exotic stuff it's hard to find these days: sea slugs, stewed snake — fantastic! Not only Hong Kong exiles like me think that way either — Europeans love it too. Ian is as crazy about the food in there as me."

"Is your boss eating with us tonight?"

Fung shook his head: "Afraid not, Pete. One of his Beijing appointments was brought forward by several hours. I had to rearrange his schedule. Instead of flying to China tomorrow, he went to Beijing tonight."

"When does he arrive in Hong Kong?"

"He doesn't, he heads straight off to London from Beijing." Fung sighed. "It's a shame, because I know how much Ian was looking forward to meeting local businessmen, but …" Fung threw up his arms in a what-can-you-do gesture. "The Chinese part of the trip must take precedence."

"You're not going to China with him?"

233

He shook his head. "I wanted to visit my father here. And of course I was also eager to correct all those mistakes I made last time you and I spoke."

Ah yes! the famous mistakes. I had grown tired of the dance he had led me over these celebrated screw-ups. It was time to make the music stop. I stared at him levelly. I said aggressively, "Which are?"

"Are what, Pete?" he responded easily, refusing to let me provoke him.

"You still haven't explained what you got wrong."

He raised his hands in a gesture which urged me to relax. "I'm going to, Pete, I'm going to. Because I want to help you find this girl, I really do." He paused to swat a mosquito; it must have sneaked into the car when he opened the window to toss away his cigarette. Then, in a more sombre tone than any he had used so far, he said, "When you called me in Bangkok, I told you that the phone number you gave me was for Ian's private line."

It wasn't really a question, yet he looked at me in a way which suggested that he expected a response. So I nodded at him curtly. He responded to my nod with a more elaborate one of his own. Then he leaned closer and touched me on the knee. His voice grew ever more sonorous. In the weighty tones of a man delivering vital evidence in court, the sort of stuff which might hang a person, he said, "Well, actually, Pete, it isn't. I got a bit mixed up — it's the general office number."

Then he sat back, stared ahead and said nothing for a while — perhaps the effort of delivering such a staggering piece of news had exhausted him. Or perhaps he was deliberately winding me up. In fact there was no perhaps about it, he was definitely winding me up.

I didn't give a contemptuous snort of laugher, but I came close. It wasn't so much being shocked by his failure to divulge anything important — I'd sensed ten minutes ago that all his eagerness to correct mistakes was just a game — more the fact I was disappointed he hadn't played the game better. Surely such a slick operator could have dreamt up something better than that phone number mix-up.

"And that's it?" I said.

He nodded. "But as I pointed out to you earlier, your missing girl never rang Ian on either his private line or the general office number — the phone company made a mistake with her bill."

"That's all you have to tell me?"

"I wanted to set the record straight."

"Wouldn't a phone call have been easier?"

He looked at me as if I'd just suggested mass murder might be an interesting hobby to pursue: "Absolutely and definitely not, Pete! For important matters it's *always* better to talk face to face. That way there's much less chance of ... We're here!"

I glanced out of the window. Our driver had parked opposite the police station on Hollywood Road.

"I thought we were going to a restaurant," I said.

Fung nodded. "But I thought it would be a good idea for us to walk the final part of the way. It'll help us to build up an appetite."

Sited between mansions on the Peak, the hill-top enclave where Hong Kong's rich and famous live because the air there is less humid, and the sweaty working-class tenements below, Mid-Levels is a large and diverse area. Parts of it contain homes built before the Second World War. These blocks often have few

235

elevators and air-conditioning units, but plenty of cockroaches and blocked toilets. They are frequently sited near shops that sell noodles and bowls of evil-smelling offal.

In other parts of Mid-Levels, modern apartment blocks tower into the sky. Although cheaper than mansions on the Peak, these apartments are still way too expensive for most Hong Kongers. Shops in this area of Mid-Levels often sell antiques and paintings. Restaurants serve up small portions of nouvelle French cuisine, or Indian food that costs four times what it costs a few kilometres away in Wan Chai, or 'authentic' Chinese stuff lusted after by home-sick exiles like Fung. There are trendy wine bars and trendy clubs where you can rub shoulders with trendy TV and film stars.

We had come to this trendy part.

We walked up Hollywood Road, turned left on to Shelley Street and then swung right on to Staunton Street, which is the heart of Soho's restaurant area. An aroma of crushed garlic and freshly ground coffee, wafted through the air. Across the road young people in designer gear congregated outside a European-style bar, sipping cappuccinos and red wine, or swigging *San Miguel* beer from the bottle. In the purple-black sky, an airliner that resembled a spent firework began its descent into Lantau's airport.

The restaurant owner was waiting for us in the downstairs lobby. He looked to be in his early fifties: a short and extremely fat man, whose dinner jacket fitted too tightly, and whose bald head shone so brightly under the restaurant's ceiling lights that it looked as though he had given it a coating of wax. He greeted Fung like a long-lost son: slapping him repeatedly on the shoulder, laughing uproariously at his jokes — Fung must have left a really big tip last time. Or was the owner scared that if he failed to show his guest enough respect, Fung would inform his father and dad's 14K Triad heavies would pay the restaurant a visit?

Moving with surprising grace for such a fat man — almost like a ballroom dancer — the owner waltzed us across the deep-pile blue carpet and over to a staircase that was lined with photographs signed by some of his famous customers. There were pictures of male and female pop stars, of movie actors and actresses, football players, business tycoons — as well as a large framed shot of Ian Jeffries and Stephen Fung.

We climbed the stairs to the first floor landing, turned left and entered the restaurant proper. The owner escorted us to a table by the window, which he assured us was the best that he had. Would he ever offer his good friend Mister Fung anything less?

"Is Ah Chow working tonight?" Fung asked.

The owner nodded.

"In that case I must have a quick word with him." Fung squeezed my shoulder. "Don't run away, Pete, I'll be back in a moment."

He strode off in the direction of the kichen.

"Mister Fung wants to discuss important matters with our head chef," the owner explained after Fung had gone. "He wants to ask if our head chef has any special dishes he can prepare for you tonight."

"Mister Fung takes his food seriously, huh?"

"Oh yes indeed, sir." The owner beamed proudly, revealing that one of his bottom teeth was made of gold. "And he only ever eats here when he's in Hong Kong. He never goes anywhere else."

I reached into my pocket for the picture of Kam Sau that Alan Yip had given me.

"Has he ever eaten here with this girl?"

"No sir."

"You haven't looked closely at her yet," I said.

"But Mister Fung *never* comes to my restaurant with any lady, sir; only with his superior."

"You mean his boss?" I said. "Mister Ian Jeffries?"

The owner nodded.

"Does his boss like the food here as much as Mister Fung?"

"So Mister Fung tells me."

"What does his boss tell you?"

"I don't know, sir, I don't speak English."

I frowned. "Mister Jeffries speaks Cantonese."

"Who told you, sir?"

"No one told me, but I read somewhere that—"

"We're in luck, Pete!"

Fung had returned.

"Has Ah Chow proved able to meet all your special requirements?" the owner asked.

Fung nodded: "But he needs to check something with you first."

"Then please excuse me. Enjoy your dinner."

Polished skull gleaming beneath the ceiling lights like a new bowling ball, the restaurant owner strode off to the kitchen. Fung and I sat down. He flicked a speck of dust from the collar of his purple shirt then sighed.

"It's a real shame Ian couldn't be here with us to-night. He loves the authentic Chinese cooking in this place almost as much as ..." Fung broke off suddenly and threw a glance over my shoulder. "What the fuck is *he* doing in here?"

"Who?"

"Four tables behind you," Fung said, "chatting with the Indian guy."

I half-turned in my seat. John Yip's pock-faced aide sat at a table with a middle-aged Indian man. So much for that deal I had struck with Snakefingers. My safe-breaker friend had promised me faithfully he would follow Yip's aide and then report back on his every movement. But Snakefingers had played his usual game of double-cross.

Fung frowned. "He works for Johnny Yip. But why so buddy-buddy with our Indian friend?" He leaned closer. His voice fell to a conspiratorial whisper. "That Indian guy is Alan Yip's main business rival."

I didn't need Fung to tell me. I had recognised the man immediately. He was the Bollywood movie producer who had featured in the magazine I'd read during my flight over to China — the man who had so unwillingly bent the knee to 'King' Alan Yip in a joke picture that the magazine's photographer had rigged up.

Fung nudged me. "He's seen us. Seems a little bit surprised, doesn't he?"

To call John Yip's side-kick 'a bit surprised' was putting it mildly: he gulped as though he had swallowed a turkey-cock whole. I turned away from him and gazed at Fung, who continued to frown darkly. He seemed genuinely perplexed. As though never in his wildest dreams had he expected to encounter friend Johnny's aide in here. Perhaps it was a coincidence. After all, coincidences happened every day. Could our encounter with John Yip's aide be one of them?

It was possible: about as possible as the ceiling opening and Ian Jeffries parachuting in to join us for dinner.

This encounter had been carefully planned. Fung had not dragged me away from my office to tell me some far-fetched stories about him and the phone company screwing up Jeffries' phone numbers. He had wanted to show me John Yip's aide and the Bollywood producer enjoying a cosy chat.

My mind flashed back to when film-maker Alan Yip had swaggered into my office to demand that I find his secretary Kam Sau, and recover confidential documents she had stolen. I knew now that Kam Sau had never stolen any documents. Someone else had broken into Yip's safe and then ...

"I didn't mention it to my friend the chef when I spoke to him," Fung said, breaking into my thoughts. "But how about we ask him to serve us up some nice fat juicy sea slugs? They're another speciality in here and they're ... Hey! Are you listening?"

I was listening to him, but not intently. I was too busy silently cursing myself for all the mistakes I had made since that meeting with Alan Yip. I had screwed up almost everything. No longer, though. Tonight's events had finally opened my eyes.

I wanted to cancel the meal. To rush back to my office and make urgent phone calls. But if I dashed out of the restaurant now I would be making the killer aware that I knew the truth — I knew why Joe Chan and the others had been murdered.

I knew the killer's identity.

I didn't want to make him aware. Not until I could prove that what I knew was the truth. So I stayed put and told Fung his fat juicy sea slugs would be perfect; in fact he could order anything — rat bollocks, stewed snake, deep-fried lizard, or any other 'authentic' Cantonese dish that happened to take his fancy. He ordered his fat sea slugs and then we made small talk while waiting for our so-called food to arrive. Ten minutes into our wait, John Yip's aide and the Bollywood producer rose to leave. As he hurried towards the exit, Yip's aide threw a glance in my direction. He looked scared. Probably he thought I would rush over and grab him. But I stayed in my seat. Now was not yet the time to challenge anyone. I needed to wait until I was fully prepared.

As if on cue, the instant the aide and his Bollywood friend disappeared from view, our waiter appeared with Fung's 'authentic' food. I grabbed one look at the shiny sea slugs slithering around on the virginal-white plate and took this as *my* cue to leave. I threw Fung some line about suddenly feeling unwell. He knew it was a lie, of course, but he didn't care if I stayed — he had achieved what he wanted to achieve in bringing me here.

It was almost midnight when I reached my office. I plugged in my laptop and did some Internet searches. Then I rang up the safe house in Cebu, uttering a silent prayer that it would be Giselle who answered; Kam Sau would hang up the moment she realised it was me. My luck was in. Giselle took the call. I said I needed her to ask Kam Sau some questions.

"She's next door watching TV. Why don't you ask her yourself?"

I explained that Kam Sau still didn't trust me and it would be better if she spoke to someone she did trust.

"What sort of questions?"

"Ask her if Joe Chan spoke English," I said. "Then ask her if a friend was with John Yip the first time that he met Ah Fah. The friend is called …"

241

I told her the name. Then I waited while she talked with Kam Sau. The wait took longer than I expected. But finally Giselle came back on the line.

"Yeah, that guy was with John Yip."

"What about Chan?"

"Kam Sau says he only spoke Cantonese."

"Good. Now I want you to do one more thing."

"What?"

I spent a few minutes explaining.

"Can you do it, Giselle?"

"Yeah, I can do it," she replied. Then she added in a hesitant voice, "Only I … Well, is this one phone call really so important, huh? I mean what will me talking to him really do?"

"It will help me trap a killer."

35

DAWN CAME EARLY.

A cold, dirty-grey dawn it spread its chill embrace across snowbound fields, icy fingers stretching out to shake the rice farmers awake. I needed no such encouragement. For the past three hours I had been awake — and afraid. The car's heater was broken and cold clawed my bones like a tiger, but fear made me sweat. The sweat dripped from my brow; it oozed over my shoulder blades and underneath the leather holster cradling the 9mm snub-nosed Makarov; it carved an arc across my chest; it rolled over my stomach and nestled in my groin.

I stared through the scratched windscreen. The kidnapper was about forty metres away, a hazy, dreamlike figure who seemed to float in the glow of the car's headlamps. I shoved the car door open and stumbled out on to the icy road. The kidnapper got within about ten metres of me and then halted; a slim silhouette who seemed to be cut from grey tissue paper.

"Got the money?" he rasped.

"In the car," I said, "half a million in small notes."

The kidnapper's body shimmied in the bronzed mist of the lamps. There was a dull click and my arm was half-moving to the Makarov, before I realised he was only lighting a cigarette.

"Good," he said. "I can see Buddha has fated us to stay friends."

"Where's the woman?"

"In my car," he said, "half a mile down the road." He seized a pull from his cigarette then blew smoke into the freezing early-morning air. "She's fine and she'll stay fine — providing there are no tricks."

"There'll be no tricks."

"So step away from the car, Peter."

His voice had changed — it was a voice I knew well. When I looked at him closer I saw that his face had also changed and was now one I recognised: the face of my father, Paddy Duggan.

"Wait five minutes until after I've driven off," Paddy commanded. "Then, and only then, you get her."

He stepped out of the light to walk to my car, boots crunching the packed snow. The car door opened then closed. The engine spluttered. Wheels churned against slush. I waited five minutes and then trudged down the deserted road. Wind sliced across the fields like a razor, but I didn't feel it as I strained to glimpse Paddy's car. After ten minutes I had seen nothing.

He lied! There's no car!

Then I saw it. A dark-red lifeboat all alone in a grey-white sea of snow and ice; Paddy's car was where he had said it would be; everything would be all right.

I was about fifteen metres away from the car when it exploded. Frozen ground rose to club me in the face. I tasted glass fragments, shards of metal; saw blue-yellow flames shoot high into a leaden sky. I smelled burning gasoline, scorched rubber; the singed hair of my nostrils. I tried to get up, but my body belonged to someone whose legs had been chopped off. Above the roar of flames came the screams of my mother burning to death.

I SNAPPED AWAKE, covered in sweat. I grabbed deep breaths to calm myself — relax, Peter; it was only a bad dream. But why *this* dream, I wondered, as I hauled myself from the sweat-soaked bed. Tomorrow would mark the fifteenth anniversary of mother's death, so I was bound to dream of Paddy — whenever the anniversary drew near he always haunted me: but why the burning car?

Eight years had passed since I had last woken up screaming as Paddy roasted mother in his car. Two days later I had made the worst screw-up of my career, my arrogance and stupidity almost killing a girl. Was I being warned that I risked messing up again? Was my dream telling me I'd been arrogant and foolish to use Giselle to trap the killer?

I shuffled into the bathroom and stood under the shower jet, turned the cold water on full and tried to blast all my worries away. No good. The water only made me shiver. After five minutes I got dried and returned to the living room, cleaner and cooler, but still troubled by that dream about Paddy.

Why had mother married him? More to the point, why had she continued to love him? Because she *had* loved the selfish son of a bitch, even after he deserted us. There had been countless times as a child when I had witnessed her devotion. I would be in the kitchen, watching her cleaning dishes, when she would hear footsteps in the corridor. Her gaze would move to the door and she would get all misty-eyed, hoping the footsteps were Paddy's — yes, she had loved him.

Why? He was the reason she had died of cancer. He had left us without a cent, forcing mother to labour for years in an asbestos-ridden factory in Kwai Chung. Why had she continued to love him? I had often wanted to ask her but had known she would find the question painful to answer. So I had never pressed her. I'd asked people who had worked with Paddy, though. They had told me that the booze had changed him; sober he'd been a gentle soul, but drink had unleashed demons.

He must have been sober when he had first met mother. An intelligent woman like her would never have married a drunk; yes, he must have been another man in those days. People changed, though. Look at me. After seeing how Paddy had treated mother, I'd vowed to be different. And what had I done? Broken promise after promise; treated Suk Fan thoughtlessly; put career before family. About the only difference between me and Paddy was that, in my case, the wife had left her husband. But Suk Fan had given me plenty of chances before storming out.

My mobile rang.

I thought it might be Giselle, calling to say the killer had entered my trap. It turned out to be John Yip's secretary. She said he wanted me to stop searching for Kam Sau. I asked her to let me speak to him, but she said he was busy. Then she hung up. Yip's aide had obviously rushed off last night and told his boss about our restaurant encounter. But if Yip thought that by

246

sacking me he would stop me unmasking the killer, he was wrong. It was only be a matter of time before I had definite proof. I had set a trap. The killer would step into it. Then I would unmask him.

My phone rang again: Giselle this time? No, it was my daughter. Kathy sounded sleepy.

"Where are you, dad? Why aren't you answering your home number?"

"I had to leave home early," I lied. "I had a breakfast meeting with a contact. What's wrong?"

She yawned: "Nothing's wrong. I just wanted to know when we're visiting the temple."

"I'll pick you up at twelve. Is your mother there?"

"Taking a shower; I'll tell her the temple time."

She hung up.

I got dressed. Then I walked over to the window and tugged back the thick blue curtains to check on the weather. Sunlight so sharp it had sliced through the pollution haze glinted off buses and cars as they sped along Gloucester Road and off sludge-coloured water n Causeway Bay's typhoon shelter. Rows of gleaming cabin cruisers bobbed at anchor in the shelter.

I was at the Excelsior Hotel, in a twelfth-floor room that over-looked the typhoon shelter. I had come here last night. After persuading Giselle to help me lay that trap it had been impossible for me to return home. The killer's thugs would have rushed to my flat immediately after Giselle had called him.

The diamond-hard sunlight dazzled me. I drew the curtains. A mosquito buzzed my face; I swiped at it, but missed. I decided to turn the air-conditioner to the super-cool level; a blast of freezing air should chase away this nuisance and any of his annoying pals who had sneaked into the room. Before I could reach up to adjust the air-conditioner's dial, my phone rang again.

"Think you're clever do you, Duggan?"

It was a man's voice; hard and sneering.

"You're not, you're fucking stupid."

I stiffened: "Who is this?"

"Did you really think we wouldn't find out where they lived?"

My throat went dry: "Where who lives?"

"You're so clever. Work it out."

"Who are you? What do you want?"

"We want your wife and—"

"No," I shouted. "Leave my family alone."

"We're outside her flat now, Duggan. In another minute we'll be inside."

"I'll kill you!" I screamed.

36

BEFORE THE TAXI had come to a stop I was kicking open the door and leaping out onto the pavement — then sprinting for Suk Fan's apartment fifty metres away.

I skidded to a halt in front of her block — shoved open the double glass entrance doors and half-charged, half-fell into the lobby. The old security guard dozing at his desk jolted awake.

"Hey! What the—"

"Are they all right?" I gasped.

"Are who all right?"

I strode over to the lift, thumped the button to open the metal doors.

"If he's hurt them, I'll—"

"No good battering the lift, chief. Doors won't open any quicker."

I thumped the button harder.

The lift doors stayed shut.

"Come on, come on," I snapped, "get it working."

"I can't — it's broken. The engineer's on his way to fix it, but he won't arrive until ..."

I no longer listened to him. I was running for the door that led to the fire escape; wrenching the door open then charging up the stairs two, sometimes three at a time, ignoring the strain on my lungs and pain in my chest. At the sixth floor, I kicked open the swing doors and lurched on to the corridor — Suk Fan's flat was the second on the left.

I got ready to charge at the door in order to break the lock. No need. The door lay open.

I moved inside the flat.

"Suk Fan! Kathy!"

No reply.

"Suk Fan! Kathy!"

Still no answer.

I looked around. There were no signs of a struggle: no broken furniture, upended chairs, smashed crockery — everything seemed normal. For an instant I wondered if I had imagined it all. Was it like one of those Paddy Duggan nightmares? Would I soon wake up, shaking and covered in sweat?

No. The lock on the door was broken. Those thugs had broken it. They had snatched Kathy and Suk Fan. And you're to blame, Duggan, I told myself, it's your fault. You thought you were clever, didn't you? You were so confident of trapping the killer. Look where your lousy confidence has got you — he's grabbed your wife and daughter. You don't know where he's taken them. You haven't got a clue where he's ...

I swallowed hard.

Supposing that he had not taken them anywhere!

Supposing they were here in the flat: sprawled out in a bloody mess on the floor of one of the bedrooms. Or in the bathroom, or the kitchen, or ... With a sense of dread, I searched the bedrooms, and then the kitchen and bathroom — Kathy and Suk Fan were nowhere.

I breathed a sigh of relief.

But what had I to feel relieved about? The fact that I hadn't found any bodies didn't mean they were safe. They had been snatched by a man who had ordered three deaths. A cold-blooded killer who would not hesitate to make Kathy and Suk Fan his fourth and fifth victims. And I had no idea where they were. Not a clue where ….

"Hey! What are you doing here?"

I spun round. A middle-aged fat woman stood framed in the doorway, frowning heavily. She clutched yellow plastic shopping bags in both her hands.

"Who are you?" she demanded to know.

"Kathy's father."

"So where are Suk Fan and Kathy? And why is the door broken like that?"

"I know it looks suspicious," I said. "But …"

She dropped the shopping bags and ran for the safety of her apartment — probably to call the police. Why had she not returned twenty minutes ago? A neighbour's presence in the corridor might have deterred those thugs from breaking in. And why had I not arrived earlier — why the stupid decision to take a taxi? I had thought it would be faster. I should have used my own car, though. Then I would have arrived in time to … Of course I wouldn't have arrived in time. The thugs had snatched Suk Fan and Kathy twenty minutes ago. No way could I have stopped them. How had they smuggled my wife and daughter out of the building without alerting the security guard? It wouldn't have been difficult. That character in the lobby had probably been asleep like he had been when I'd burst in. Even if he had been awake Kathy and Suk Fan would never have dared to alert him. Not with loaded guns pressed against their backs.

My mobile rang. I yanked it from my pocket.

"You should enter the fucking Olympics! Run as fast there as you did from that taxi and you'll—"

"Where are they, you bastard?"

"Try looking out of the window."

I strode to the window, yanked back the flowered curtains and gazed on to the street. About fifty metres away, standing beside a silver Mercedes, were Kathy and Suk Fan. Two hoodlums, both of them wearing darkened glasses, also stood beside the Mercedes.

"What do you want from me?"

"We want you to see they're alive. And to tell you they'll stay alive — if you're a good boy and do as you're told."

I felt a cold fist closing over my heart. "What do you really want from me?"

"We want those tapes that bitch in the Philippines gave you."

"First you let my wife and daughter go; they have nothing to do with this."

"We'll let them go *after* you give us the stuff."

"I don't have the tapes with me."

"Then you'd better get them."

"It'll take time."

"You've got two hours."

"I need longer."

"Two hours, Duggan. Someone will phone you then with details of how to make the delivery. And don't try to screw us around either. Or your wife and kid suffer."

"I want to speak to them," I said. "I need to make sure they're all right."

"All you need to make sure of is that you're ready for our next call. Two hours."

"Put them on the line," I said. "I want …"

But the line had gone dead.

37

I WAS AN arrogant son of a bitch and my wife and daughter had paid for my arrogance. When I had phoned Giselle in the Philippines, I had been sure it would only be a matter of time. The killer was bound to enter my trap. Giselle only had to follow orders.

"I say I've found two tapes?"

"Yes."

"Of him raping her?"

"You say you found them in Kam Sau's room. He's already got the originals. He'll assume yours are copies Joe Chan made for security."

"He'll offer to buy them?"

"Yes."

"I say no?"

"You say the dead girl was like a sister. You don't want blood money. You want him arrested."

"That's why I've given the tapes to you?"

"And if he asks why not to the police, you say girls in your job like to keep cops at a distance."

"And I called him because I wanted to personally let him know he was screwed?"

"That's right. You wanted to tell him how he would suffer for murdering your friend. You wanted to savour the moment."

Her voice quavered: "But just supposing …"

"What?"

"Supposing … I mean … Supposing he doesn't believe this stuff?"

"Tell him everything I've told you, Giselle, and it'll work — trust me."

She had trusted me. She had made the call. But the plan had failed. My stupidity and arrogance had put Kam Sau's and Kathy's lives in danger.

There was a sharp knock at the door.

A husky voice said, "Open up, Pete, it's me."

I opened the door: Frank Ching stood outside. I had contacted Frank two hours ago and told him everything. I needed help, but no way would I call the police; I was too afraid they would screw up. I trusted Frank, though; I trusted him with my life.

"Did you get it?" I said.

Frank tapped the black attaché case he was holding. "In here."

He padded into the room and sat on the bed. He lifted the case onto his lap, slipped the locks. His case was a hard-topped model, the sort that executives used to carry important documents. No documents were in this case, though. It contained a sub-machinegun with a pistol-type grip and curved magazine.

"Heckler and Koch MP 5K," Frank said. "Fires a nine-millimetre bullet from a thirty-round magazine at nine hundred rounds a minute."

I can count on one hand the times when I've carried a gun. If a criminal is unarmed you don't need a gun to arrest him. Even when he is armed, it only increases danger. If he knows you have no gun, he'll know you can't shoot him if he makes a dash for freedom — his instinct will be to run. Pull out an automatic and he'll feel cornered; he's likely to blaze away.

There are times, though, when you have to change your ways. Today was one of them. I had asked Frank to exhaust his connections and find me a small hand-gun — preferably a Colt .38 — that I could strap to my ankle. I like to carry a gun there rather than on my shoulder, because it's easier to reach an ankle holster when you're in a car. With shoulder holsters, the seat belt often gets in the way. Ankle holsters also make it easier to grab the gun if you're knocked on your back — you pull your knees to your chest as you roll.

So why had Frank brought this monster?

"I wanted something I could hide," I said, "an ankle holster and a .38 revolver."

Frank shook his head. "They're bound to search you. They'd find that revolver in two seconds flat."

I pointed at the Heckler. "If I can't hide a Colt .38, how do I hide something as big as that?"

"You *don't* hide it."

"What?"

"This is a special model used by the American Secret Service," Frank explained. "You fire it from *inside* the case. A trigger's built into the case handle here." He tapped the handle. "You press it and the bullets come through this hole in the side of the case."

"They'll still find the gun when they open the case."

"You don't let them open it."

"I can't stop them. They'll snatch if off me then open it themselves."

"It's got a combination lock."

I stared at him in disbelief. "They're professional killers, Frank! Me refusing to tell them the combination won't make them walk away all nice and polite. They'll rip out my finger nails!"

He waved away my objections. "Remember what you said on the phone? You told me expects you to bring video tapes."

I nodded.

"That's why the case is perfect," Frank said. "You tell him the tapes are inside, but say you won't unlock the case until you see your wife and daughter. If he threatens you, you say the tapes in the case aren't the only ones — you gave copies to a friend who'll contact the cops if anything happens to you. He'll back down, Pete — he'll show you Kam Sau and Kathy. Then you point the case, pull the trigger … It'll be over in a few seconds. You'll take them by surprise."

I took the case from him; it felt surprisingly light. I tested the trigger mechanism; it seemed easy to operate.

"Where did you get this thing?"

"My security friend; you met him at the race track."

I remembered the man; a tall character in dark glasses who had been formally dressed in a suit and tie. Frank had said the man supplied big-shots with body-guards, to protect them from kidnap gangs.

"How did your friend get it?"

"They advertise stuff like this on the Internet these days — not expensive either. That one you're holding there cost less than fifteen hundred American dollars."

"It's all tried and tested?"

"The American Secret Service swears by them," Frank said; "that's why, when you see their President

Obama on TV, the characters beside him are all carrying briefcases. But if you don't like it, I've brought you an alternative."

He reached into his jacket pocket and pulled out a metal disc that was about three inches in diameter.

"Looks like a cowboy belt buckle from the front," Frank said. "Turn it over like this, though, and there's a five-shot revolver fixed to the back."

He tapped what was the smallest gun I'd ever seen; the barrel was barely an inch long. Surely this could not be a serious weapon.

"A stud on the front of the belt buckle releases the gun," Frank said. "But it hasn't got much stopping power. It only takes a twenty-two calibre bullet so you need to fire at point-blank range."

Stopping power would not be the only problem. The buckle was too big. It might work in Texas, but not Hong Kong. No one here sported huge belt buckles. Wear this to my rendezvous with those thugs and it would set alarms bell ringing.

I returned the buckle to Frank.

"I'll stick with the case; how about you?"

He unzipped his canvas jacket to reveal a shoulder holster. "Walther PPK," he said, tapping the black leather holster. He reached into his jacket again and pulled out what looked like a green dumbbell. It was about six inches long and had three large holes bored into the sides. "I've also got two of these."

"Dumbbells?"

"American X84 stun grenades," Frank said. "Give off a blinding flash and make a deafening noise. My security firm friend swears by them. Reckons they're invaluable in hostage situations and … What's wrong?"

"You told him?" I shook my head in disbelief. "You told him about Suk Fan and Kathy?" My voice rose in anger. "Are you completely crazy? They're in enough danger without you opening your big—"

"Calm down, Pete!"

"I told you to keep your mouth shut," I snapped.

"That's what I did," Frank shot back. "Do you think I'm stupid enough to give the *real* reason why I wanted the stuff? I said I needed it for a police demonstration."

I took a deep breath.

"Sorry, Frank, I must be the most ungrateful bastard alive."

"It's all right," he said. "I know what you must be going through."

"You're putting yourself on the line for me and here I am snapping and snarling. You know I don't mean it, though. It's just …" I swallowed hard to try and get rid of the dryness in my throat. "You know what I mean."

He nodded. "There's just you and me, and we don't know what we're up against" He paused. Then he said haltingly, "That's why … Well I … Shouldn't we get in touch with police headquarters and—"

"No."

"With more help we could—"

"No," I said. "Too many cops are on the take from the 14K. You're the only one I can trust, Frank."

He fired up a cigarette, something that he only ever did when he was scared. He took a deep pull to relax himself then blew out a cloud of silvery-blue smoke. Then he said, "So where and when do you meet him?"

I checked my watch: ten past eleven.

"Someone will call soon with details."

"Will it be Ian Jeffries himself?"

259

I frowned. "Jeffries?"

"Will he call you himself?" Frank said. "Or will one of those Ke Ge Bo hit-men do his dirty work?"

I shook my head. "Either I didn't make it clear when we spoke on the phone, or you've misunderstood."

It was Frank's turn to frown. "I don't get you."

"Stephen Fung is the killer."

38

"JOE CHAN SPOKE no English and Ian Jeffries can't string a sentence together in Cantonese," I said. "Yet according to the phone company's records, Chan made a nine-minute call to Jeffries' office in England. Would you chat for nine minutes to a man who you couldn't understand?"

"He called Fung?"

I nodded. "Your Ke Ge Bo friend spoke the truth the other day when he said they had nothing to do with those three murders — the killers are from the 14K Triad; Fung got his dad's hoodlums to cover up what happened at that party."

Frank looked unconvinced: "Three murders just to cover up a sex scandal!"

"It was more than a sex scandal," I said. "He raped that girl, Frank. And Chan filmed it! If those video tapes ever got out, Fung was staring at a long prison sentence."

Frank shook his head. "That stuff about Chan not understanding Jeffries doesn't stand up. Ian Jeffries is a China scholar — speaks good Cantonese."

"No he doesn't," I said. "I checked on the computer last night. It was Chinese culture he studied at university, not language. He can't string a sentence together in Mandarin or Cantonese — Fung raped that girl and Fung ordered those three murders."

"I read it in the newspaper," Frank insisted. "I read that Jeffries—"

I interrupted.

"I read the stuff about him speaking Cantonese too," I said. "The newspapers got it wrong, Frank. It wouldn't be the first time they screwed up. Some of them ran corrections a few days after the original story. Only the corrections were so small that if you had blinked you would have missed them."

"So why did your missing secretary say that it was Jeffries who raped her friend?"

It was becoming oppressively hot in the room. I reached up to the air-conditioning unit on the wall. I turned the dial to a cooler level.

I said, "She still hoped to cut a deal with Fung and was scared me knowing the truth might stop her getting rich. Fung was the man in the bedroom, though. That's why I got my Filipina friend to call him last night. She said she'd found copies of the tapes — the ones of him raping Ah Fah — and had sent them to me. I wanted Fung to break cover, see. I thought it was a clever way to force him into the open. But it wasn't clever, it was dumb, because now he's grabbed my wife and ..."

My throat felt dry. My heart raced. I forced myself to breathe more slowly and more deeply. Gradually, my heart beat returned to something like normal.

"So where does John Yip come into all this?" Frank asked. "Why get Snakefingers to burgle your office?"

"It was during a visit to the film studios to see John Yip that Fung first met Ah Fah," I explained. "He was smitten. He got John Yip to invite her to that party."

"But why did Yip have your office turned over?"

"To discover how close I had got to finding out that he was a thief."

Frank frowned: "Thief?"

"He stole those documents from his father's safe."

"I thought it was your missing secretary."

I shook my head. "John Yip sold the documents to a Bombay film producer — the man who is his father's chief business rival. Stephen Fung got to know about what had happened. Fung used that knowledge to force John Yip to do his bidding and …"

There was a knock on the door.

"Who is it?" I called out.

"Maid service," a woman answered. "Come to clean up your room."

"Later," I said. "Come back in an hour."

I waited until I was sure she had gone. Then I said, "But at first Alan Yip is sure that Kam Sau is his thief. It's understandable, I guess. His papers go missing then his secretary does a vanishing act — he puts two and two together and makes three. He hires me to find Kam Sau. Fung doesn't want me to find her, though; because he's scared she'll tell me the truth about who raped Ah Fah. He orders John Yip to phone and warn me off the case. When that fails to make me quit, Fung gets his father to put the squeeze on Alan Yip."

"Alan Yip sacks you?"

"He's as keen on avoiding broken legs as the next man," I said. "He's not going to disobey a direct order from the 14K Triad boss because … What's wrong?"

"I still don't understand that other John Yip stuff," Frank said. "Why would he make a phone call warning you to stop searching for that missing girl — then next minute hire you to find her?"

"Because after phoning me, he suddenly has second thoughts," I said. "He's terrified his father will discover the truth about who really stole those documents — he thinks that by keeping the focus on Kam Sau he'll divert suspicion away from himself."

I paused to brush sweat from my brow; it was still too hot in the room. I reached over and moved the air-conditioning unit's dial to the super-cold mark. Would it stop me sweating? Perhaps my sweating had nothing to do with the room's warmth. Maybe it was caused by the fear I might never see Suk Fan and Kathy again.

I said, "Fung is angry about his old school friend hiring me. He threatens to reveal the truth about who stole those documents unless John Yip comes into line. Bringing me face to face with Yip's aide and that Bombay producer last night was part of the threat — Fung letting Yip know he'll bury him if Yip disobeys orders. Yip got the message. He sacked me first thing this morning."

"I still don't get it."

"I just told you, Frank. He sacked me because—"

Frank waved his hand dismissively. "I mean that call Fung ordered John Yip to make — the one warning you off the case. Why did he need to have Yip phone you? Why couldn't Fung phone himself?"

"Because he plans for every eventuality," I explained. "He knows John Yip can link him to that dead girl in China. As far as Fung is concerned, this makes Yip a threat — he combats the threat by involving Yip in the cover-up. That way, Yip's going to be sure to keep his mouth shut. He'll be in so deep that if he ever tells the truth he'll hurt himself as well as Fung and …"

The ring of my mobile interrupted me.

"Have you got it, Duggan?"

It was the same sneering, hard voice that I had heard in Suk Fan's apartment.

I swallowed dryly. "I've got it."

"Good. Now listen carefully."

"I want to speak to my wife and daughter."

"Relax, Duggan, they're safe. They'll stay safe too — providing you follow orders. Now listen up carefully. Here's what you do."

39

PORTUGESE SAILORS FIRST weighed anchor off the coast of Macau in the sixteenth century. So as a European trading colony it predates Hong Kong by three hundred-odd years.

Yet Hong Kong has never afforded Macau the respect for old age that forms such a traditional and vital part of Chinese culture. In fact it has constantly overshadowed its elderly neighbour. Hong Kong has more hotels, more restaurants, more office towers, more cars, more noise, more pollution — more of everything.

Apart from casinos.

Because of fears that it could spawn more organised crime gangs, all gambling apart from on the government's Mark Six lottery, or on government-regulated horse racing, was outlawed in Hong Kong years ago. Recognising this had created a pent-up demand for casinos among gambling-mad Hong Kongers, Macau businessmen built some. In fact they built lots of them. Recently American tycoons have got in on the act, financing glitzy new 'super' casino-and-hotel complexes like those to be found in Las Vegas. Which is why there now seem to be casinos and gambling dens on almost every Macau street, and why Macau has taken over from Las Vegas as the world's gambling capital.

I stood in one of these new 'super' casinos. But I hadn't come to gamble. I had rushed here to save my wife and daughter from a killer.

I waved a hand to clear the thick fog of cigarette smoke away from my face. As the grey-yellow tobacco mist slowly lifted, pasty-faced men and women hovered like phantoms before me. Judging from their haunted appearances, most of them had already gambled away next month's wages. It was always the same sad story. On the sixty-kilometre journey across the South China Sea, the Hong Kong gamblers would have been dreaming of winning enough in the casinos to buy a luxury yacht, or a mansion on the Peak. Yet most of them would wake up tomorrow broken and dispirited.

I pushed my way past a blackjack game. Two women were hunched over the green baize table, staring at their playing cards with eyes that were pools of despair. Probably they were only in their twenties, yet both of them looked closer to forty. The word 'loser' was stamped all over their sad, sweat-stained faces. Tomorrow they would be home in Hong Kong, begging the Yau Ma Tei money-lenders for three or four thousand dollars to help them survive the month. The money-lenders would charge big interest. If the women failed to repay the loans on time, Triad thugs would pay them a visit.

Beyond the blackjack table, red and yellow lights flashed on a regiment of buzzing and beeping arcade machines. An army of old crones in drab, Mao-style pyjama uniforms stood on duty beside the ranks of machines, pumping dollar coins into them in a robot-like fashion. But I had not come here for slot machines or blackjack. The roulette wheel in the corner was my destination: that was where I was due to rendezvous with Fung's gunman.

A crowd of gamblers, four or five deep, surrounded the good-looking young Filipino croupier as he got ready to spin the roulette wheel. But none of them wore a yellow shirt. I checked my watch: ten past nine. I was on time. Where was the gunman? My gaze raked the crowd again. I still couldn't see him. Had he lied during that phone call? Supposing Stephen Fung never planned to return my wife and daughter? Supposing that he …

"No more bets!" the croupier cried out in a loud voice. "Stand back, please! Stand back!"

He spun the wheel.

The crowd held its breath. A leathery-faced old woman standing on my right touched a jade Buddha pendant for luck. Another woman, this one middle-aged, nervously chewed her top lip. Grubby-faced, unshaven men who looked as if they had not slept for days gazed with desperation-soaked eyes at the spinning wheel, as if by doing so they would somehow will the white ball into the correct slot and win themselves a fortune.

The spinning stopped.

"Stand back!" shouted the croupier. "Stand back!"

The little white ball rolled five times around the roulette wheel's rim, making a low whirring sound, before slowing down and trickling into slot twenty-seven, then bouncing out and landing in another slot three places away. The roulette area erupted into confusion: yells of glee from a few lucky winners clashed with groans from the mass of people who had lost. There was an explosion of glass as one group of losers hurled their drinks to the floor. Men and women cursed in Cantonese and Mandarin — a few even swore in English.

I saw the man in the yellow shirt.

A tall and raw-boned figure, he had lank greasy hair and a pock-marked face. We had met before. He had pulled a gun on me at Kam Sau's flat, and with another hoodlum had chased me and my bargirl friend Giselle through Wan Chai's streets. He nodded brusquely as we made eye contact. Then he turned, equally as brusquely, on his heels and strode towards the casino's exit.

I strode after him. He shoved open double glass doors and headed towards a silver-skinned Mercedes, parked about twenty metres away. I followed him. Two men sat in the car. I had never seen the fat, swarthy-faced driver, but I knew the broken-nosed character who sat beside him. He was the other thug who had chased me and Giselle in Wan Chai.

Yellow Shirt yanked open one of the rear doors.

"Get in, Duggan."

I climbed in and rested the case gun on my lap. I said a silent prayer that Frank did not follow so close behind us that he aroused suspicion. At the same time, I did not want him to stay so far away that he lost contact. Against three killers on my own, I had no chance.

Yellow Shirt got in beside me. He leaned so close that I could smell stale sweat and bad breath. He jabbed something hard against my ribs.

"It's a loaded Makarov," he said in a low, threatening voice. "There's a silencer on the barrel too — no one will hear if I squeeze the trigger. Any tricks from you and I will squeeze it. Understood?"

"I understand."

His gun-free hand moved roughly over my chest and legs. Satisfied that I had come unarmed, he sat back and placed his head against the grey leather of the seat rest. But the Makarov still pressed against me.

"Keep both your hands where I can see them," he ordered. "And look ahead. Are the tapes in the case?"

I nodded.

"Open it and show me."

"Not until I see my wife and daughter."

He reached over with his gun-free hand and yanked the case off my lap. He tried to open it.

"There's a combination lock," I said. "And no one gets the number until—"

I grunted with pain as he drove the Makarov's barrel into my ribcage.

"I want that combination."

"Not until I know my family is safe."

"I want it now."

"No."

He shoved his face up close to mine. So close that hot saliva from his lips sprayed against my left cheek.

"I warned you about tricks," he hissed. "There's a silencer on the gun that's pressed against your guts. If I squeeze the trigger, no one will hear a thing."

I shook my head. "The case stays locked until I see that they're both safe."

"You'll never see them safe," he said. "I'm going to kill you, Duggan." He ground the Makarov even harder against my ribs. "I'm going to do it now."

40

I BRACED FOR a bullet that never came.

He eased the pressure on my ribs. "On second thoughts, I'd better wait," he said. "There's someone who wants to say goodbye first." He nodded brusquely to the driver. "Get us moving, Ah Kwan."

The driver started up the engine and pressed on the accelerator. We moved away from the kerb. The driver steered left at the first set of traffic lights, then right at one of the pawn shops that are everywhere in Macau — full of Rolex watches and jewellery traded by gamblers for cash that will give them a last chance to get rich in the casinos.

We moved on to the silver humpbacked bridge that spans the Pearl River Estuary and links Macau to Taipa and Coloane. Beneath us, the sea glinted blade-grey in the moonlight; yellow and orange lights glowed on China-bound ferries and cargo ships as they ploughed through the water. We crossed the bridge into Taipa. Not too many cars were on the roads here and we made good progress. After another five minutes we reached Coloane.

We halted at traffic lights. Headlamps washed over us as a car pulled up behind. Was Frank the driver? Yellow Shirt frowned as he studied the lamps' glare in the rear-view mirror. I stiffened. For a moment I was afraid he would accuse me of organising a tail. To my relief, he kept silent.

The traffic lights turned green. We moved off.

Five minutes more and we were heading down a steep and winding hill, the Mercedes bucking like a runaway bronco as our driver negotiated the severely pockmarked road. We turned right at the bottom of the hill and moved on to the waterfront. Fifty metres away the red and orange lights on a pier shone like gaudy jewels set in a bed of black velvet. Our driver parked ten metres from the pier, but kept the engine running.

Yellow Shirt kicked the door open and climbed out.

"Now you," he commanded.

I got out; Broken Nose too. The driver stayed put. With a screech of burning rubber, he spun the Mercedes around and headed back to Macau. As I watched the car's taillights disappear up the hill, I wiped bulbs of sweat from my face; although late at night the air remained as sticky as treacle.

Or did fear make me sweat?

To try and calm myself, I seized a deep breath. Bad move. The air stank of diesel oil, dried fish. On their own each smell might have been bearable; together they reeked of vomit and made my stomach churn.

Sampans bobbed about in the oily black sea on either side of the pier. Lights gleamed dully on several of these small boats, but I glimpsed no one on board; perhaps everyone there had gone to sleep. The sampans were anchored in the sea about twenty-five metres away. Only one boat had been tied up to the pier. A pleasure junk that would take office parties cruising at weekends and on bank holidays, it was about thirty feet long and made of polished wood.

I watched Broken Nose stride towards it. Then I glanced away, in the direction of the hill we had just driven down. At the top of this hill two cars sped past, powerful headlamps cleaving bronze channels in the aubergine-coloured night air. Was Frank one of the drivers? Would he park out of sight and then return to help me?

Broken Nose stepped nimbly on to the junk and moved quickly to the captain's cabin. He unlocked the door and disappeared inside. Yellow Shirt jabbed me in the back with his Makarov and ordered me on board. He followed close behind. When we were both on board he pointed at a pair of thick mooring ropes that secured the junk to the pier.

"Cast off."

Holding the Heckler case gun in one hand, I reached to the pier with my other hand and unhooked the first rope from its iron mooring pillar. I hauled the heavy, greasy rope on board then repeated the procedure with the second rope. Yellow Shirt made a brusque hand signal to Broken Nose. The junk gave a violent shudder as Broken Nose fired up the engine. We began to drift away from the pier.

Frank could not help now.

I was alone.

But not unarmed. I still had the attaché case. A 9mm Heckler and Koch sub-machinegun lay inside. These two didn't know that I was armed — I could take them by surprise. A quick swing of the attaché case, flick of the trigger … I could handle them. Not yet, though. Not until I'd made sure Kathy and Suk Fan were safe.

"Where are my wife and daughter?"

"Relax, Duggan, you'll see them when we're at sea."

So they were here on board. Where? In the living quarters probably; I half-turned and stared at the door that led to the junk's interior. It was shut now, but I would soon open it. I began to move towards it — the door stood only five feet away. One more step and …

Bullets smacked the doorframe above my head.

"Get away from there!" Yellow Shirt ordered. "Move over to the handrail!"

"If you've harmed a single hair on—"

"Ah Liu told you to relax, Pete."

The living quarters' door had swung open: Stephen Fung stood nonchalantly by the entrance, a can of beer in his left hand. He took a leisurely drink then lobbed the can overboard. He wore an orange Polo shirt, black canvas trousers and Timberland boat shoes. He seemed relaxed; the perfect picture of a man enjoying the type of pleasure cruise these junks had been designed for. At least he would have looked the perfect picture — had he not gripped a snub-nosed Colt .45 in his right hand.

He smiled his broad, public relations-type smile. Without that gun he held at waist level, he might be a party host welcoming a favoured guest on board. In the same fake-friendly tone he had used at our restaurant meeting, he said, "What say you open that nice shiny case, Pete, and hand me my tapes?"

"Where are my wife and daughter, you bastard?"

He smiled more broadly. "Our guest seems a little bit hard of hearing, Ah Liu. Maybe you should open the case for him."

Yellow Shirt shook his head: "It's got a combination lock, boss."

"And no one learns the number," I said, "until I see my family and make sure they're safe."

Fung stiffened. The public relations smile fell away from his lips. He raised the Colt so that it pointed at my chest. I swallowed dryly.

"Open the fucking case."

"Killing me gets you nowhere," I blurted out. "I left copies with a friend — anything happens to me and those tapes go public."

He moved a step closer. He stood only eight feet away now. Close enough to see the veins standing out on his neck. To glimpse the tiger-like fury in his eyes.

"Kathy! Suk Fan!" I yelled.

A muffled reply came from the living quarters. I couldn't make out what had been said, but I knew who had said it — that was my wife and daughter in there.

"Kathy! Suk …"

Bang! Bang!

Bullets splintered the planking by my feet.

"Next time it won't be the deck," Fung said.

But his threats had come too late to stop me learning what I had been desperate to learn — Kathy and Suk Fan were alive in there. Were they unguarded? Had Fung only brought Yellow Shirt and Broken Nose with him tonight? Or did a third gunman guard my wife and daughter? If this third gunman existed, it didn't matter how fast I swung my case gun from one target to another here on deck: I might kill Fung and the other two, but that still left a third gunman in the living quarters. Killing Fung might cause this third gunman to shoot Kathy and Suk Fan.

"Have your guard inside bring my wife and daughter on deck," I said. "Then we can trade."

"You have ten seconds to open that case."

"Be sensible," I urged him. "Do the trade."

"Now it's eight seconds."

"Think of it as just another business deal," I said. "I give you all the tapes I brought tonight, as well as the copies I've made — you return my wife and daughter and let us all leave safely."

Fung made no reply.

"Well?" I asked. "Do we have a deal?"

Still no answer; for a moment he didn't even look at me; he half-turned and stared intently in the direction of the shore. Yellow Shirt still covered me with his gun, though. I stared in the same direction as Fung had stared, puzzled by what had attracted his attention. Eventually, I realised that he had seen nothing. He had merely decided to take time out to consider my deal.

The sea grew choppier: salt water sprayed my face and stung my eyes. We lay about four hundred metres out. Lights on those few sampans anchored by the pier had grown so dim that I could scarcely see them. The lights on the pier itself had grown equally dull. Apart from these few red and orange pinpricks, darkness swamped the shore. Until the full moon slipped out from behind an aubergine-coloured cloud and painted everything silver-grey. On the hill above the waterfront, I spotted the silhouette of a parked car. Had Frank driven it there?

"Supposing that I agree to your business deal?" Fung said suddenly, turning away from the shore to face me. "What is there to stop you from releasing those videos once you're back in Hong Kong?"

276

"I have to protect my family," I said. "I know jailing you wouldn't keep them safe. Even from a prison cell you'd still be able to contact your Triad friends."

His gaze scoured my face, searching for signs that I had told him the truth. After about five or six seconds, he nodded brusquely at his chief gunman.

"Ah Liu will bring them out."

He had just pronounced his own death sentence.

If Yellow Shirt needed to fetch Kathy and Suk Fan it meant no third man guarded them. It meant I only had to take out Fung and his two gunmen here on deck — then turn the boat around and return to the pier.

Broken Nose should be easiest; he was busy steering; I could leave him until I had dealt with the others. But supposing I failed with the others? Fung and Yellow Shirt were armed and stood only a few feet away — one in front, one behind me. Target one of them and I gave the other a clear shot at me. Unless I narrowed the odds by half-turning and … Yes, standing sideways-on like this cut the time it would take me to swing the case from one to the other — not by much but anything was better than nothing. And I had the element of surprise. They still thought I had come here unarmed.

"But he only brings them out here *after* you open that briefcase," Fung said. "So flip the locks and …"

He fell silent and stared out to sea once more. He had just heard the same noise that I had heard; the unmistakable husky throb of an engine. It came from the direction of shore. How far from shore it was hard to tell, because no boat lights shone in the darkness.

"No problems, boss," Yellow Shirt said reassuringly, "probably just a fishing sampan."

"Bullshit! That engine's way too powerful."

"So maybe it's a powerboat," Yellow Shirt suggested. "The locals use them to smuggle stuff over to China. They keep the lights off to avoid the coastguards."

Fung thought about it for a moment then nodded, satisfied it was a smugglers' boat that he had heard. He returned his attention to me.

"Open the case, Duggan."

It was now or never.

But I mustn't rush anything — if I did I risked making a fatal mistake. I did everything coldly and precisely, exactly how Frank had showed me in the hotel room. I turned the attaché case until the Heckler's concealed barrel pointed at Fung's chest: I slipped off the safety: placed my finger on the trigger mechanism in the case's handle: took a deep, calming breath. I had it all clear in my mind: shoot Fung first, then Yellow Shirt, then deal with Broken Nose and then … Would it really work, though? Would I be fast enough to get all three? Yes, I told myself, it would work. It would only take a split second to swing the attaché case from Fung to his gunman. I had the perfect weapon: ultra-fast, totally reliable. All I had to do was keep pressing the trigger as I swung the case. The Heckler spewed out ammunition at nine hundred rounds a minute.

"Hurry up," Fung snapped. "Open it."

I squeezed the trigger.

41

THE BULLETS HIT Fung in the chest: the impact lifted him off his feet and sent him splashing into the water. I turned to Yellow Shirt: aimed the case-gun, squeezed the trigger.

The case-gun jammed.

I stared in disbelief: first at the jammed case-gun then at an unharmed Yellow Shirt. How could this be happening? The Heckler was precision-made, ultra-reliable — it never jammed. Yellow Shirt was stunned too. We gaped in blank astonishment at each other. Unable to grasp what had happened, unsure what to do next; both of us locked in a trance.

He broke from the trance first.

He took a step forward.

My brain told me to throw the case at him — knock the pistol from his hand, dive for his legs — but my body refused to obey. I saw his eyes narrow as he took careful aim with the Makarov. Saw his facial muscles contract as he squeezed the trigger.

My brain screamed a final warning.

Get away!

I dropped the case, flung myself in a rugby tackle at his legs. Too slowly: I felt a blow on my left shoulder, as if someone had punched me. Then a searing heat, as if a red-hot poker had been pressed against me; and not only against my shoulder, my left leg was on fire too. Had two bullets hit me?

The furnace-like heat vanished as suddenly as it had appeared, replaced by an icy cold numbness. The deck rose to slap me in the face. I tried to struggle to my feet, but it felt like a tree lay on top of me.

Bang!

A bullet hit the deck. I wouldn't be as lucky again, though: the next shot would hit me.

Crawl away! Move! Move!

Impossible: that was no longer a single tree on top of me but a whole forest. No way could I shift it. I could only lie helplessly and await that fatal bullet. Wait for blackness to engulf me.

No bullet came.

No blackness.

What came was a deafening blast a million times louder than a gun-shot. Then the world exploded into brilliant white light. I screwed my eyes shut against the blinding glare. When I re-opened them, the world had changed.

Orange-white mist lit up the boat like one of Alan Yip's *kung fu* film-sets. Nothing on this set seemed any longer to involve me; I was a man watching the action not taking part. Was this how it felt to die — had I joined mother in the after-life? Did everything in the after-life happen in a ghostly silence and super slow-motion? But if I had died, why was Yellow Shirt still trying to kill me?

280

He moved closer.

In this strange orange-white, misty world, he seemed to float not walk. Float slowly. So slowly that at this rate it would be days before he stood over me to deliver the fatal shot. For a moment he kept his stone-hard, killer's gaze fixed on me. Then he looked away for a moment and down at the snub-nosed Makarov. A puzzled look spread across his face as he stared at the gun — he looked like a man who had forgotten how to fire it.

He stumbled. His arms flailed windmill style as he struggled to keep his balance. A dark patch appeared on his tee-shirt in the area around his chest. The patch grew bigger and bigger, until the whole front of his tee-shirt was stained purple where it had once been yellow.

All this time he continued to fall.

He no longer flailed his arms to try and keep his balance; both arms now remained by his sides. In the new, slow-motion world that the orange-white fog had created, it seemed to take a week for him to fall half-way to the deck. As he fell, his body turned sideways; it was as if a huge invisible hand had reached out to flip him over in mid-air. Finally, his head hit the deck. Even in my brain-dulled state I knew that he was dead.

I glanced over to the captain's cabin. The cabin door was opening, but so slowly that it seemed to take an hour before the second gunman emerged. He shouted at me. In this ghostly new world, as silent as it was slow, I couldn't hear him. Then he jumped up and started to move backwards through the air. He clawed at the mist the way that a drowning man claws water. But no matter how hard he tried he couldn't stop himself moving backwards. What finally halted him was the cabin door when the back of his head smashed into it. He slid down to the boat's deck. His legs and arms twitched. Then he lay still. A man whose face I couldn't see — he was an orange-white blur — stepped over the second gunman. Were three of Fung's thugs on board? But why would this third hoodlum kill his friend? It made no sense.

The man drew closer. It wasn't one of Fung's thugs. It was my friend, Frank Ching. How had Frank got on board? He leaned over, shouted in my ear. I couldn't hear him. Then he was standing up and leaving me; I grabbed his arm — I didn't want to be left alone.

He signalled that he wouldn't be gone for long. Reluctantly, I released my grip. He moved over to the junk's living quarters. I uttered a silent prayer that he would return soon — I needed help. That furnace–like pain I had experienced after being shot, but which had then quickly vanished, was back: flames flickered down the whole left side of my body.

Frank opened the door of the living quarters and went inside. He was probably only gone from my view for fifteen seconds, but it seemed half an hour before he reappeared. Kathy and Suk Fan were with him. Then they were walking over to me, reaching down and putting their arms around me.

But all I could feel were those flames.

Suk Fan brought her face up close to mine and said something. I couldn't hear her, though, I could only see her. Then I couldn't see her. Not clearly. My vision became more blurred: the yellow-white mist swallowed her. Bit by bit, my wife slipped away from me. I saw less and less of her, until she was so far away, so swallowed up by the mist, that I no longer saw her at all: only hard, burning white light.

42

I WOKE UP to find an elderly, white-coated doctor standing beside my bed. He informed me that I had been unconscious for a day and a half but that everything was going to be all right. Surgeons had removed the bullet that Stephen Fung's gunman had pumped into my left shoulder. The doctor was confident of me making a full and speedy recovery.

He said that if I had woken up an hour ago my wife and daughter would have been sitting by the bed, but they had gone home to get some rest. He called them on his mobile phone and delivered the good news. Then he passed the phone over to me. Kathy said they would be at the hospital within the next hour. I told her to rest up a bit first, but she told me to shut my mouth. Then she passed the phone to Suk Fan. There were various questions I could have asked my wife: I could have asked if Fung's gunmen had hurt either her or Kathy, or whether they were suffering from shock.

Instead, I said, "Are you coming back home to stay?"

Rather than answer my question, Suk Fan told me that neither her nor Kathy was suffering from shock;

they were both a lot stronger than I thought they were. She said a few other things to me, too; things that I forgot about almost as soon as she had mentioned them. But she didn't answer my question about returning home.

So I asked it again.

"Are you coming back?"

"I don't know, Peter, I'll need to have a long hard think about everything first."

"It'll be different this time."

"I have to go now. Kathy says we need to get the taxi. We'll talk more at the hospital."

The line went dead.

After about half an hour, Frank Ching came in — Kathy had phoned him to say I was conscious. Frank sat on the chair beside my bed and then explained how he had managed to get on board Fung's junk.

"I parked the car on that road at the top of the hill," Frank said. "About fifty metres from where Fung had his boat moored. Then I ran down to the waterfront and found a local who owned a speedboat — one of those super-fast jobs locals in that area use to smuggle stuff over to China." Frank shifted on the chair to make himself more comfortable. "I paid this guy a thousand dollars to hire the boat for the night, and then steered it over to Fung's junk. It was so dark that Fung and those other two never saw either me or the boat until it was too late to do anything about it."

The orange-white flashes which had lit up the junk like a film set had been caused by Frank hurling his American army stun grenades. Frank showed me some newspapers he had bought. I expected Stephen Fung's face to be plastered all over the front pages. To my amazement, none of the newspapers contained a word about Fung's death or our gun-battle.

"No one knows he's dead yet," Frank explained. "I weighed down his two gunmen first and dumped their bodies overboard. Then I found Fung's body floating in the water near the junk and weighted him down too — I figured that if no one finds them, then no one can ever pin anything on us."

What would happen when Fung had been missing for a few more days, though? When his powerful father, or influential boss Ian Jeffries, realised that something was seriously wrong? I neither knew, nor cared. Not now, anyway. All I cared about was persuading Suk Fan to come home. So I said nothing about Ian Jeffries or Fung's father. I simply sat and listened to Frank, as he switched from reassuring me about Fung to telling me about my journalist friend Jack Spalding. Jack was in this same hospital that I was in, but on a different floor. He was making a good recovery, Frank said; he should be out of hospital in a week. Then Frank left, saying that he did not want to tire me out.

So now I'm alone again.

Not for long, though, only for a few minutes. It's five-thirty. Suk Fan and Kathy will arrive soon. What answer will Suk Fan give about coming home? I'll have to wait and find out. Not for long, though, because I can hear footsteps in the corridor. The footsteps are getting louder. Now the door to my room is opening. Suk Fan and Kathy are coming in. Kathy is grinning. My wife is smiling.

Lightning Source UK Ltd.
Milton Keynes UK
17 December 2009
147661UK00001B/16/P